ORACLE NIGHT

Paul Auster was born in New Jersey in 1947. After attending
Columbia University, he lived in France for four years. Since 1974
he has published poems, essays, novels, screenplays and transla-
tions. He lives in Brooklyn, New York.

PAUL AUSTER
Oracle Night

faber and faber

First published in the United States in 2004
by Henry Holt and Company, LLC
115 West 18th Street
New York, New York 10011

First published in Great Britain in 2004
by Faber and Faber Limited
3 Queen Square London WC1N 3AU

This paperback edition first published in 2005

Typeset by Faber and Faber Limited
Printed in England by Mackays of Chatham plc, Chatham, Kent

A CIP record for this book
is available from the British Library

ISBN 978–0–571–21697–0

4 6 8 10 9 7 5

for Q.B.A.S.G.
(in memory)

I had been sick for a long time. When the day came for me to leave the hospital, I barely knew how to walk anymore, could barely remember who I was supposed to be. Make an effort, the doctor said, and in three or four months you'll be back in the swing of things. I didn't believe him, but I followed his advice anyway. They had given me up for dead, and now that I had confounded their predictions and mysteriously failed to die, what choice did I have but to live as though a future life were waiting for me?

I began with small outings, no more than a block or two from my apartment and then home again. I was only thirty-four, but for all intents and purposes the illness had turned me into an old man – one of those palsied, shuffling geezers who can't put one foot in front of the other without first looking down to see which foot is which. Even at the slow pace I could manage then, walking produced an odd, airy lightness in my head, a free-for-all of mixed-up signals and crossed mental wires. The world would bounce and swim before my eyes, undulating like reflections in a wavy mirror, and whenever I tried to look at just one thing, to isolate a single object from the onrush of whirling colors – a blue scarf wrapped around a woman's head, say, or the red taillight of a passing delivery truck – it would immediately begin to break apart and dissolve, disappearing like a drop of dye in a glass of water. Everything shimmied and wobbled, kept darting off in different directions, and for the first several weeks I had trouble telling where my body stopped and the rest of the world began. I bumped into walls and trash bins, got tangled up in dog leashes and scraps of floating paper, stumbled on the smoothest sidewalks. I had lived in New York all my life, but I didn't understand the streets and crowds anymore, and every time I went out on one of my little excursions, I felt like a man who had lost his way in a foreign city.

Summer came early that year. By the end of the first week of June, the weather had turned stagnant, oppressive, rank: day after day of torpid, greenish skies; the air clogged with garbage fumes and exhaust; heat rising from every brick and concrete slab. Still, I pushed on, forcing myself down the stairs and out into the streets every morning, and as the jumble in my head began to clear and my strength slowly returned, I was able to extend my walks into some of the more far-flung crevices of the neighborhood. Ten minutes became twenty minutes; an hour became two hours; two hours became three. Lungs gasping for air, my skin perpetually awash in sweat, I drifted along like a spectator in someone else's dream, watching the world as it chugged through its paces and marveling at how I had once been like the people around me: always rushing, always on the way from here to there, always late, always scrambling to pack in nine more things before the sun went down. I wasn't equipped to play that game anymore. I was damaged goods now, a mass of malfunctioning parts and neurological conundrums, and all that frantic getting and spending left me cold. For comic relief, I took up smoking again and whiled away the afternoons in air-conditioned coffee shops, ordering lemonades and grilled cheese sandwiches as I listened in on conversations and worked my way through every article in three different newspapers. Time passed.

On the morning in question – September 18, 1982 – I left the apartment somewhere between nine-thirty and ten o'clock. My wife and I lived in the Cobble Hill section of Brooklyn, midway between Brooklyn Heights and Carroll Gardens. I usually went north on my walks, but that morning I headed south, turning right when I came to Court Street and continuing on for six or seven blocks. The sky was the color of cement: gray clouds, gray air, gray drizzle borne along by gray gusts of wind. I have always had a weakness for that kind of weather, and I felt content in the gloom, not the least bit sorry that the dog days were behind us. About ten minutes after starting out, in the middle of the block between Carroll and President, I spotted a stationery store on the other side of the street. It was wedged in between a shoe-repair shop and a twenty-four-hour bodega, the only bright façade in a row of shabby, undistinguished buildings. I gathered that it hadn't been there long, but in spite of its newness, and in spite of the clever display in the window (towers of ballpoints, pencils, and rulers arranged to suggest the New York skyline), the Paper Palace looked too small to contain much of interest. If I decided to cross the street and go in, it must have been because I secretly wanted to start working again – without knowing it, without being aware of the urge that had been gathering inside me. I hadn't written anything since coming home from the hospital in May – not a sentence, not a word – and hadn't felt the slightest inclination to do so. Now, after four months of apathy and silence, I suddenly got it into my head to stock up on a fresh set of supplies: new pens and pencils, new notebook, new ink cartridges and erasers, new pads and folders, new everything.

A Chinese man was sitting behind the cash register in front. He appeared to be a bit younger than I was, and when I glanced through the window as I entered the store, I saw that he was hunched over a pad of paper, writing down columns of figures with a black mechanical pencil. In spite of the chill in the air that day, he was dressed in a short-sleeved shirt – one of those flimsy, loose-fitting summer things with an open collar – which accentuated the thinness of his coppery arms. The door made a tinkling sound when I pulled it open, and the man lifted his head for a moment to give me a polite nod of greeting. I nodded back, but before I could say anything to him, he lowered his head again and returned to his calculations.

The traffic out on Court Street must have hit a lull just

then, or else the plate glass window was exceedingly thick, but as I started down the first aisle to investigate the store, I suddenly realized how quiet it was in there. I was the first customer of the day, and the stillness was so pronounced that I could hear the scratching of the man's pencil behind me. Whenever I think about that morning now, the sound of that pencil is always the first thing that comes back to me. To the degree that the story I am about to tell makes any sense, I believe this was where it began – in the space of those few seconds, when the sound of that pencil was the only sound left in the world.

I made my way down the aisle, pausing after every second or third step to examine the material on the shelves. Most of it turned out to be standard office- and school-supply stuff, but the selection was remarkably thorough for such a cramped place, and I was impressed by the care that had gone into stocking and arranging such a plethora of goods, which seemed to include everything from six different lengths of brass fasteners to twelve different models of paper clip. As I rounded the corner and began moving down the other aisle toward the front, I noticed that one shelf had been given over to a number of high-quality imported items: leather-bound pads from Italy, address books from France, delicate rice-paper folders from Japan. There was also a stack of notebooks from Germany and another one from Portugal. The Portuguese notebooks were especially attractive to me, and with their hard covers, quadrille lines, and stitched-in signatures of sturdy, unblottable paper, I knew I was going to buy one the moment I picked it up and held it in my hands. There was nothing fancy or ostentatious about it. It was a practical piece of equipment – stolid, homely, serviceable, not at all the kind of blank book you'd think of offering some-one as a gift. But I liked the fact that it was cloth-bound, and I also liked the shape: nine and a quarter by seven and a quar-ter inches, which made it slightly shorter and wider than most notebooks. I can't explain why it should have been so,

4

but I found those dimensions deeply satisfying, and when I held the notebook in my hands for the first time, I felt something akin to physical pleasure, a rush of sudden, incomprehensible well-being. There were just four notebooks left on the pile, and each one came in a different color: black, red, brown, and blue. I chose the blue, which happened to be the one lying on top.

It took about five more minutes to track down the rest of the things I'd come for, and then I carried them to the front of the shop and placed them on the counter. The man gave me another one of his polite smiles and started punching the keys on his cash register, ringing up the amounts of the various items. When he came to the blue notebook, however, he paused for a moment, held it up in the air, and ran his fingertips lightly over the cover. It was a gesture of appreciation, almost a caress.

'Lovely book,' he said, in heavily accented English. 'But no more. No more Portugal. Very sad story.'

I couldn't follow what he was saying, but rather than put him on the spot and ask him to repeat it, I mumbled something about the charm and simplicity of the notebook and then changed the subject. 'Have you been in business long?' I asked. 'It looks so new and clean in here.'

'One month,' he said. 'Grand opening on August ten.'

As he announced this fact, he seemed to stand up a little straighter, throwing out his chest with boyish, military pride, but when I asked him how business was going, he gently placed the blue notebook on the counter and shook his head. 'Very slow. Many disappointments.' As I looked into his eyes, I understood that he was several years older than I'd thought at first – at least thirty-five, perhaps even forty. I made some lame remark about hanging in there and giving things a chance to develop, but he merely shook his head again and smiled. 'Always my dream to own store,' he said. 'Store like this with pens and paper, my big American dream. Business for all people, right?'

'Right,' I said, still not exactly sure what he was talking about.

'Everybody make words,' he continued. 'Everybody write things down. Children in school do lessons in my books. Teachers put grades in my books. Love letters sent in envelopes I sell. Ledgers for accountants, pads for shopping lists, agendas for planning week. Everything in here important to life, and that make me happy, give honor to my life.'

The man delivered his little speech with such solemnity, such a grave sense of purpose and commitment, I confess that I felt moved. What kind of stationery store owner was this, I wondered, who expounded to his customers on the metaphysics of paper, who saw himself as serving an essential role in the myriad affairs of humanity? There was something comical about it, I suppose, but as I listened to him talk, it didn't once occur to me to laugh.

'Well put,' I said. 'I couldn't agree with you more.'

The compliment seemed to lift his spirits somewhat. With a small smile and a nod of the head, the man resumed punching the keys of the cash register. 'Many writers here in Brooklyn,' he said. 'Whole neighborhood full of them. Good for business maybe.'

'Maybe,' I said. 'The problem with writers is that most of them don't have much money to spend.'

'Ah,' he said, looking up from the cash register and breaking into a big smile that exposed a mouthful of crooked teeth. 'You must be writer yourself.'

'Don't tell anyone,' I answered, trying to keep the tone playful. 'It's supposed to be a secret.'

It wasn't a very funny remark, but the man seemed to think it was hilarious, and for the next little while it was all he could do not to collapse in a fit of laughter. There was a strange, staccato rhythm to his laugh – which seemed to fall somewhere between talking and singing – and it rushed out of his throat in a series of short mechanical trills: *Ha ha ha. Ha ha ha. Ha ha ha.* 'No tell nobody,' he said, once the outburst had subsided. 'Top secret. Just between you and me. Sew up my lips. *Ha ha ha.*'

He went back to his work at the cash register, and by the time he'd finished packing my things into a large white shopping bag, his face had turned serious again. 'If one day you write story in blue Portugal book,' he said, 'make me very glad. My heart fill with joy.'

I didn't know how to answer that, but before I could think of anything to say, he extracted a business card from his shirt pocket and handed it to me across the counter. The words PAPER PALACE were printed in bold letters at the top. The address and telephone number followed, and then, in the lower right-hand corner, there was a last piece of information that read: *M. R. Chang, Proprietor.*

'Thank you, Mr. Chang,' I said, still looking down at the card. Then I slipped it into my own pocket and pulled out my wallet to pay the bill.

'Not mister,' Chang said, smiling his big smile again. 'M. R. Sound more important like that. More American.'

Once again, I didn't know what to say. A few ideas about what the initials stood for flashed through my mind, but I kept them to myself. Mental Resources. Multiple Readings. Mysterious Revelations. Some comments are best left unsaid, and I didn't bother to inflict my dismal wisecracks on the poor man. After a brief, awkward silence, he handed me the white shopping bag and then bowed by way of thanks.

'Good luck with your store,' I said.

'Very small palace,' he said. 'Not much stuff. But you tell me what you want, I order for you. Anything you want, I get.'

'Okay,' I said, 'it's a deal.'

I turned to leave, but Chang scuttled out from behind the counter and cut me off at the door. He seemed to be under the impression that we had just concluded a matter of highly important business, and he wanted to shake my hand. 'Deal,' he said. 'Good for you, good for me. Okay?'

'Okay,' I repeated, letting him shake my hand. I found it absurd to be making so much of so little, but it didn't cost me anything to play along. Besides, I was eager to get going, and the less I said, the sooner I would be on my way.

'You ask, I find. Whatever it is, I find for you. M. R. Chang deliver the goods.'

He pumped my arm two or three more times after that, and then he opened the door for me, nodding and smiling as I slid past him into the raw September day.[1]

I had been planning to stop in for breakfast at one of the local diners, but the twenty-dollar bill I had put in my wallet before starting out had been reduced to three singles and a smattering of coins – not even enough for the $2.99 special when you figured in the tax and tip. If not for the shopping bag, I might have gone on with my walk anyway, but there seemed to be no point in lugging that thing around the neighborhood with me, and since the weather was in a fairly nasty state by then (the once-fine drizzle had turned into a steady downpour), I opened my umbrella and decided to go home.

---

1. Twenty years have elapsed since that morning, and a fair amount of what we said to each other has been lost. I search my memory for the missing dialogue, but I can come up with no more than a few isolated fragments, bits and pieces shorn from their original context. One thing I'm certain of, however, is that I told him my name. It must have happened just after he found out I was a writer, since I can hear him asking me who I was – on the off chance he ran across something I had published. 'Orr' is what I said to him, giving my last name first, 'Sidney Orr.' Chang's English wasn't good enough for him to understand my response. He heard Orr as *or*, and when I shook my head and smiled, his face seemed to crumple up in embarrassed confusion. I was about to correct the error and spell out the word for him, but before I could say anything his eyes brightened again and he began making furious little rowing gestures with his hands, thinking that perhaps the word I'd said to him was *oar*. Again, I shook my head and smiled. Utterly defeated now,

8

It was a Saturday, and my wife had still been in bed when I'd left the apartment. Grace had a regular nine-to-five job, and the weekends were her only chance to sleep in, to indulge in the luxury of waking up without an alarm clock. Not wanting to disturb her, I had crept out as quietly as I could, leaving a note for her on the kitchen table. Now I saw that a few sentences had been added to the note. *Sidney: Hope you had fun on your walk. I'm going out to do some errands. Shouldn't be long. See you back at the ranch. Love, G.*

I went into my workroom at the end of the hall and unpacked my new supplies. It was hardly bigger than a closet in there – just enough space for a desk, a chair, and a miniature bookcase with four narrow shelves – but I found it sufficient for my needs, which had never been more elaborate than to sit in the chair and put words on pieces of paper. I had gone into the room several times since my discharge from the hospital, but until that Saturday morning in September – what I prefer to call *the morning in question* – I don't think I had sat down once in the chair. Now, as I lowered my sorry, debilitated ass onto the hard wooden seat, I felt like someone who had come home from a long and difficult journey, an unfortunate traveler who had returned to claim his rightful place in the world. It felt good to be there again, good to want to be there again, and in the wake of the happiness that washed over me as I settled in at my old desk, I decided to mark the occasion by writing something in the blue notebook.

Chang emitted a loud sigh and said: 'Terrible tongue, this English. Too tricky for my poor brain.' The misunderstanding continued until I lifted the blue notebook from the counter and wrote out my name in block letters on the inside front cover. That seemed to produce the desired result. After so much effort, I didn't bother to tell him that the first Orrs in America had been Orlovskys. My grandfather had shortened the name to make it sound more American – just as Chang had done by adding the decorative but meaningless initials, M. R., to his.

I put a fresh ink cartridge in my fountain pen, opened the notebook to the first page, and looked at the top line. I had no idea how to begin. The purpose of the exercise was not to write anything specific so much as to prove to myself that I still had it in me to write – which meant that it didn't matter what I wrote, just so long as I wrote something. Anything would have served, any sentence would have been as valid as any other, but still, I didn't want to break in that notebook with something stupid, so I bided my time by looking at the little squares on the page, the rows of faint blue lines that crisscrossed the whiteness and turned it into a field of tiny identical boxes, and as I let my thoughts wander in and out of those lightly traced enclosures, I found myself remembering a conversation I'd had with my friend John Trause a couple of weeks earlier. The two of us rarely talked about books when we were together, but that day John had mentioned that he was rereading some of the novelists he had admired when he was young – curious to know if their work held up or not, curious to know if the judgments he'd made at twenty were the same ones he would make today, more than thirty years down the road. He ran through ten writers, through twenty writers, touching on everyone from Faulkner and Fitzgerald to Dostoyevsky and Flaubert, but the comment that stuck most vividly in my mind – and which came back to me now as I sat at my desk with the blue notebook open in front of me – was a small digression he'd made concerning an anecdote in one of Dashiell Hammett's books. 'There's a novel in this somewhere,' John had said. 'I'm too old to want to think about it myself, but a young punk like you could really fly with it, turn it into something good. It's a terrific premise. All you need is a story to go with it.'[2]

---

2. John was fifty-six. Not young, perhaps, but not old enough to think of himself as old, especially since he was aging well and still looked like a man in his mid- to late forties. I had known him for three years by then, and our friendship was a direct result of my

He was referring to the Flitcraft episode in the seventh chapter of *The Maltese Falcon*, the curious parable that Sam Spade tells Brigid O'Shaughnessy about the man who walks away from his life and disappears. Flitcraft is a thoroughly conventional fellow – a husband, a father, a successful businessman, a person without a thing to complain about. One afternoon as he's walking to lunch, a beam falls from a construction site on the tenth floor of a building and nearly lands on his head. Another inch or two, and Flitcraft would have been crushed, but the beam misses him, and except for a little chip of sidewalk that flies up and hits him in the face, he walks away unhurt. Still, the close call rattles him, and he can't push the incident from his mind. As Hammett puts it: 'He felt like somebody had taken the lid off life and let him look at the works.' Flitcraft realizes that the world isn't the sane and orderly place he thought it was, that he's had it all wrong from the beginning and never understood the first

---

marriage to Grace. Her father had been at Princeton with John in the years immediately following the Second World War, and although the two of them worked in different fields (Grace's father was a District Federal Court judge in Charlottesville, Virginia), they had remained close ever since. I therefore met him as a family friend, not as the well-known novelist I had been reading since high school – and whom I still considered to be one of the best writers we had.

He had published six works of fiction between 1952 and 1975, but nothing now for more than seven years. John had never been fast, however, and just because the break between books had been somewhat longer than usual, that didn't mean he wasn't working. I had spent several afternoons with him since my release from the hospital, and sprinkled in among our conversations regarding my health (about which he was deeply concerned, unflagging in his solicitude), his twenty-year-old son, Jacob (who had caused him much anguish of late), and the struggles of the floundering Mets (an abiding mutual obsession), he had dropped enough hints about his current activities to suggest that he was thoroughly wrapped up in something, devoting the better part of his time to a project that was well under way – and perhaps now coming to an end.

thing about it. The world is governed by chance. Randomness stalks us every day of our lives, and those lives can be taken from us at any moment – for no reason at all. By the time Flitcraft finishes his lunch, he concludes that he has no choice but to submit to this destructive power, to smash his life through some meaningless, wholly arbitrary act of self-negation. He will fight fire with fire, as it were, and without bothering to return home or say good-bye to his family, without even bothering to withdraw any money from the bank, he stands up from the table, goes to another city, and starts his life all over again.

In the two weeks since John and I had discussed that passage, it hadn't once crossed my mind that I might want to take up the challenge of fleshing out the story. I agreed that it was a good premise – good because we have all imagined letting go of our lives, good because at one moment or another we have all wanted to be someone else – but that didn't mean I had any interest in pursuing it. That morning, however, as I sat at my desk for the first time in almost nine months, staring at my newly acquired notebook and struggling to come up with an opening sentence that wouldn't embarrass me or rob me of my courage, I decided to give the old Flitcraft episode a shot. It was no more than an excuse, a search for a possible way in. If I could jot down a couple of reasonably interesting ideas, then at least I could call it a beginning, even if I broke off after twenty minutes and never did another thing with it. So I removed the cap from my pen, pressed the point against the top line of the first page in the blue notebook, and started to write.

The words came quickly, smoothly, without seeming to demand much effort. I found that surprising, but as long as I kept my hand moving from left to right, the next word always seemed to be there, waiting to come out of the pen. I saw my Flitcraft as a man named Nick Bowen. He's in his mid-thirties, works as an editor at a large New York publishing house, and is married to a woman named Eva.

12

Following the example of Hammett's prototype, he is necessarily good at his job, admired by his colleagues, financially secure, happy in his marriage, and so on. Or so it would appear to a casual observer, but as my version of the story begins, trouble has been stirring in Bowen for some time. He had grown bored with his work (although he is unwilling to admit it), and after five years of relative stability and contentment with Eva, his marriage has come to a standstill (another fact he hasn't had the courage to face). Rather than dwell on his burgeoning dissatisfaction, Nick spends his spare time at a garage on Desbrosses Street in Tribeca, engaged in the long-term project of rebuilding the engine of a broken-down Jaguar he bought in the third year of his marriage. He is a top young editor at a prestigious New York company, but the truth is that he prefers working with his hands.

As the story opens, the manuscript of a novel has arrived on Bowen's desk. A short work bearing the suggestive title of *Oracle Night*, it was supposedly written by Sylvia Maxwell, a popular novelist from the twenties and thirties who died nearly two decades ago. According to the agent who sent it in, this lost book was composed in 1927, the year Maxwell ran off to France with an Englishman named Jeremy Scott, a minor artist of the period who later worked as a set designer for British and American films. The affair lasted eighteen months, and when it was over Sylvia Maxwell returned to New York, leaving the novel behind with Scott. He held on to it for the rest of his life, and when he died at the age of eighty-seven, a few months before my story begins, a clause was found in his will that bequeathed the manuscript to Maxwell's granddaughter, a young American woman named Rosa Leightman. It was through her that the book was given to the agent – with explicit instructions that it be sent to Nick Bowen first, before anyone else had a chance to read it.

The package arrives at Nick's office on a Friday afternoon,

just minutes after he has left for the weekend. When he returns on Monday morning, the book is sitting on his desk. Nick is an admirer of Sylvia Maxwell's other novels, and therefore he is eager to get started on this one. A moment after he turns to the first page, however, the telephone rings. His assistant informs him that Rosa Leightman is in the reception area, asking if she can see him for a few minutes. Send her in, Nick says, and before he is able to finish reading the opening sentences of the book (*The war was nearly over, but we didn't know that. We were too small to know anything, and because the war was everywhere, we didn't . . .*), Sylvia Maxwell's granddaughter enters his office. She is dressed in the simplest clothes, has almost no makeup on, wears her hair in a short, unfashionable cut, and yet her face is so lovely, Nick finds, so achingly young and unguarded, so much (he suddenly thinks) an emblem of hope and uncoiled human energy, that he momentarily stops breathing. That is precisely what happened to me the first time I saw Grace – the blow to the brain that left me paralyzed, unable to draw my next breath – so it wasn't difficult for me to transpose those feelings onto Nick Bowen and imagine them in the context of that other story. To make matters even simpler, I decided to give Grace's body to Rosa Leightman – even down to her smallest, most idiosyncratic features, including the childhood scar on her kneecap, her slightly crooked left incisor, and the beauty mark on the right side of her jaw.[3]

---

3. I happened to meet Grace in a publisher's office as well, which might explain why I chose to give Bowen the job I did. It was January 1979, not long after I had finished my second novel. My first novel and an earlier book of stories had been brought out by a small publisher in San Francisco, but now I had moved on to a larger, more commercial house in New York, Holst & McDermott. About two weeks after I signed the contract, I went to the office to see my editor, and at some point during our conversation we started discussing ideas for the cover of the book. That was when Betty Stolowitz picked up the phone on her desk and said to me, 'Why

As for Bowen, however, I expressly made him someone I was not, an inversion of myself. I am tall, and so I made him short. I have reddish hair, and so I gave him dark brown hair. I wear size eleven shoes, and so I put him in size eight and a half. I didn't model him on anyone I knew (not consciously, at any rate), but once I had finished putting him together in my mind, he became astonishingly vivid to me – almost as if I could see him, almost as if he had entered the room and were standing next to me, looking down at the desk with his hand on my shoulder and reading the words I was writing . . . watching me bring him to life with my pen.

At last, Nick gestures for Rosa to sit down, and she settles into a chair on the opposite side of the desk. A long hesitation follows. Nick has begun breathing again, but he

------

don't we get Grace in here and see what she thinks?' It turned out that Grace worked in the art department at Holst & McDermott and had been given the job of designing the dust jacket for *Self-Portrait with Imaginary Brother* – which was what my little book of whims, reveries, and nightmare sorrows was called.

Betty and I went on talking for another three or four minutes, and then Grace Tebbetts walked into the room. She stayed for about a quarter of an hour, and by the time she walked out again and returned to her office, I was in love with her. It was that abrupt, that conclusive, that unexpected. I had read about such things in novels, but I had always assumed the authors were exaggerating the power of the first look – that endlessly talked-about moment when the man gazes into the eyes of his beloved for the first time. To a born pessimist like myself, it was an altogether shocking experience. I felt as if I had been thrust back into the world of the troubadours, reliving some passage from the opening chapter of *La Vita Nova* (. . . *when first the glorious Lady of my thoughts was made manifest to my eyes*), inhabiting the stale tropes of a thousand forgotten love sonnets. *I burned. I longed. I pined. I was rendered mute.* And all this happened to me in the dullest of precincts, under the harsh fluorescent glare of a late-twentieth-century American office – the last place on earth where one would think to stumble upon the passion of one's life.

There is no accounting for such an event, no objective reason to explain why we fall for one person and not another. Grace was a good-looking woman, but even in those first tumultuous seconds of

can't think of anything to say. Rosa breaks the ice by asking if he found time to finish the book over the weekend. No, he answers, it came in too late. I didn't get it until this morning.

Rosa looks relieved. That's good, she says. There's been talk that the novel is a hoax, that it wasn't written by my grandmother. I couldn't be sure myself, so I hired a handwriting expert to examine the original manuscript. His report came in on Saturday, and he says it's genuine. Just so you know. *Oracle Night* was written by Sylvia Maxwell.

It sounds as if you liked the book, Nick says, and Rosa says yes, she was very moved by it. If it was written in 1927, he continues, then it came after *The Burning House* and *Redemption* but before *Landscape with Trees* – which would

---

our first encounter, as I shook her hand and watched her settle into a chair by Betty's desk, I could see that she was not inordinately beautiful, not one of those movie star goddesses who overpower you with the dazzle of their perfection. No doubt she was becoming, striking, pleasant to behold (however one chooses to define those terms), but fierce as my attraction was, I also knew that it was more than just a physical attraction, that the dream I was starting to dream was more than just a momentary surge of animal desire. Grace struck me as intelligent, but as the meeting wore on and I listened to her talk about her ideas for the cover, I understood that she wasn't a terribly articulate person (she hesitated frequently between thoughts, confined her vocabulary to small, functional words, seemed to have no gift for abstraction), and nothing she said that afternoon was particularly brilliant or memorable. Other than making a few friendly remarks about my book, she gave no sign to suggest that she was even remotely interested in me. And yet there I was in a state of maximum torment – *burning* and *longing* and *pining*, a man trapped in the snares of love.

She was five feet eight inches tall and weighed a hundred and twenty-five pounds. Slender neck, long arms and long fingers, pale skin, and short dirty-blond hair. That hair, I later realized, bore some resemblance to the hair shown in the drawings of the hero of *The Little Prince* – choppy juts of spikes and curls – and perhaps the association enhanced the somewhat androgynous aura that Grace

have made it her third novel. She was still under thirty then, wasn't she?

Twenty-eight, Rosa says. The same age I am now.

The conversation goes on for another fifteen or twenty minutes. Nick has a hundred things to do that morning, but he can't bring himself to ask her to leave. There is something so forthright about this girl, so lucid, so lacking in self-deception, that he wants to go on looking at her for a little while and absorb the full impact of her presence – which is beautiful, he decides, precisely because she is unaware of it, because of her absolute disregard of the effect she has on others. Nothing of consequence is said. He learns that Rosa is the daughter of Sylvia Maxwell's oldest son (who was a product of Maxwell's second marriage, to theater director

---

projected. The mannish clothes she was wearing that afternoon must have played their part in creating the image as well: black jeans, white T-shirt, and a pale blue linen jacket. About five minutes into her visit, she removed the jacket and draped it over the back of her chair, and when I saw her arms, those long, smooth, infinitely feminine arms of hers, I knew there would be no rest for me until I was able to touch them, until I had earned the right to put my hands on her body and run them over her bare skin.

But I want to go deeper than Grace's body, deeper than the incidental facts of her physical self. Bodies count, of course – they count more than we're willing to admit – but we don't fall in love with bodies, we fall in love with each other, and if much of what we are is confined to flesh and bone, there is much that is not as well. We all know that, but the minute we go beyond a catalogue of surface qualities and appearances, words begin to fail us, to crumble apart in mystical confusions and cloudy, insubstantial metaphors. Some call it *the flame of being*. Others call it *the internal spark* or *the inner light of selfhood*. Still others refer to it as *the fires of quiddity*. The terms always draw on images of heat and illumination, and that force, that essence of life we sometimes refer to as soul, is always communicated to another person through the eyes. Surely the poets were correct to insist on this point. The mystery of desire begins by looking into the eyes of the beloved, for it is only there that one can catch a glimpse of who that person is.

17

Stuart Leightman) and that she was born and raised in Chicago. When Nick asks her why she was so keen on having the book sent to him first, she says she knows nothing about the publishing business, but Alice Lazarre is her favorite living novelist, and when she found out that Nick was her editor, she decided he was the man for her grandmother's book. Nick smiles. Alice will be pleased, he says, and a few minutes later, when Rosa finally stands up to make her exit, he pulls some books off a shelf in his office and gives her a stack of Alice Lazarre first editions. I hope you're not disappointed in *Oracle Night*, Rosa says. Why should I be disappointed? Nick asks. Sylvia Maxwell was a first-rate novelist. Well, Rosa says, this book is different from the others. In what way? Nick asks. I don't know, Rosa

———

Grace's eyes were blue. A dark blue flecked with traces of gray, perhaps some brown, perhaps some hints of hazelish contrast as well. They were complex eyes, eyes that changed color according to the intensity and timbre of the light that fell on them at a given moment, and the first time I saw her that day in Betty's office, it occurred to me that I had never met a woman who exuded such composure, such tranquillity of bearing, as if Grace, who was not yet twenty-seven at the time, had already moved on to some higher state of being than the rest of us. I don't mean to suggest that there was anything withheld about her, that she floated above her circumstances in some beatific haze of condescension or indifference. On the contrary, she was quite animated throughout the meeting, laughed readily, smiled, said all the appropriate things, and made all the appropriate gestures, but underneath a professional engagement in the ideas that Betty and I were proposing to her, I felt a startling absence of inner struggle, an equilibrium of mind that seemed to exempt her from the usual conflicts and aggressions of modern life: self-doubt, envy, sarcasm, the need to judge or belittle others, the scalding, unbearable ache of personal ambition. Grace was young, but she had an old and weathered soul, and as I sat with her that first day in the offices of Holst & McDermott, looking into her eyes and studying the contours of her lean, angular body, that was what I fell in love with: the sense of calm that enveloped her, the radiant silence burning within.

says, in every way. You'll find out for yourself when you read it.

There were other decisions to be made, of course, a host of significant details that still had to be conjured up and worked into the scene – for purposes of fullness and authenticity, for narrative ballast. How long has Rosa been living in New York? for example. What does she do there? Does she have a job and, if so, is the job important to her or simply a means of generating enough money to cover the rent? What about the status of her love life? Is she single or married, attached or unattached, on the prowl or patiently waiting for the right person to come along? My first impulse was to make her a photographer, or perhaps an assistant film editor – work that was connected to images, not words, just as Grace's job was. Definitely unmarried, definitely never married, but perhaps involved with someone, or, even better, perhaps recently broken up after a long, tortured affair. I didn't want to dwell on any of those questions for the time being, nor on similar questions relating to Nick's wife – profession, family background, taste in music, books, and so on. I wasn't writing the story yet, I was merely sketching out the action in rough strokes, and I couldn't afford to bog myself down in the minutiae of secondary concerns. That would have forced me to stop and think, and for the moment I was only interested in forging ahead, in seeing where the pictures in my mind were going to take me. It wasn't about control; it wasn't even about making choices. My job that morning was simply to follow what was happening inside me, and in order to do that I had to keep the pen moving as fast as I could.

Nick is not a rogue or a seducer of women. He has not made a habit of cheating on his wife during the course of their marriage, and he is not aware of having any designs on Sylvia Maxwell's granddaughter now. But there is no question that he feels attracted to her, that he has been pulled in by the iridescence and simplicity of her manner, and the moment she stands up and leaves the office, it flashes through his mind – an unbidden thought, the figurative thunderclap of lust – that he would probably do anything to go to bed with this woman, even to the point of sacrificing his marriage. Men produce such thoughts twenty times a day, and just because a person experiences a momentary flicker of arousal doesn't mean he has any intention of acting on the impulse, but still, no sooner does Nick play out the thought in his head than he feels disgusted with himself, stung by a sensation of guilt. To appease his conscience, he calls his wife at her office (law firm, brokerage house, hospital – to be determined later) and announces that he is going to book a reservation at their favorite downtown restaurant and take her to dinner that night.

They meet there at eight o'clock. Things go pleasantly enough through drinks and the appetizer course, but then they begin to discuss some minor household matter (a broken chair, the imminent arrival of one of Eva's cousins in New York, a thing of no importance), and soon they have fallen into an argument. Not a vehement one, perhaps, but enough irritation enters their voices to destroy the mood. Nick apologizes and Eva accepts; Eva apologizes and Nick accepts; but the conversation has gone flat, and there is no recapturing the harmony of just a few minutes ago. By the time the main course is delivered to the table, they are both sitting there in silence. The restaurant is packed, humming with animation, and as Nick absently casts his eyes around the room, he catches sight of Rosa Leightman, sitting at a corner table with five or six other people. Eva notices him looking off in that direction and asks if he's seen someone he knows. That girl, Nick says. She was in my office this morning. He goes on to tell her something about Rosa, mentions the novel written by her grandmother, Sylvia Maxwell, and then tries to change the subject, but Eva has turned her head by then and is looking across the room at Rosa's table. She's very beautiful, Nick says, don't you think? Not bad, Eva answers. But strange hair, Nicky, and really terrible clothes. It doesn't matter, Nick says. She's alive – more alive than anyone I've met in months. She's the kind of woman who could turn a man inside out.

It's an awful thing for a man to say to his wife, especially to a wife who feels her husband has begun to drift away from her. Well, Eva says defensively, too bad you're stuck with me. Would you like me to go over there and ask her to join us? I've never seen a man turned inside out before. Maybe I'll learn something.

Realizing the thoughtless cruelty of what he's just said, Nick tries to undo the damage. I wasn't talking about myself, he replies. I just meant a man – any man. Man in the abstract.

After dinner, Nick and Eva return to their place in the West Village. It's a tidy, well-appointed duplex on Barrow Street – John Trause's apartment, in fact, which I appropriated for my Flitcraftian tale as a silent bow to the man who'd suggested the idea to me. Nick has a letter to write, some bills to pay, and as Eva prepares herself for bed, he sits down at the dining room table to attend to these small tasks. It takes him three quarters of an hour, but even though it's getting late now, he feels restless, not yet ready for sleep. He pokes his head into the bedroom, sees that Eva is still awake, and tells her he's going out to mail the letters. Just down to the box at the corner, he says. I'll be back in five minutes.

That's when it happens. Bowen picks up his briefcase (which still contains the manuscript of *Oracle Night*), tosses in the letters, and goes out on his errand. It is early spring, and a stiff wind is blowing through the city, rattling the street signs, and stirring up bits of paper and debris. Still brooding about his disturbing encounter with Rosa that morning, still trying to make sense of the doubly disturbing accident of having seen her again that night, Nick walks to the corner in a fog, scarcely paying attention to where he is. He removes the letters from his briefcase and slips them into the mailbox. Something inside him has been broken, he tells himself, and

21

for the first time since his troubles with Eva began, he's willing to admit the truth of his situation: that his marriage has failed, that his life has come to a dead end. Rather than turn around and immediately head home, he decides to go on walking for a few more minutes. He continues down the street, turns at the corner, walks down another street, and then turns again at the next corner. Eleven stories above him, the head of a small limestone gargoyle attached to the façade of an apartment building is slowly breaking loose from the rest of its body as the wind continues to attack the street. Nick takes another step, and then another step, and at the moment the gargoyle head is finally dislodged, he walks straight into the trajectory of the falling object. Thus, in slightly modified form, the Flitcraft saga begins. Hurtling down within inches of Nick's head, the gargoyle grazes his right arm, knocks the briefcase out of his hand, and then shatters into a thousand pieces on the sidewalk.

The impact throws Nick to the ground. He is stunned, disoriented, afraid. At first, he has no idea what has happened to him. A split second of alarm as the stone touched his sleeve, an instant of shock as the briefcase flew out of his hand, and then the noise of the gargoyle head exploding against the pavement. Several moments go by before he can reconstruct the sequence of events, and when he does, he picks himself up from the sidewalk understanding that he should be dead. The stone was meant to kill him. He left his apartment tonight for no other reason than to run into that stone, and if he's managed to escape with his life, it can only mean that a new life has been given to him – that his old life is finished, that every moment of his past now belongs to someone else.

A taxi rounds the corner and comes down the street in his direction. Nick raises his hand. The taxi stops, and Nick climbs in. Where to? the driver asks. Nick has no idea, and so he speaks the first word that enters his head. The airport, he says. Which one? the driver asks. Kennedy, La Guardia, or

Newark? La Guardia, Nick says, and off they go to La Guardia. When they get there, Nick walks up to the ticket counter and asks when the next flight is leaving. Flight to where? the ticket salesman asks. Anywhere, Nick says. The salesman consults the schedule. Kansas City, he says. There's a flight that begins boarding in ten minutes. Fine, Nick says, handing the salesman his credit card, give me a ticket. One way or round-trip? the salesman asks. One way, Nick says, and half an hour later he's sitting on a plane, flying through the night toward Kansas City.

That was where I left him that morning – suspended in midair, winging madly toward an uncertain, implausible future. I wasn't sure how long I'd been at it, but I could feel myself beginning to run out of gas, so I put down my pen and stood up from the chair. All in all, I had covered eight pages in the blue notebook. That would suggest at least two or three hours' work, but the time had passed so quickly, I felt as if I'd been in there for only a few minutes. When I left the room, I headed down the hall and went into the kitchen. Unexpectedly, Grace was standing by the stove, preparing a pot of tea.

'I didn't know you were home,' she said.

'I got back a while ago,' I explained. 'I've been sitting in my room.'

Grace looked surprised. 'Didn't you hear me knock?'

'No, I'm sorry. I must have been pretty wrapped up in what I was doing.'

'When you didn't answer, I opened the door and peeked inside. But you weren't there.'

'Of course I was. I was sitting at my desk.'

'Well, I didn't see you. Maybe you were somewhere else. In the bathroom maybe.'

'I don't remember going to the bathroom. As far as I know, I was sitting at my desk the whole time.'

Grace shrugged. 'If you say so, Sidney,' she answered. She was clearly in no mood to pick a quarrel. Intelligent woman that she was, she gave me one of her glorious, enigmatic smiles and then turned back to the stove to finish preparing the tea.

The rain stopped at some point in the middle of the afternoon, and several hours later a battered blue Ford from one of the local car services drove us across the Brooklyn Bridge for our biweekly dinner with John Trause. Since my return from the hospital, the three of us had made a point of getting together every other Saturday night, alternating meals at our place in Brooklyn (where we cooked for John) with elaborate culinary blowouts at Chez Pierre, an expensive new restaurant in the West Village (where John always insisted on picking up the tab). The original program for that night had been to meet at the bar of Chez Pierre at seven-thirty, but John had called earlier in the week to say that something was wrong with his leg and that he would have to cancel. It turned out to be an attack of phlebitis (an inflammation of the vein brought on by the presence of a blood clot), but then John had called back on Friday afternoon to tell us that he was feeling a little better. He wasn't supposed to walk, he said, but if we didn't mind coming to his apartment and ordering in Chinese food, maybe we could have our dinner after all. 'I'd hate to miss seeing you and Gracie,' he said. 'Since I have to eat something anyway, why don't we all do it here together? As long as I keep my leg up, it really doesn't hurt too much anymore.'[4]

---

4. John was the only person in the world who still called her *Gracie*. Not even her parents did that anymore, and I myself, who had been involved with her for more than three years, had never once addressed her by that diminutive. But John had known her all her life – literally from the day she was born – and a number of special privileges had accrued to him over time, elevating him from the rank of family friend to unofficial blood relation. It was as if he had achieved the status of favorite uncle – or, if you will, godfather-without-portfolio.

I had stolen John's apartment for my story in the blue notebook, and when we got to Barrow Street and he opened the door to let us in, I had the strange, not altogether unpleasant feeling that I was entering an imaginary space, walking into a room that wasn't there. I had visited Trause's apartment countless times in the past, but now that I had spent several hours thinking about it in my own apartment in Brooklyn, peopling it with the invented characters of my story, it seemed to belong as much to the world of fiction as to the world of solid objects and flesh-and-blood human beings. Unexpectedly, this feeling didn't go away. If anything, it grew stronger as the night went on, and by the time the Chinese food arrived at eight-thirty, I was already beginning to settle into what I would have to call (for want of a better term) a state of double consciousness. I was both a part of what was going on around me and cut off from it, drifting freely in my mind as I imagined myself sitting at my desk in Brooklyn, writing about this place in the blue notebook, and sitting in a chair on the top floor of a Manhattan duplex, firmly anchored in my body, listening to what John and Grace were saying to each other and even adding some

_____

John loved Grace, and Grace loved him back, and because I was the man in Grace's life, John had welcomed me into the inner circle of his affections. During the period of my collapse, he had sacrificed much of his time and energy to helping Grace through the crisis, and when I finally recovered from my brush with death, he started turning up at the hospital every afternoon to sit by my bed and keep me company – to keep me (as I later realized) in the land of the living. When Grace and I went to visit him for dinner that night (September 18, 1982), I doubt that anyone in New York was closer to John than we were. Nor was anyone closer to us than John. That would explain why he considered our Saturday nights so important and hadn't wanted to break the date, in spite of the problem with his leg. He lived alone, and since he rarely circulated in public, seeing us had become his principal form of social entertainment, his only real chance to indulge in a few hours of uninterrupted conversation.

remarks of my own. It's not unusual for a person to be so preoccupied as to appear absent – but the point was that I wasn't absent. I was there, fully engaged in what was happening, and at the same time I wasn't there – for the there wasn't an authentic there anymore. It was an illusory place that existed in my head, and that's where I was as well. In both places at the same time. In the apartment and in the story. In the story in the apartment that I was still writing in my head.

John appeared to be in a lot more pain than he was willing to admit. He was leaning on a crutch when he opened the door, and as I watched him limp up the stairs and then hobble back to his place on the sofa – a big sagging affair festooned with a pile of pillows and blankets for propping up his leg – he was wincing noticeably, suffering with every step he took. But John wasn't about to make a big production of it. He had fought in the Pacific as an eighteen-year-old private at the end of World War II, and he belonged to that generation of men who considered it a point of honor never to feel sorry for themselves, who recoiled in disdain whenever anyone tried to fuss over them. Other than making a couple of cracks about Richard Nixon, who had given the word *phlebitis* a certain comic resonance in the days of his administration, John stubbornly refused to talk about his infirmity. No, that's not quite correct. After we entered the upstairs room, he allowed Grace to help him onto the sofa and to reposition the pillows and blankets, apologizing for what he called his 'moronic decrepitude.' Then, once he had settled into his spot, he turned to me and said, 'We're quite a pair, aren't we, Sid? You with your wobbles and nosebleeds, and now me with this leg. We're the goddamn gimps of the universe.'

Trause had never been overly attentive to his appearance, but that night he looked particularly disheveled to me, and from the rumpled condition of his blue jeans and cotton sweater – not to speak of the grayish tinge that had spread over the bottoms of his white socks – I gathered he'd been wearing that outfit for several days in a row. Not surprisingly, his hair was mussed, and the back strands had been flattened and stiffened after lying on the sofa for so many hours in the past week. The truth was that John looked haggard, considerably older than he had ever looked to me before, but when a man is in pain, and no doubt losing much sleep because of that pain, he can hardly be expected to look his best. I wasn't alarmed by what I saw, but Grace, who was normally the most unruffled person I knew, seemed flustered and upset by John's condition. Before we could get down to the business of ordering the food, she grilled him for ten solid minutes about doctors, medicines, and prognoses, and then, once he'd assured her he wasn't going to die, she moved on to a host of practical concerns: grocery shopping, cooking, trash removal, laundry, the daily routine. Madame Dumas had it all under control, John said, referring to the woman from Martinique who had been cleaning his apartment for the past two years, and when she wasn't available, her daughter came instead. 'Twenty years old,' he added, 'and very intelligent. Nice to look at, too, by the way. She doesn't walk so much as glide around the room, as if her feet weren't touching the floor. It gives me a chance to practice my French.'

The matter of John's leg aside, he seemed glad to be with us, and he talked more than he usually did on such occasions, rattling on steadily for most of the evening. I can't be certain, but I believe it was the pain that loosened his tongue and kept him going. The words must have provided a distraction from the tumult coursing through his leg, a frenzied sort of relief. That, and the vast quantities of alcohol he consumed as well. As each new bottle of wine was uncorked, John was the first to hold out his glass, and of the three bottles we drank that night, roughly half the contents wound up in his system. That makes a bottle and a half of wine, along with the two glasses of straight Scotch he drank toward the end. I had seen him drink that much a few times in the past, but no matter how well lubricated John became, he never appeared to be drunk. No slurred speech, no glassiness in the eyes. He was a big person – six-two, a shade under two hundred pounds – and he could hold it.

'About a week before this leg thing started,' he said, 'I got a call from Tina's brother Richard.[5] I hadn't heard from him in a long time. Not since the day of the funeral, in fact, which means we're talking about eight years – more than eight years. I'd never had much to do with her family while we were married, and now that she wasn't there anymore, I hadn't bothered to stay in touch with them. Nor they with me, for that matter – not that I particularly cared. All those Ostrow brothers, with their cruddy furniture store on Springfield Avenue and their boring wives and their mediocre children. Tina had about eight or nine first cousins, but she was the only one with any spirit, the only one who'd had the gumption to break out of that little New Jersey world and try to make something of herself. So it surprised me when Richard called the other day. He lives in

5. Tina was John's second wife. His first marriage had lasted ten years (from 1954 to 1964) and had ended in divorce. He never talked about it in my presence, but Grace had told me that no one in her family had been particularly fond of Eleanor. The Tebbetts had seen her as a stuck-up Bryn Mawr girl from a long line of Massachusetts bluebloods, a 'cold fish' who had always looked down her nose at John's working-class Paterson, New Jersey, family. No matter that Eleanor was a respected painter whose reputation was nearly as important as John's. They weren't surprised when the marriage ended, and not one of them was sorry to see her go. The only pity, Grace said, was that John had been forced to remain in contact with her. Not through any desire on his part, but because of the ongoing antics of their troubled, wildly unstable son, Jacob.

Then he had met Tina Ostrow, a dancer-choreographer twelve years younger than he was, and when he married her in 1966, the Tebbetts clan applauded the decision. They felt confident that John had finally found the woman he deserved, and time proved them

Florida now, he said, and had come to New York on a business trip. Would I be interested in going out to dinner with him? Somewhere nice, he said, his treat. Since I didn't have any other plans, I accepted. I don't know why I did, but there wasn't any compelling reason not to, and so we arranged to meet the next night at eight o'clock.

'You have to understand about Richard. He'd always struck me as a featherweight, a person without substance. He was born a year after Tina, which would make him about forty-three now, and except for a few moments of glory as a high school basketball player, he'd stumbled around for most of his life, flunking out of two or three colleges, moving from one dismal job to the next, never marrying, never really growing up. A sweet disposition, I suppose, but shallow and uninspired, with a kind of slack-jawed dopiness that always got on my nerves. About the only thing I ever liked about him was his devotion to Tina. He loved her every bit as much as I did – that's certain, an uncontestable fact – and I'm not going to deny that he was a good brother to her, an exemplary brother. You were at the funeral, Gracie. You

---

right. The small and vibrant Tina was an adorable person, Grace said, and she had loved John (in Grace's words) 'to the point of worship.' The only problem with the marriage was that Tina didn't live long enough to see her thirty-seventh birthday. Uterine cancer slowly took her from him over the course of eighteen months, and after John buried her, Grace said, he shut down for a long time, 'just froze up and sort of stopped breathing.' He moved to Paris for a year, then to Rome, then to a small village on the northern coast of Portugal. When he returned to New York in 1978 and settled into the apartment on Barrow Street, it had been three years since his last novel had been published, and the rumor was that Trause hadn't written a word since Tina's death. Four more years had passed since then, and still he hadn't produced anything – at least not anything he was willing to show anyone. But he was working. I knew he was working. He'd told me as much himself, but I didn't know what kind of work it was, for the simple reason that I hadn't found the nerve to ask.

remember what happened. Hundreds of people showed up, and every person in the chapel was sobbing, moaning, wailing in horror. It was a flood of collective grief, suffering on a scale I'd never witnessed before. But of all the mourners in that room, Richard was the one who suffered the most. He and I together, sitting in the front pew. When the service was over, he nearly passed out when he tried to get to his feet. It took all my strength to hold him up. I literally had to throw my arms around his body to stop him from falling to the floor.

'But that was years ago. We lived through that trauma together, and then I lost track of him. When I agreed to have dinner the other night, I was expecting to have a dull time of it, to slog my way through a couple of hours of awkward conversation and then dash for the door and head home. But I was wrong. I'm happy to report that I was wrong. It always stimulates me to discover new examples of my own prejudice and stupidity, to realize that I don't know half as much as I think I do.

'It started with the pleasure of seeing his face. I'd forgotten how much he resembled his sister, how many features they had in common. The set and slant of the eyes, the rounded chin, the elegant mouth, the bridge of the nose – it was Tina in a man's body, or little flashes of her at any rate, darting out at random moments. It overwhelmed me to be with her again like that, to feel her presence again, to feel that a part of her had lived on in her brother. A couple of times Richard turned in a certain way, gestured in a certain way, did a certain something with his eyes, and I was so moved that I wanted to lean across the table and kiss him. Smack on the lips – a full-bore osculation. You'll probably laugh, but I'm actually sorry now that I didn't.

'Richard was still Richard, the selfsame Richard of yore – but better, somehow, more comfortable in his own skin. He's gotten himself married and has two little girls. Maybe that's helped. Maybe being eight years older has helped, I don't know. He's still grinding away at one of those sad-sack jobs of his – computer parts salesman, efficiency consultant, I forget what it was – and he still spends every evening in front of the television set. Football games, sitcoms, cop shows, nature specials – he loves everything about television. But he never reads, never votes, never even bothers to pretend to have an opinion about what's going on in the world. He's known me for sixteen years, and in all that time he hasn't once taken the trouble to open one of my books. I don't mind, of course, but I mention it in order to show how lazy he is, how thoroughly lacking in curiosity. And yet I enjoyed being with him the other night. I enjoyed listening to him talk about his favorite TV programs, about his wife and two daughters, about his ever-improving tennis game, about the advantages of living in Florida over New Jersey. Better climate, you understand. No more snowstorms and icy winters; summer every day of the year. So ordinary, children, so fucking complacent, and yet – how shall I put it? – utterly at peace with himself, so contented with his life that I almost envied him for it.

'So there we were, eating an unremarkable dinner in an unremarkable midtown restaurant, talking about nothing of any great importance, when Richard suddenly looked up from his plate and began to tell me a story. That's why I've been telling you all this – in order to get to Richard's story. I don't know if you'll agree with me, but it strikes me as one of the most interesting things I've heard in a long time.

'Three or four months ago, Richard was in his garage at home, looking for something in a cardboard box, when he came across an old 3-D viewer. He vaguely remembered that his parents had bought it when he was a kid, but he couldn't recall the circumstances or what they'd used it for. Unless he'd blanked out the experience, he was fairly certain he'd never looked through it, had never even held it in his hands. When he lifted it out of the box and started to examine it, he saw that it wasn't one of those cheap, flimsy things used for looking at ready-made pictures of tourist sites and pretty scenery. It was a solid, well-built optical instrument, a prize relic from the 3-D craze of the early fifties. The fad didn't last long, but the idea was to take your own 3-D pictures with a special camera, develop them as slides, and then look at them through the viewer, which served as a kind of three-dimensional photo album. The camera was missing, but Richard found a box of slides. There were just twelve of them, he said, which seemed to suggest his parents had shot only one roll of film with their novelty camera – and then had stowed it away somewhere and forgotten all about it.

'Not knowing what to expect, Richard put one of the slides in the viewer, pressed down on the background illuminator button, and had a look. In one instant, he said, thirty years of his life were erased. It was 1953, and he was in the living room of his family's house in West Orange, New Jersey, standing among the guests at Tina's sixteenth birthday party. He remembered everything now: the Sweet Sixteen bash, the caterers unpacking their food in the kitchen and lining up champagne glasses on the counter, the ringing of the doorbell, the music, the din of voices, the chignon knot in Tina's hair, the whooshing of her long yellow dress. One by one, he put each slide in the viewer and looked at all twelve of them. Everyone was there, he said. His mother and father, his cousins, his aunts and uncles, his sister, his sister's friends, and even himself, a scrawny fourteen-year-old with his protruding Adam's apple, flattop haircut, and red clip-on bow tie. It wasn't like looking at normal photographs, he explained. It wasn't even like looking at home movies – which always disappoint you with their jerky images and washed-out colors, their sense of belonging to the remote past. The 3-D pictures were incredibly well preserved, supernaturally sharp. Everyone in them looked alive, brimming with energy, present in the moment, a part of some eternal now that had gone on perpetuating itself for close to thirty years. Intense colors, the minutest details shining in utmost clarity, and an illusion of surrounding space, of depth. The longer he looked at the slides, Richard said, the more he felt that he could see the figures breathing, and every time he stopped and went on to the next one, he had the impression that if he'd looked a little longer – just one more moment – they actually would have started to move.

'After he'd looked at each slide once, he looked at them all again, and the second time around it gradually occurred to him that most of the people in the pictures were now dead. His father, killed by a heart attack in 1969. His mother, killed by kidney failure in 1972. Tina, killed by cancer in 1974. And of his six aunts and uncles in attendance that day, four of them dead and buried as well. In one picture, he was standing on the front lawn with his parents and Tina. It was just the four of them – arms linked, leaning into one another, a row of four smiling faces, ridiculously animated, mugging for the camera – and when Richard put that one into the viewer for the second time, his eyes suddenly filled with tears. That was the one that did him in, he said, the one that was too much for him. He was standing on the lawn with three ghosts, he realized, the only survivor from that afternoon thirty years ago, and once the tears started, there was nothing he could do to stop them. He put down the viewer, lifted his hands over his face, and began to sob. That was the word he used when he told me the story: *sob*. 'I sobbed my guts out,' he said. 'I completely lost it.'

'This was Richard, remember – a man with no poetry in him, a man with the sensitivity of a doorknob – and yet once he found those pictures, he couldn't think about anything else. The viewer was a magic lantern that allowed him to travel through time and visit the dead. He would look at the pictures in the morning before he left for work, and he would look at them in the evening after he came home. Always in the garage, always by himself, always away from his wife and children – obsessively returning to that afternoon in

1953, unable to get enough of it. The spell lasted for two months, and then one morning Richard went into the garage and the viewer didn't work. The machine had jammed up, and he couldn't depress the button anymore to turn on the light. He'd probably used it too much, he said, and since he didn't know how to fix it, he assumed the adventure was over, that the marvelous thing he'd discovered had been taken away from him for good. It was a catastrophic loss, the cruelest of deprivations. He couldn't even look at the slides by holding them up to the light. Three-D pictures aren't conventional photographs, and you need the viewer to translate them into coherent images. No viewer, no image. No image, no more time travel into the past. No more time travel, no more joy. Another round of grief, another round of sorrow – as if, after bringing them back to life, he had to bury the dead all over again.

'That was the situation when I saw him two weeks ago. The machine was broken, and Richard was still trying to come to grips with what had happened to him. I can't tell you how touched I was by his story. To see this bumbling, ordinary man turned into a philosophical dreamer, an anguished soul longing for the unattainable. I told him I'd do anything I could to help. This is New York, I said, and since everything in the world can be found in New York, there has to be someone in the city who can fix it. Richard was a little embarrassed by my enthusiasm, but he thanked me for the offer, and that was where we left it. The next morning, I got busy. I called around, did some research, and within a day or two I'd tracked down the owner of a camera shop on West Thirty-first Street who thought he could do it. Richard was back in Florida by then, and when I called him that night to tell him the news, I thought he'd be excited, that we'd immediately start talking about how to pack up the viewer and ship it to New York. But there was a long pause on the other end of the line. "I don't know, John," Richard finally said. "I've thought about it a lot since I saw you, and maybe it's not such a good idea for me to be looking at those pictures all the time. Arlene was getting pretty upset, and I wasn't really paying much attention to the girls. Maybe it's better this way. You have to live in the present, right? The past is past, and no matter how much time I spend with those pictures, I'm never going to get it back."'

That was the end of the story. A disappointing end, John felt, but Grace disagreed with him. After communing with the dead for two months, Richard had put himself in danger, she said, and was perhaps running the risk of falling into a serious depression. I was about to say something then, but just as I opened my mouth to offer my opinion, I got another one of my infernal nosebleeds. They had started a month or two before I was put in the hospital, and even though most of my other symptoms had cleared up by now, the nosebleeds had persisted – always striking at the most inopportune moments, it seemed, and never failing to cause me intense embarrassment. I hated not to be in control of myself, to be sitting in a room as I was that night, for example, taking part in a conversation, and then suddenly to notice that blood was pouring out of me, splattering onto my shirt and pants, and not being able to do a damn thing to stop it. The doctors had told me not to worry – there were no medical consequences, no signs of impending trouble – but that didn't make me feel any less helpless or ashamed. Every time my nose gushed blood, I felt like a little boy who'd wet his pants.

I jumped out of the chair, pressed a handkerchief against my face, and hustled toward the nearest bathroom. Grace asked if I wanted any help, and I must have given her a somewhat peevish answer, although I can't remember what I said. 'Don't bother,' perhaps, or 'Leave me alone.' Something with enough irritation in it to amuse John, in any case, for I can distinctly remember hearing him laugh as I left the room. 'Old Faithful strikes again,' he said. 'Orr's menstruating schnozz. Don't let it get you down, Sidney. At least you know you're not pregnant.'

35

There were two bathrooms in the apartment, one on each level of the duplex. Normally, we would have spent the evening downstairs in the dining room and living room, but John's phlebitic leg had pushed us up to the second floor, since that was where he was spending most of his time now. The upstairs room was a kind of supplementary parlor, a cozy little spot with large bay windows, bookshelves lining three of the walls, and built-in spaces for stereo equipment and TV – the perfect enclave for a recovering invalid. The bathroom on that floor was just off John's bedroom, and in order to reach the bedroom I had to walk through his study, the place where he wrote. I switched on the light when I entered that room, but I was too involved with my nose-bleed to pay any attention to what was in it. I must have spent fifteen minutes in the bathroom squeezing my nostrils and tilting back my head, and until those old remedies began to work, so much liquid flowed out of me that I wondered if I wouldn't have to go to the hospital for an emergency transfusion. How red the blood looked against the whiteness of the porcelain sink, I thought. How vividly imagined that color was, how aesthetically shocking. The other fluids that came out of us were dull in comparison, the palest of squirts. Whitish spittle, milky semen, yellow pee, green-brown mucus. We excreted autumn and winter colors, but running invisibly through our veins, the very stuff that kept us alive, was the crimson of a mad artist – a red as brilliant as fresh paint.

After the attack was over, I lingered at the sink for a while, doing what I could to make myself presentable again. It was too late to remove the spots from my clothes (which had hardened into small rusty circles that smeared across the fabric when I tried to rub them out), but I gave my hands and face a thorough washing and wet down my hair, using John's comb to complete the job. I was feeling a bit less sorry for myself by then, a bit less battered. My shirt and pants were still adorned with ugly polka dots, but the river wasn't

36

flowing anymore, and the stinging in my nose had mercifully abated.

As I walked through John's bedroom and entered his
study, I glanced over at his desk. I wasn't really looking
there, just casting my eyes around the room as I headed for
the door, but lying out in full view, surrounded by an assort-
ment of pens, pencils, and messy stacks of paper, there was
a blue hardbound notebook – remarkably similar to the one
I'd bought in Brooklyn that morning. A writer's desk is a
holy place, the most private sanctuary in the world, and
strangers aren't allowed to approach it without permission.
I had never gone near John's desk before, but I was so startled, so curious to know if that notebook was the same as
mine, that I forgot my discretion and went over to have a
look. The notebook was closed, lying faceup on a small dictionary, and the moment I bent down to examine it, I saw
that it was the exact double of the one lying on my desk at
home. For reasons that still baffle me, I became enormously
excited by this discovery. What difference did it make what
kind of notebook John used? He had lived in Portugal for a
couple of years, and no doubt they were a common item
over there, available in any run-of-the-mill stationery store.
Why shouldn't he be writing in a blue hardbound notebook
that had been manufactured in Portugal? No reason, no reason at all – and yet, given the deliciously pleasant sensations
I'd felt that morning when I'd bought my own blue notebook, and given that I'd spent several productive hours
writing in it earlier that day (my first literary efforts in close
to a year), and given that I'd been thinking about those
efforts all through the evening at John's, it hit me as a
startling conjunction, a little piece of black magic.

I wasn't planning to mention it when I returned to the sitting room. It was too nutty, somehow, too idiosyncratic and
personal, and I didn't want to give John the impression that
I was in the habit of snooping into his things. But when I
walked into the room and saw him lying on the sofa with his

leg up, staring at the ceiling with a grim, defeated look in his eyes, I suddenly changed my mind. Grace was downstairs in the kitchen, washing dishes and disposing of leftovers from our take-out meal, and so I sat down in the chair she had been occupying, which happened to be just to the right of the sofa, a couple of feet from John's head. He asked if I was feeling any better. Yes, I replied, much better, and then I leaned forward and said to him, 'The strangest thing happened to me today. When I was out on my morning walk, I went into a store and bought a notebook. It was such an excellent notebook, such an attractive and appealing little thing, that it made me want to write again. And so the minute I got home, I sat down at my desk and wrote in it for two straight hours.'

'That's good news, Sidney,' John said. 'You're starting to work again.'

'The Flitcraft episode.'

'Ah, even better.'

'We'll see. It's just some rough notes so far, nothing to get excited about. But the notebook seems to have charged me up, and I can't wait to write in it again tomorrow. It's dark blue, a very pleasant shade of dark blue, with a cloth strip running down the spine and a hard cover. Made in Portugal, of all places.'

'Portugal?'

'I don't know which city. But there's a little label on the inside back cover that says MADE IN PORTUGAL.'

'How on earth did you find one of those things here?'

'There's a new shop in my neighborhood. The Paper Palace, owned by a man named Chang. He had four of them in stock.'

'I used to buy those notebooks on my trips down to Lisbon. They're very good, very solid. Once you start using them, you don't feel like writing in anything else.'

'I had that same feeling today. I hope it doesn't mean I'm about to become addicted.'

'Addiction might be too strong a word, but there's no question that they're extremely seductive. Be careful, Sid. I've been writing in them for years, and I know what I'm talking about.'

'You make it sound as if they're dangerous.'

'It depends on what you write. Those notebooks are very friendly, but they can also be cruel, and you have to watch out that you don't get lost in them.'

'You don't look lost to me – and I just saw one lying on your desk when I left the bathroom.'

'I bought a big supply before I moved back to New York. Unfortunately, the one you saw is the last one I have, and I've almost filled it up. I didn't know you could get them in America. I was thinking of writing to the manufacturer and ordering some more.'

'The man in the shop told me that the company's gone out of business.'

'Just my luck. But I'm not surprised. Apparently there wasn't much of a demand for them.'

'I can pick one up for you on Monday, if you want.'

'Are there any blue ones left?'

'Black, red, and brown. I bought the last blue one.'

'Too bad. Blue is the only color I like. Now that the company's gone, I guess I'll have to start developing some new habits.'

'It's funny, but when I looked over the pile this morning, I went straight for the blue myself. I felt drawn to that one, as if I couldn't resist it. What do you think that means?'

'It doesn't mean anything, Sid. Except that you're a little off in the head. And I'm just as off as you are. We write books, don't we? What else can you expect from people like us?'

Saturday nights in New York are always crowded, but that night the streets were even more packed than usual, and what with one delay and another, it took us over an hour to get home. Grace managed to flag down a cab right outside John's door, but when we climbed in and told the driver we were going to Brooklyn, he made some excuse about being low on gas and wouldn't accept the fare. I wanted to make a stink about it, but Grace took hold of my arm and gently pulled me out of the cab. Nothing materialized after that, so we walked over to Seventh Avenue, threading our way past gangs of raucous, drunken kids and half a dozen demented panhandlers. The Village was percolating with energy that night, a madhouse jangle that seemed ready to erupt into violence at any moment, and I found it exhausting to be out among those crowds, trying to keep my balance as I clung to Grace's arm. We stood at the corner of Barrow and Seventh for a good ten minutes before an empty taxi approached us, and Grace must have apologized six times for having forced me out of the other one. 'I'm sorry I didn't let you put up a fight,' she said. 'It's my fault. The last thing you need is to be standing out in this chill, but I hate to argue with stupid people. It makes me too upset.'

But Grace wasn't only upset by stupid cabdrivers that night. A few moments after we got into the second taxi, she inexplicably began to cry. Not on a large scale, not with some breathless outrush of sobs, but the tears started gathering in the corners of her eyes, and when we stopped at Clarkson for a red light, the glare of the street lamps swept into the cab, and I could see the tears glistening in the brightness, welling up in her eyes like small expanding crystals. Grace never broke down like that. Grace never cried or gave way to excessive shows of feeling, and even at her most stressful moments (during my collapse, for example, and all through the desperate early weeks of my stay in the hospital), she seemed to have an inborn talent for holding herself together, for facing up to the darkest truths. I asked her what was wrong, but she only shook her head and turned away. When I put my hand on her shoulder and asked again, she shrugged me off – which was something she had never done before. It wasn't a terribly hostile gesture, but again, it was unlike Grace to act that way, and I admit that I felt a little stung by it. Not wanting to impose myself on her or let her know I'd been hurt, I withdrew to my corner of the backseat and waited in silence as the cab inched southward along Seventh Avenue. When we came to the intersection at Varick and Canal, we were stalled in traffic for several minutes. It was a monumental jam-up: honking cars and trucks, drivers shouting obscenities at one another, New York mayhem in its purest form. In the middle of all that ruckus and confusion, Grace abruptly turned to me and apologized. 'It's just that he looked so terrible tonight,' she said, 'so done-in. All the men I love are falling apart. It's getting to be a little hard to take.'

I didn't believe her. My body was on the mend, and it seemed implausible that Grace would have been so disheartened by John's fleeting leg ailment. Something else was troubling her, some private torment she wasn't willing to share with me, but I knew that if I kept on hounding her to open up, it would only make things worse. I reached out and put my arm around her shoulder, then drew her slowly toward me. There was no resistance in her this time. I felt her muscles relax, and a moment later she was curling up beside me and leaning her head against my chest. I put my hand on her forehead and began stroking her hair with the flat of my palm. It was an old ritual of ours, the expression of some wordless intimacy that continued to define who we were together, and because I never grew tired of touching Grace, never grew tired of having my hands on some part of her body, I kept on doing it, repeating the gesture dozens of times as we made our way down West Broadway and crept toward the Brooklyn Bridge.

We didn't say anything to each other for several minutes. By the time the cab turned left on Chambers Street and started to approach the bridge, every ramp was clogged with traffic, and we could hardly advance at all. Our driver, whose name was Boris Stepanovich, muttered curses to himself in Russian, no doubt lamenting the folly of trying to cross over to Brooklyn on a Saturday night. I leaned forward and talked to him through the money slot in the scarred Plexiglas partition. Don't worry, I said, your patience will be rewarded. Oh? he said. And what means that? A big tip, I answered. As long as you get us there in one piece, you'll have your biggest tip of the night.

Grace let out a small laugh when she heard the malapropism – *What means that?* – and I took it as a sign that her funk was lifting. I settled back into the seat to resume stroking her head, and as we mounted the roadway of the bridge, crawling along at one mile an hour, suspended over the river with a blaze of buildings behind us and the Statue of Liberty off to our right, I started to talk to her – to talk for no other reason than to talk – in order to hold her attention and prevent her from drifting away from me again.

'I made an intriguing discovery tonight,' I said.

'Something good, I hope.'

'I discovered that John and I have the same passion.'

'Oh?'

'It turns out that we're both in love with the color blue. In particular, a defunct line of blue notebooks that used to be made in Portugal.'

'Well, blue is a good color. Very calm, very serene. It sits well in the mind. I like it so much, I have to make a conscious effort not to use it on all the covers I design at work.'

'Do colors really convey emotions?'

'Of course they do.'

'And moral qualities?'

'In what way?'

'Yellow for cowardice. White for purity. Black for evil. Green for innocence.'

'Green for envy.'

'Yes, that too. But what does blue stand for?'

'I don't know. Hope, maybe.'

'And sadness. As in, I'm feeling blue. Or, I've got the blues.'

'Don't forget *true blue*.'

'Yes, you're right. Blue for loyalty.'

'But red for passion. Everyone agrees on that.'

'The Big Red Machine. The red flag of socialism.'

'The white flag of surrender.'

'The black flag of anarchism. The Green Party.'

'But red for love and hate. Red for war.'

'You carry the colors when you go into battle. That's the phrase, isn't it?'

'I think so.'

'Are you familiar with the term *color war*?'

'It doesn't ring any bells.'

'It comes from my childhood. You spent your summers riding horses in Virginia, but my mother sent me to a sleepaway camp in upstate New York. Camp Pontiac, named after the Indian chief. At the end of the summer, they'd divide everyone into two teams, and for the next four or five days different groups from the two sides would compete against one another.'

'Compete at what?'

'Baseball, basketball, tennis, swimming, tug-of-war – even egg-and-spoon races and singing contests. Since the camp colors were red and white, one side was called the Red Team and the other was called the White Team.'

'And that's color war.'

'For a sports maniac like me, it was terrific fun. Some years I was on the White Team and other years on the Red. After a while, though, a third team was formed, a kind of secret society, a brotherhood of kindred souls. I haven't thought about it in years, but it was very important to me at the time. The Blue Team.'

'A secret brotherhood. It sounds like silly boys' stuff to me.'

'It was. No . . . actually it wasn't. When I think about it now, I don't find it silly at all.'

43

'You must have been different then. You never want to join anything.'

'I didn't join, I was chosen. As one of the charter members, in fact. I felt very honored.'

'You're already on Red and White. What's so special about Blue?'

'It started when I was fourteen. A new counselor came to the camp that year, someone a little older than the rest of the people on the staff – who were mostly nineteen- and twenty-year-old college students. Bruce . . . Bruce something . . . the last name will come to me later. Bruce had his BA and had already finished a year at Columbia Law School. A scrawny, gnomish little guy, a strict nonathlete working at a camp devoted to sports. But sharp-witted and funny, always challenging you with difficult questions. Adler. That's it. Bruce Adler. Commonly known as the Rabbi.'

'And he invented the Blue Team?'

'Sort of. To be more exact, he re-created it as an exercise in nostalgia.'

'I don't follow.'

'A few years earlier, he'd worked as a counselor at another camp. The colors of that camp were blue and gray. When color war broke out at the end of summer, Bruce was put on the Blue Team, and when he looked around and saw who was on the team with him, he realized it was everyone he liked, everyone he most respected. The Gray Team was just the opposite – filled with whining, unpleasant people, the dregs of the camp. In Bruce's mind, the words *Blue Team* came to stand for something more than just a bunch of rinky-dink relay races. They represented a human ideal, a tight-knit association of tolerant and sympathetic individuals, the dream of a perfect society.'

'This is getting pretty strange, Sid.'

'I know. But Bruce didn't take it seriously. That was the beauty of the Blue Team. The whole thing was kind of a joke.'

'I didn't know rabbis were allowed to make jokes.'

'They probably aren't. But Bruce wasn't a rabbi. He was just a law student with a summer job, looking for a little entertainment. When he came to work at our camp, he told one of the other counselors about the Blue Team, and together they decided to form a new branch, to reinvent it as a secret organization.'

'How did they choose you?'

'In the middle of the night. I was fast asleep in my bed, and Bruce and the other counselor shook me awake. "Come on," they said, "we have something to tell you," and then they led me and two other boys into the woods with flashlights. They had a little campfire going, and so we sat around the fire and they told us what the Blue Team was, why they had selected us as charter members, and what qualifications they were looking for – in case we wanted to recommend other candidates.'

'What were they?'

'Nothing specific, really. Blue Team members didn't conform to a single type, and each one was a distinct and independent person. But no one was allowed in who didn't have a good sense of humor – however that humor might have expressed itself. Some people crack jokes all the time; others can lift an eyebrow at the right moment and suddenly everyone in the room is rolling on the floor. A good sense of humor, then, a taste for the ironies of life, and an appreciation of the absurd. But also a certain modesty and discretion, kindness toward others, a generous heart. No blowhards or arrogant fools, no liars or thieves. A Blue Team member had to be curious, a reader of books, and aware of the fact that he couldn't bend the world to the shape of his will. An astute observer, someone capable of making fine moral distinctions, a lover of justice. A Blue Team member would give you the shirt off his back if he saw you were in need, but he would much rather slip a ten-dollar bill into your pocket when you weren't looking. Is it beginning to make sense? I can't pin it down for you and say it's one thing or another.

45

It's all of them at once, each separate part interacting with all the others.'

'What you're describing is a good person. Pure and simple. My father's term for it is *honest man*. Betty Stolowitz uses the word *mensch*. John says *not an asshole*. They're all the same thing.'

'Maybe. But I like *Blue Team* better. It implies a connection among the members, a bond of solidarity. If you're on the Blue Team, you don't have to explain your principles. They're immediately understood by how you act.'

'But people don't always act the same way. They're good one minute and bad the next. They make mistakes. Good people do bad things, Sid.'

'Of course they do. I'm not talking about perfection.'

'Yes you are. You're talking about people who've decided they're better than other people, who feel morally superior to the rest of us common folk. I'll bet you and your friends had a secret handshake, didn't you? To set you apart from the riffraff and the dumbbells, right? To make you think you had some special knowledge no one else was smart enough to have.'

'Jesus, Grace. It was just a little thing from twenty years ago. You don't have to break it down and analyze it.'

'But you still believe in that junk. I can hear it in your voice.'

'I don't believe in anything. Being alive – that's what I believe in. Being alive and being with you. That's all there is for me, Grace. There's nothing else, not a single thing in the whole goddamn world.'

It was a dispiriting way for the conversation to end. My not-so-subtle attempt to tease her out of her dark mood had worked for a while, but then I'd pushed her too far, accidentally touching on the wrong subject, and she'd turned on me with that caustic denunciation. It was entirely out of character for her to talk with such belligerence. Grace seldom got herself worked up over issues of that sort, and whenever we'd had similar discussions in the past (those floating, meandering dialogues that aren't about anything, that just dance along from one random association to the next), she'd tended to be amused by the notions I'd toss out at her, rarely taking them seriously or presenting a counterargument, content to play along and let me spout my meaningless opinions. But not that night, not on the night of the day in question, and because she was suddenly fighting back tears again, engulfed by the same unhappiness that had swept over her at the beginning of the ride, I understood that she was in genuine distress, unable to stop brooding about the nameless thing that was tormenting her. There were a dozen questions I wanted to ask, but again I held back, knowing that she wouldn't confide in me until she was good and ready to talk – assuming she ever was.

We had made it over the bridge by then and were traveling down Henry Street, a narrow thoroughfare flanked by red-brick walkups that led from Brooklyn Heights to our place in Cobble Hill, just below Atlantic Avenue. It wasn't personal, I realized. Grace's little outburst hadn't been against me so much as a reaction to what I'd said – a spark produced by an accidental collision between my comments and her own train of thought. *Good people do bad things.* Had Grace done something wrong? Had someone close to her done something wrong? It was impossible to know, but someone felt guilty about something, I decided, and even though my words had triggered Grace's defensive remarks, I was fairly certain they had nothing to do with me. As if to prove that point, a moment after we crossed Atlantic Avenue and headed into the final leg of the journey, Grace reached out her hand and took hold of the back of my neck, then pulled me toward her and pressed her mouth against mine, slowly pushing in her tongue for a long, provocative kiss – *a full-bore osculation*, as Trause had put it. 'Make love to me tonight,' she whispered. 'The second we walk through the door, tear off my clothes and make love to me. Break me in two, Sid.'

*

47

We slept late the next morning, not climbing out of bed until eleven-thirty or twelve. One of Grace's cousins was in town for the day, and they were planning to meet at the Guggenheim at two, then work their way down to the Met for a few hours in the permanent collection. Looking at paintings was Grace's preferred weekend activity, and she scrambled out of the house at one in reasonably tranquil spirits.[6] I offered to walk her to the subway, but she was already running late by then, and since the station was a good distance from the house (all the way up on Montague Street), she didn't want me to overexert myself by having to walk so many blocks at too fast a pace. I accompanied her down the stairs and out onto the street, but at the first corner we said good-bye and walked off in opposite directions.

---

6. Much of her graphic work was inspired by looking at art, and before my collapse at the beginning of the year, we had often spent our Saturday afternoons wandering in and out of galleries and museums together. In some sense, art had made our marriage possible, and without the intervention of art, I doubt that I would have found the courage to pursue her. It was fortunate that we had met in the neutral surroundings of Holst & McDermott, a so-called work environment. If we had been thrown together in any other way – at a dinner party, for example, or on a bus or a plane – I wouldn't have been able to contact her again without exposing my intentions, and I instinctively felt that Grace had to be approached with caution. If I tipped my hand too early, I was almost certain I would lose my chance with her forever.

Luckily, I had an excuse to call. She had been assigned to work on the cover of my book, and under the pretext of having a new idea to discuss with her, I rang up her office two days after our initial meeting and asked if I could come in and see her. 'Anytime you like,' she said. *Anytime* proved to be difficult to arrange. I had a regular job then (teaching history at John Jay High School in Brooklyn), and I couldn't make it to her office before four o'clock. As it happened, Grace's agenda was clogged with late-afternoon appointments for the rest of the week. When she suggested that we meet the following Monday or Tuesday, I told her I was going out of town to give a reading (which happened to be true, but I probably would have said it even if it

Grace sped up Court Street toward the Heights, and I ambled down a few blocks to Landolfi's Candy Store and bought a pack of cigarettes. That was the extent of my constitutional for the day. I was eager to return to the blue notebook, and so rather than take my usual walk around the neighborhood, I immediately turned around and went home. Ten minutes later, I was in the apartment, sitting at my desk in the room at the end of the hall. I opened the notebook, turned to the page where I had left off on Saturday, and settled down to work. I didn't bother to read over what I had written so far. I just picked up the pen and started to write.

Bowen is on the plane, flying through the dark toward Kansas City. After the whirlwind of falling gargoyles and

---

wasn't), so Grace relented and offered to squeeze in some time for me after work on Friday. 'I have to be somewhere at eight,' she said, 'but if we met for an hour or so at five-thirty, it shouldn't be a problem.'

I had stolen the title of my book from a 1938 pencil drawing by Willem de Kooning. *Self-Portrait with Imaginary Brother* is a small, delicately rendered piece that depicts two boys standing side by side, one a year or two older than the other, one in long pants, the other in knickers. Much as I admired the drawing, it was the title that interested me, and I had used it not because I wanted to refer to de Kooning but because of the words themselves, which I found highly evocative and which seemed to fit the novel I had written. In Betty Stolowitz's office earlier that week, I had suggested putting de Kooning's drawing on the cover. Now I was planning to tell Grace that I thought it was a bad idea – that the pencil strokes were too faint and wouldn't be visible enough, that the effect would be too muted. But I didn't really care. If I had argued against the drawing in Betty's office, I would have been for it now. All I wanted was a chance to see Grace again – and art was my way in, the one subject that wouldn't compromise my true purpose.

Her willingness to see me after office hours gave me hope, but at the same time the news that she was going out at eight o'clock all but destroyed that hope. There was little question that she had an appointment with a man (attractive women are always with a man on Friday night), but it was impossible to know how deeply connected

reckless dashes to the airport, a sense of growing calm, a serene blankness within. Bowen doesn't question what he is doing. He has no regrets, doesn't rethink his decision to leave town and abandon his job, feels not the slightest pang of remorse about walking out on Eva. He knows how hard it will be on her, but he manages to persuade himself that she'll be better off without him in the end, that once she recovers from the shock of his disappearance, it will be possible for her to begin a new, more satisfying life. Hardly an admirable or sympathetic position, but Bowen is in the grip of an idea, and that idea is so large, so much bigger than his own paltry wants and obligations, that he feels he has no choice but to obey it – even at the cost of acting irresponsibly, of doing things that would have been morally repug-

---

she was to him. It could have been a first date, and it could have been a quiet dinner with her fiancé or live-in boyfriend. I knew she wasn't married (Betty had told me as much after Grace left her office following our first meeting), but the range of other intimacies was boundless. When I asked Betty if Grace was involved with anyone, she said she didn't know. Grace kept her private life to herself, and no one in the company had the smallest inkling of what she did outside the office. Two or three editors had asked her out since she'd started working there, but she'd turned them all down.

I quickly learned that Grace was not someone who shared confidences. In the ten months I knew her before we were married, she never once divulged a secret or hinted at any prior entanglements with other men. Nor did I ever ask her to tell me something she didn't seem willing to talk about. That was the power of Grace's silence. If you meant to love her in the way she demanded to be loved, then you had to accept the line she'd drawn between herself and words.

(Once, in an early conversation I had with her about her childhood, she reminisced about a favorite doll her parents had given her when she was seven. She named her Pearl, carried her everywhere for the next four or five years, and considered her to be her best friend. The remarkable thing about Pearl was that she was able to talk and understood everything that was said to her. But Pearl never uttered a word in Grace's presence. Not because she couldn't speak, but because she chose not to.)

nant to him just one day before. 'Men died at haphazard,' is how Hammett expressed the idea, 'and lived only while blind chance spared them. . . . In sensibly ordering his affairs [Flitcraft] had got out of step, and not into step, with life. He knew before he had gone twenty feet from the fallen beam that he would never know peace again until he had adjusted himself to this new glimpse of life. By the time he had eaten his luncheon he had found his means of adjustment. Life could be ended for him at random by a falling beam: he would change his life at random by simply going away.'

I didn't have to approve of Bowen's actions in order to write about them. Bowen was Flitcraft, and Flitcraft had done the same thing to his own wife in Hammett's novel.

There was someone in her life at the time I met her – I'm sure of that – but I never learned his name or how seriously she felt about him. Quite seriously, I would imagine, for the first six months proved to be a tempestuous time for me, and they ended badly, with Grace telling me she wanted to break it off and that I shouldn't call her anymore. Through all the disappointments of those months, however, all the ephemeral victories and tiny surges of optimism, the rebuffs and capitulations, the nights when she was too busy to see me and the nights when she allowed me to share her bed, through all the ups and downs of that desperate, failed courtship, Grace was always an enchanted being for me, a luminous point of contact between desire and the world, the implacable love. I kept my word and didn't call her, but six or seven weeks later she contacted me out of the blue and said she had changed her mind. She didn't offer any explanation, but I gathered that the man who had been my rival was now out of the picture. Not only did she want to start seeing me again, she said, but she wanted us to get married. *Marriage* was the one word I had never spoken in her presence. It had been in my head from the first moment I saw her, but I had never dared to say it, for fear it would frighten her off. Now Grace was proposing to me. I had resigned myself to living out the rest of my life with a shattered heart, and now she was telling me I could live with her instead – in one piece, my whole life in one piece with her.

That was the premise of the story, and I wasn't about to back down from the bargain I'd made with myself to stick to the premise of the story. At the same time, I understood that there was more to it than just Bowen and what happens to him after he boards the plane. There was Eva to consider as well, and no matter how wrapped up I became in following Nick's adventures in Kansas City, I wouldn't be doing the story justice unless I returned to New York and explored what was happening to her. Her fate was just as important to me as her husband's. Bowen is in search of indifference, a tranquil affirmation of things-as-they-are, whereas Eva is at war with those things, a victim of circumstances, and from the moment Nick fails to return from his errand around the corner, her mind becomes a storm field of conflicting emotions: panic and fear, sorrow and anger, despair. I relished the prospect of entering that misery, of knowing that I would be able to live those passions with her and write about them in the days ahead.

Half an hour after the plane takes off from La Guardia, Nick opens his briefcase, slides out the manuscript of Sylvia Maxwell's novel, and begins to read. That was the third element of the narrative that was taking shape in my head, and I decided that it should be introduced as early as possible – even before the plane lands in Kansas City. First, Nick's story; then, Eva's story; and finally, the book that Nick reads and continues to read as their stories unfold: the story within the story. Nick is a literary man, after all, and therefore someone susceptible to the power of books. Little by little, by force of the attention he brings to Sylvia Maxwell's words, he begins to see a connection between himself and the story in the novel, as if in some oblique, highly metaphorical way, the book were speaking intimately to him about his own present circumstances.

At that point, I had only the dimmest notion of what I wanted *Oracle Night* to be, no more than the first tentative tracings of an outline. Everything still had to be worked out concerning the plot, but I knew that it was supposed to be a brief philosophical novel about predicting the future, a fable about time. The protagonist is Lemuel Flagg, a British lieutenant blinded by a mortar explosion in the trenches of World War I. Bleeding from his wounds, disoriented and howling in pain, he wanders off from the battle and loses contact with his regiment. Thrashing forward, stumbling, with no idea where he is, he enters the Ardennes Forest and collapses to the ground. Later that same day, his unconscious body is discovered by two French children, an eleven-year-old boy and a fourteen-year-old girl, François and Geneviève. They are war orphans who live on their own in an abandoned hut in the middle of the woods – pure fairy-tale characters in a pure fairy-tale setting. They carry Flagg home and nurse him back to health, and when the war ends a few months later, he takes the children back to England with him. It is Geneviève who narrates the story, looking back from the vantage of 1927 at the strange career and eventual suicide of her adoptive father. Flagg's blindness has given him the gift of prophecy. In sudden trancelike fits, he falls to the ground and begins flailing about like an epileptic. The seizures last from eight to ten minutes, and for the length of the time they endure, his mind is overrun with images of the future. The spells come upon him without warning, and there is nothing he can do to stop them or control them. His talent is both a curse and a blessing. It brings him wealth and influence, but at the same time the attacks cause him intense physical pain – not to speak of mental pain, since many of Flagg's visions furnish him with knowledge of things he would prefer not to know. The day of his mother's death, for example, or the site of a train wreck in India where two hundred people will be killed. He struggles to lead an unobtrusive life with his children, but the astonishing accuracy of his predictions (which range from weather forecasts to the results of Parliamentary elections to the scores of cricket test matches) turns him into one of the most celebrated men in postwar Britain. Then, at the peak of his fame, things begin to go wrong for him in love, and his talent ends up destroying him. He falls for a woman named Bettina Knott, and for two years she reciprocates his love, even to the point of accepting his proposal of marriage. On the night before their wedding, however, Flagg has another one of his spells, during which he is visited by the knowledge that Bettina will betray him before the year is out. His predictions have never been wrong, and therefore he knows the marriage is doomed. The tragedy is that Bettina is innocent, utterly free of guilt, since she has not yet met the man she will betray her husband with. Unable to face the anguish that destiny has prepared for him, Flagg stabs himself in the heart and dies.

The plane lands. Bowen puts the half-read manuscript back into his briefcase, walks out of the terminal, and finds a cab. He knows nothing about Kansas City. He has never been there, has never met anyone who lives within a hundred miles of the place, and would be hard-pressed to point to it on a blank map. He asks the driver to take him to the best hotel in town, and the driver, a corpulent black man with the unlikely name of Ed Victory, bursts out laughing. I hope you're not superstitious, he says.

Superstitious? Nick replies. What's that got to do with it?

You want the best hotel. That would be the Hyatt Regency. I don't know if you read the papers, but there was a big disaster at the Hyatt about a year ago. The suspended walkways came loose from the ceiling. They crashed down into the lobby, and over a hundred people got themselves killed.

Yes, I remember that. There was a photo on the front page of the *Times*.

The place is open again now, but some folks feel pretty squeamish about staying there. If you're not squeamish, and if you're not superstitious, that's the hotel I'd recommend.

All right, Nick says. The Hyatt it is. I've already been

struck by lightning once today. If it wants to hit me again, it will know where to find me.[7]

Ed laughs at Nick's answer, and the two men continue talking as they drive into the city. It turns out that Ed is about to retire from the taxi business. He's been at it for thirty-four years, and tonight is his last night on the job. This is his last shift, his last airport run, and Bowen is his last fare – the final passenger who will ever travel in his cab. Nick asks what he plans on doing now to keep himself occupied, and Edward M. Victory (for that is the man's full name) reaches into his shirt pocket, pulls out a business card, and hands it to Nick. BUREAU OF HISTORICAL PRESERVATION is what the card says – with Ed's name, address, and phone number printed at the bottom. Nick is about to ask what the words mean, but before he can form the question, the car pulls up in front of the hotel, and Ed holds out his hand to receive the last fare that will ever be given to him. Bowen adds a twenty-dollar tip to the amount, wishes the now-retired taxi driver good luck, and walks through the revolving doors into the lobby of the ill-fated hotel.

Because he is low on cash and has to pay with a credit card, Nick registers under his own name. The reconstructed

---

7. Kansas City was an arbitrary choice for Bowen's destination – the first place that popped into my head. Possibly because it was so remote from New York, a town locked in the center of the heartland: Oz in all its glorious strangeness. Once I had Nick on his way to Kansas City, however, I remembered the Hyatt Regency catastrophe, which was a real event that had taken place fourteen months earlier (in July 1981). Close to two thousand people had been gathered in the lobby at the time – an immense open-air atrium of some seventeen thousand square feet. They were all looking up, watching a dance contest that was being held in one of the upstairs walkways (also referred to as 'floating walkways' or 'skyways'), when the wide flange beams supporting the structure broke loose from their moorings and collapsed, crashing down into the lobby four stories below. Twenty-one years later, it is still considered one of the worst hotel disasters in American history.

lobby looks as if it's just a few days old, and Nick can't help thinking that he and the hotel are more or less in the same situation: both of them trying to forget their pasts, both of them trying to begin a new life. The glittering palace with its transparent elevators and immense chandeliers and burnished metallic walls, and he with nothing but the clothes on his back, two credit cards in his wallet, and a half-read novel in his leather bag. He splurges on a suite, rides the elevator up to the tenth floor, and doesn't come down again for thirty-six hours. Naked under his hotel robe, he eats room service meals, stands by the window, studies himself in the bathroom mirror, and reads Sylvia Maxwell's book. He finishes it that first night before going to bed, and then he spends the entire next day reading it again, and then again, and then a fourth time, plowing through its two hundred and nineteen pages as if his very life depended on it. The story of Lemuel Flagg affects him deeply, but Bowen doesn't read *Oracle Night* because he is looking to be moved or entertained, and he doesn't immerse himself in the novel in order to put off making a decision about what to do next. He knows what he has to do next, and the book is the only means at hand with which to do it. He has to train himself not to think about the past. That's the key to the whole mad adventure that started for him when the gargoyle crashed to the sidewalk. If he has lost his old life, then he must act as if he has just been born, pretend that he is no more burdened by the past than an infant is. He has memories, of course, but those memories are no longer relevant, no longer a part of the life that has begun for him, and whenever he finds himself drifting into thoughts about his old life in New York – which has been erased, which is nothing more than illusion now – he does everything in his power to turn his mind from the past and concentrate on the present. That is why he reads the book. That is why he keeps reading the book. He must lure himself away from the false memories of a life that no longer belongs to him, and because the manuscript demands total surrender in order to be read, an unremitting attentiveness of both body and mind, he can forget who he was when he is lost in the pages of the novel.

On the third day, Nick finally ventures outside. He walks down the street, enters a men's clothing store, and spends the next hour browsing among the racks, shelves, and bins. Little by little, he pieces together a new wardrobe for himself, loading up on everything from pants and shirts to underwear and socks. When he hands the clerk his American Express card to pay the bill, however, the machine rejects the card. The account has been canceled, the clerk informs him. Nick is thrown by this unexpected development, but he pretends to take it in his stride. It doesn't matter, he says. I'll pay with my Visa card. But when the clerk swipes that one through the machine, it proves to be invalid as well. It's an embarrassing moment for Nick. He wants to make a joke about it, but no funny remarks spring to mind. He apologizes to the clerk for having inconvenienced him and then turns around and leaves the store.

The snafu is easily explained. Bowen has already figured it out before he returns to the hotel, and once he understands why Eva canceled the cards, he grudgingly admits that he would have done the same thing in her place. A husband goes out to mail a letter and doesn't come back. What is the wife to think? Desertion is a possibility, of course, but that thought wouldn't come until later. The first response would be alarm, and then the wife would run through a catalogue of potential accidents and dangers. Hit by a truck, knifed in the back, robbed at gunpoint and then knocked on the head. And if her husband was the victim of a robbery, then the thief would have taken his wallet and walked off with his credit cards. With no evidence to support one hypothesis or another (no reports of a crime, no dead bodies found in the street), canceling the credit cards would have been a minimum precaution.

Nick has only sixty-eight dollars in cash. He has no checks

with him, and when he stops at an ATM on his way back to the Hyatt Regency, he learns that his Citibank card has been canceled as well. His situation has suddenly become quite desperate. All avenues to money have been blocked, and when the hotel finds out that the American Express card he registered with on Monday night is no longer valid, he'll be in the ugliest of predicaments, perhaps even forced to defend himself against criminal charges. He thinks about calling Eva and going home, but he can't bring himself to do it. He hasn't come all this way just to turn around and run back at the first sign of trouble, and the fact is that he doesn't want to go home; he doesn't want to go back. Instead, he takes the elevator to the tenth floor of the hotel, enters his suite, and dials Rosa Leightman's number in New York. He does it on pure impulse, without having the first idea of what he wants to say to her. Fortunately, Rosa is out, and so Nick leaves a message on her answering machine – a rambling monologue that makes little or no sense, not even to him.

I'm in Kansas City, he says. I don't know why I'm here, but I'm here now, maybe for a long time, and I need to talk to you. It would be best if we could talk in person, but it's probably too much to ask you to fly out here on such short notice. Even if you can't come, please give me a call. I'm staying at the Hyatt Regency, room Ten-forty-six. I've been through your grandmother's book several times now, and I think it's the best thing she ever wrote. Thank you for giving it to me. And thank you for coming to my office on Monday. Don't be upset when I say this, but I haven't been able to stop thinking about you. You pounded me like a hammer, and when you stood up and left the room, my brain was in little pieces. Is it possible to fall in love with someone in ten minutes? I don't know anything about you. I don't even know if you're married or live with someone, if you're free or not. But it would be so nice if I could talk to you, so nice if I could see you again. It's beautiful out here, by the way. All strange and flat. I'm standing at the window, looking out at the city. Hundreds of buildings, hundreds of roads, but everything is silent. The glass blocks out the sound. Life is on the other side of the window, but in here everything looks dead, unreal. The problem is that I can't stay at the hotel much longer. I know a man who lives at the other end of town. He's the only person I've met so far, and I'm going out to look for him in a few minutes. His name is Ed Victory. I have his card in my pocket and I'll give you his number, just in case I've checked out before you call. Maybe he'll know where I am. 816-765-4321. I'll say it again: 816-765-4321. How odd. I just noticed that the numbers go down in order, one digit at a time. I've never seen a telephone number that did that before. Do you think it means something? Probably not. Unless it does, of course. I'll let you know when I find out. If I don't hear from you, I'll call again in a couple of days. Adios.

A week goes by before she listens to the message. If Nick had called twenty minutes earlier, she would have answered the telephone, but Rosa has just left her apartment, and therefore she knows nothing about his call. At the moment Nick records his words on her machine, she is sitting in a yellow cab three blocks from the entrance to the Holland Tunnel, on her way to Newark Airport, where an afternoon flight will be taking her to Chicago. It's Wednesday. Her sister is getting married on Saturday, and because the ceremony will be held at her parents' house, and because Rosa is the maid of honor, she's going out early to help with the preparations. She hasn't seen her parents in some time, so she'll take advantage of the visit to spend a few extra days with them following the wedding. Her plan is to return to New York on Tuesday morning. A man has just declared his love to her on a telephone answering machine, and a full week will go by before she knows anything about it.

In another part of New York on that same Wednesday

afternoon, Nick's wife, Eva, has also turned her thoughts toward Rosa Leightman. Nick has been missing for roughly forty hours. With no word from the police concerning accidents or crimes that involve a man who matches her husband's description, with no ransom notes or telephone calls from would-be kidnappers, she begins to consider the possibility that Nick has absconded, that he walked out on her under his own steam. Until this moment, she has never suspected him of having an affair, but when she thinks back to what he said about Rosa in the restaurant on Monday night, and when she remembers how taken he was with her – even going so far as to confess his attraction out loud – she starts to wonder if he isn't off on some adulterous escapade, shacked up in the arms of the thin girl with the spiky blond hair.

She looks up Rosa's number in the phone book and calls her apartment. There's no answer, of course, since Rosa is already on the plane. Eva leaves a short message and hangs up. When Rosa fails to return the call, Eva dials again that night and leaves another message. This pattern is repeated for several days – a call in the morning and a call at night – and the longer Rosa's silence continues, the more enraged Eva becomes. Finally, she goes to Rosa's building in Chelsea, climbs three flights of stairs, and knocks on her apartment door. Nothing happens. She knocks again, pounding with her fist and rattling the door on its hinges, and still no one answers. Eva takes this as definitive proof that Rosa is with Nick – an irrational assumption, but by now Eva is beyond the pull of logic, frantically stitching together a story to explain her husband's absence that draws on her darkest anxieties, her worst fears about her marriage and herself. She scribbles a note on a scrap of paper and slips it under Rosa's door. *I need to talk to you about Nick,* it says. *Call me at once. Eva Bowen.*

By now, Nick is long gone from the hotel. He has found Ed Victory, who lives in a tiny room on the top floor of a boardinghouse in one of the worst parts of town, a fringe neighborhood of crumbling, abandoned warehouses and burned-out buildings. The few people wandering the streets are black, but this is a zone of horror and devastation, and it bears little resemblance to the enclaves of black poverty that Nick has seen in other American cities. He has not entered an urban ghetto so much as a sliver of hell, a no-man's-land strewn with empty wine bottles, spent needles, and the hulks of stripped-down, rusted cars. The boardinghouse is the one intact structure on the block, no doubt the last remnant of what the neighborhood used to be, eighty or a hundred years ago. On any other street, it would have passed for a condemned building, but in this context it looks almost inviting: a three-story house with flaking yellow paint, sagging steps and roof, and plywood planks hammered across every one of the nine front windows.

Nick raps on the door, but no one answers. He raps again, and a few moments later an old woman in a green terry-cloth robe and a cheap auburn wig is standing before him – disconcerted, mistrustful, asking what he wants. Ed, Bowen replies, Ed Victory. I talked to him on the phone about an hour ago. He's expecting me. For the longest time, the woman says nothing. She looks Nick up and down, dead eyes studying him as though he were some form of unclassifiable being, glancing down at the leather briefcase in his hand and then back up at his face, trying to figure out what a white man is doing in her house. Nick reaches into his pocket and produces Ed's business card, hoping to convince her he's there on a legitimate errand, but the woman is half blind, and as she leans forward to look at the card, Nick understands that she can't make out the words. He ain't in no trouble, is he? she asks. No trouble, Nick answers. Not that I know of, anyway. And you ain't no cop? the woman says. I'm here to get some advice, Nick tells her, and Ed is the only person who can give it to me. Another long pause follows, and finally the woman points to the staircase. Three-G, she says, the door on the left. Be sure and knock

61

loud when you get there. Ed's usually asleep this time of the day, and he don't hear so good.

The woman knows what she's talking about, for once Nick climbs the darkened staircase and locates Ed Victory's door at the end of the hall, he has to knock ten or twelve times before the ex-cabdriver asks him to come in. Massive and round, with his suspenders hanging off his shoulders and the top of his pants unbuttoned, Nick's sole acquaintance in Kansas City is sitting on his bed and pointing a gun straight at his visitor's heart. It's the first time anyone has pointed a gun at Bowen, but before he can become sufficiently alarmed and back out of the room, Victory lowers the weapon and puts it on the bedside table.

It's you, he says. The New York lightning man.

Expecting trouble? Nick asks, belatedly feeling the terror of a potential bullet in the chest, even though the danger has passed.

These are troubled times, Ed says, and this is a troubled place. A man can never be too careful. Especially a sixty-seven-year-old man who's none too swift afoot.

No one can outrun a bullet, Nick replies.

Ed grunts by way of response, then asks Bowen to take a seat, unexpectedly referring to a passage from *Walden* as he gestures toward the one chair in the room. Thoreau said he had three chairs in his house, Ed remarks. One for solitude, two for friendship, and three for society. I've only got the one for solitude. Throw in the bed, and maybe there's two for friendship. But there's no society in here. I had my fill of that piloting my hack.

Bowen eases himself onto the straight-backed wooden chair and glances around the small, tidy room. It makes him think of a monk's cell or a hermit's refuge: a drab, spartan place with no more than the barest essentials for living. A single bed, a single chest of drawers, a hot plate, a bar-sized refrigerator, a desk, and a bookcase with several dozen books in it, among them eight or ten dictionaries and a well-worn set of *Collier's Encyclopedia* in twenty volumes. The room represents a world of restraint, inwardness, and discipline, and as Bowen turns his attention back to Victory, who is calmly watching him from the bed, he takes in one final detail, which previously escaped his notice. There are no pictures hanging on the walls, no photographs or personal artifacts on display. The only adornment is a calendar tacked to the wall just above the bureau – from 1945, open to the month of April.

I'm in a fix, Bowen says, and I thought you might be able to help me.

It all depends, Ed replies, reaching for a pack of unfiltered Pall Malls on the bedside table. He lights a cigarette with a wooden match, takes a prolonged drag, and immediately begins to cough. Years of clogged phlegm clatters inside his shrunken bronchi, and for twenty seconds the room fills with convulsive bursts of sound. When the fit subsides, Ed grins at Bowen and says: Whenever people ask me why I smoke, I tell them it's because I like to cough.

I didn't mean to bother you, Nick says. Maybe this isn't a good time.

I'm not bothered. A man gives me a twenty-dollar tip, and two days later he shows up and tells me he's got a problem. It makes me kind of curious.

I need work. Any kind of work. I'm a good auto mechanic, and it occurred to me you might have an in at the cab company you used to work for.

A man from New York with a leather briefcase and a quality suit tells me he wants to be a mechanic. He overtips a cabbie and then claims to be broke. And now you're going to tell me you don't want to answer any questions. Am I right or wrong?

No questions. I'm the man who was struck by lightning, remember? I'm dead, and whoever I used to be makes no difference anymore. The only thing that counts is now. And right now I have to earn some money.

The people who run that outfit are a pack of knaves and fools. Forget that idea, New York. If you're really desperate, though, I might have something for you at the Bureau. You need a strong back and a good head for numbers. If you meet those qualifications, I'll hire you. At a decent wage. I might look like a pauper, but I've got bags of money, more money than I know what to do with.

The Bureau of Historical Preservation. Your business.

Not a business. It's more in the nature of a museum, a private archive.

My back is strong, and I know how to add and subtract. What kind of work are you talking about?

I'm reorganizing my system. There's time, and there's space. Those are the only two possibilities. The current setup is geographic, spatial. Now I want to switch things around and make them chronological. It's a better way, and I'm sorry I didn't think of it sooner. There's some heavy lifting involved, and my body isn't up to doing it alone. I need a helper.

And if I said I'm willing to be that helper, when would I start?

Right now if you like. Just give me a chance to button up my trousers, and I'll walk you over there. Then you can decide if you're interested or not.

I broke off then for a bite to eat (some crackers and a tin of sardines) and washed down the snack with a couple of glasses of water. It was pushing five, and although Grace had said she would be back by six or six-thirty, I wanted to squeeze in a little more time with the blue notebook before she returned, to keep on going until the last possible minute. On the way back to my study at the end of the hall, I slipped into the bathroom to have a quick pee and splash some water on my face – feeling invigorated, ready to plunge on with the story. Just as I left the bathroom, however, the front door of the apartment opened, and in stepped Grace, looking wan and exhausted. Her cousin Lily was supposed to have accompanied her to Brooklyn (to have dinner with us and spend the night on the foldout sofa in the living room, then leave early in the morning for New Haven, where she was a second-year architecture student at Yale), but Grace was alone, and before I could ask her what was wrong, she gave me a weak smile, rushed down the hall in my direction, made an abrupt left, and entered the bathroom. The moment she got there, she fell to her knees and vomited into the toilet.

After the deluge ended, I helped her to her feet and guided her into the bedroom. She looked terribly pale, and with my right arm around her shoulder and my left arm around her waist, I could feel her whole body trembling – as if small currents of electricity were passing through it. Maybe it was the Chinese food from last night, she said, but I told her I didn't think so, since I'd eaten the same dishes she had and my stomach was fine. You're probably coming down with something, I said. Yes, Grace answered, you're probably right, it must be one of those bugs – using that odd little word we all fall back on to describe the invisible contagions that float through the city and worm their way into people's bloodstreams and inner organs. But I'm never sick, Grace added, even as she passively let me take off her clothes and put her into bed. I touched her forehead, which felt neither hot nor cold, and then I fished the thermometer out of the bedside table drawer and stuck it in her mouth. Her temperature turned out to be normal. That's encouraging, I said. If you get a good night's sleep, you'll probably feel better in the morning. To which Grace replied: I have to be better. There's an important meeting at work tomorrow, and I can't miss it.

I made her a cup of weak tea and a slice of dry toast, and for the next hour or so I sat beside her on the bed, talking to her about her cousin Lily, who'd put her into a cab after the first wave of queasiness had sent her running to the women's room at the Met. After a few sips of the tea, Grace declared that the nausea was lifting – only to be overwhelmed again fifteen minutes later, which sent her on another dash to the toilet across the hall. After that second onslaught, she began to settle down, but another thirty or forty minutes went by before she was relaxed enough to fall asleep. In the meantime, we talked a little, then said nothing for a while, then talked again, and all through those minutes before she finally dropped off, I stroked her head with my open palm. It felt good to be playing nurse, I told her, even if for just a few hours. It had been the other way around for so long, I'd forgotten there could be another sick person in the house besides myself.

'You don't understand,' Grace said. 'I'm being punished for last night.'

'Punished? What are you talking about?'

'For snapping at you in the cab. I acted like a shit.'

'No you didn't. And even if you had, I doubt that God takes his revenge on people by giving them the stomach flu.'

Grace closed her eyes and smiled. 'You've always loved me, haven't you, Sidney?'

'From the first moment I saw you.'

'Do you know why I married you?'

'No. I've never been brave enough to ask.'

'Because I knew you'd never let me down.'

'You bet on the wrong horse, Grace. I've been letting you down for almost a year now. First, I drag you through hell by getting sick, and then I throw us into debt with nine hundred unpaid medical bills. Without your job, we'd be out on the street. You're carrying me on your shoulders, Ms. Tebbetts. I'm a kept man.'

'I'm not talking about money.'

'I know you're not. But you're still getting a raw deal.'

'I'm the one who owes you, Sid. More than you know – more than you'll ever know. As long as you're not disappointed in me, I can live through anything.'

'I don't understand.'

'You don't have to understand. Just keep on loving me, and everything will take care of itself.'

It was the second bewildering conversation we'd had in the past eighteen hours. Once again, Grace had been hinting at something she refused to name, some kind of inner turmoil that seemed to be dogging her conscience, and it left me at a loss, groping dumbly to figure out what was going on. And yet how tender she was that evening, how glad to accept my small ministrations, how happy to have me sit beside her on the bed. After all we'd been through together in the past year, after all her steadfastness and composure during my long illness, it seemed impossible that she could ever do anything that would disappoint me. And even if she did, I was foolish enough and loyal enough not to care. I wanted to stay married to her for the rest of my life, and if Grace had slipped at some point or done something she wasn't proud of, what difference could that make in the long run? It wasn't my job to judge her. I was her husband, not a lieutenant in the moral police, and I meant to stand by her no matter what. *Just keep on loving me.* Those were simple instructions, and unless she decided to cancel them at some future date, I intended to obey her wishes until the very end.

She fell asleep a little before six-thirty. As I tiptoed out of the room and headed toward the kitchen for another glass of water, I realized that I was glad Lily had scrapped her plan to spend the night and had caught an early train back to New Haven. It wasn't that I disliked Grace's younger cousin – in fact, I liked her very much, and enjoyed listening to her Virginia accent, which was a good deal thicker than Grace's – but having to make conversation with her all evening while Grace slept in the bedroom was a bit more than I could have coped with. I hadn't imagined I would be able to work again after they returned from Manhattan, but now that dinner was off, there was nothing to stop me from jumping back into the blue notebook. It was still early; Grace was tucked in for the night; and after my mini-meal of sardines and crackers, my hunger had been satisfied. So I walked down to the end of the hall again, took my place at my desk, and opened the notebook for the second time that day. Without once standing up from the chair, I worked steadily until three-thirty in the morning.

Time has passed. On the following Monday, seven days after Bowen's disappearance, his wife receives the final bill for the canceled American Express card. Scanning the list of charges, she comes to the last one at the bottom of the page – for the Delta Airlines flight to Kansas City the previous Monday – and suddenly understands that Nick is alive, that he must be alive. But why Kansas City? She struggles to imagine why her husband would have flown off to a place where he has no connections (no relatives, no authors in his stable of writers, no friends from the past) but can't think of a single possible motive. At the same time, she also begins to doubt her hypothesis concerning Rosa Leightman. The girl lives in New York, and if Nick has indeed run off with her, why on earth would he take her to the Midwest? Unless Rosa Leightman is originally from Kansas City, of course, but that strikes Eva as farfetched, the longest of long-shot solutions.

She has no theories, no guesswork narratives to rely on anymore, and the anger that has been roiling inside her for the past week gradually dissipates, then vanishes altogether. From the emptiness and confusion that follow, a new emotion emerges to fill her thoughts: hope, or something akin to hope. Nick is alive, and considering that the credit card statement records the purchase of only one ticket, there's a good chance that he is alone. Eva calls the Kansas City Police Department and asks for the Bureau of Missing Persons, but the sergeant who picks up the phone is less than helpful. Husbands disappear every day, he says, and unless there's evidence of a crime, there's nothing the police can do. Close to despair, finally giving vent to the strain and misery that have been mounting in her over past days, Eva tells the sergeant he's a coldhearted son-of-a-bitch and hangs up. She'll catch a plane for Kansas City, she decides, and start looking for Nick herself. Too agitated to sit still anymore, she decides to leave that very night.

She calls her answering machine at work, giving elaborate instructions to her secretary about the upcoming business of that week, then explains that she has an urgent family matter to attend to. She'll be out of town for a while, she says, but will stay in touch by phone. Until now, she has told no one about Nick's disappearance except for the New York police, who have been unable to do anything for her. But she has kept her friends and co-workers in the dark, refusing even to mention it to her parents, and when Nick's office began calling on Tuesday to find out where he was, she fended them off by saying he'd come down with an intestinal virus and was stretched out flat in bed. By the next Monday, when he should have been thoroughly recovered and back at work, she told them he was much improved, but his mother had been rushed to the hospital over the weekend after a bad fall, and he'd flown up to Boston to be with her. These lies were a form of self-protection, motivated by embarrassment, humiliation, and fear. What kind of wife was she if she couldn't account for her husband's whereabouts? The truth was a swamp of uncertainty, and the idea of confessing to anyone that Nick had deserted her did not even enter her mind.

Armed with several recent snapshots of Nick, she packs a small suitcase and heads for La Guardia, having called ahead to reserve a seat on the nine-thirty flight. When she lands in Kansas City several hours later, she finds a taxi and asks the driver to recommend a hotel, repeating almost word for word the same question her husband asked Ed Victory the previous Monday. The only difference is that she uses the word *good* instead of *best*, but for all the nuances of that distinction, the driver's response is identical. He takes her to the Hyatt, and little realizing that she's following in her husband's footsteps, Eva checks in at the front desk, asking for a single room. She isn't someone to throw away money and indulge in expensive suites, but her room is nevertheless on the tenth floor, just down the hall from where Nick stayed for the first two nights after he arrived in town. Except for the fact that her room is a mere fraction of a degree to the south of his, she has the same view of the city he had: the same expanse of buildings, the same network of roads, and the same sky of suspended clouds that he catalogued for Rosa Leightman as he stood by the window and talked into her answering machine before skipping out on the bill and leaving the place for good.

Eva sleeps badly in the unfamiliar bed, her throat dry, waking three or four times during the night to visit the bathroom, to drink another glass of water, to stare at the bright red numerals on the digital alarm clock and listen to the hum of fans whirring in the ceiling vents. She dozes off at five, sleeps uninterruptedly for about three hours, and then orders a room-service breakfast. At quarter past nine, already showered, dressed, and fortified with a full pot of black coffee, she rides the elevator to the ground floor to begin her search. All of Eva's hopes revolve around the photographs she's carrying in her bag. She will walk around the city and show Nick's picture to as many people as she can, beginning with hotels and restaurants, then stores and food markets, then taxi companies, office buildings, and God knows where else, praying that someone will recognize him and offer a lead. If nothing materializes after the first day, she will have copies made of one of the snapshots and plaster them all over town – on walls, lampposts, and telephone booths – and publish the picture in the *Kansas City Star*, along with any other papers that circulate in the region. Even as she stands in the elevator on her way down to the lobby, she imagines the text that will accompany the handbill. MISSING. Or: HAVE YOU SEEN THIS MAN? Followed by Nick's name, age, height, weight, and hair color. Then a contact number and the promise of a reward. She is still trying to figure out how much the amount should be when the elevator doors open. One thousand dollars? Five thousand dollars? Ten thousand dollars? If these stratagems fail, she tells herself, she will move on to the next step and engage the services of a private detective. Not just some ex-cop with an investigator's license, but an expert, a man who specializes in hunting down the vanished, the evaporated beings of the world.

Three minutes after Eva enters the lobby, something miraculous happens. She shows Nick's picture to the desk clerk on duty, and the young woman with the blond hair and gleaming white teeth makes a positive identification. This leads to a search through the records, and even at the sluggish pace of 1982 computers, it doesn't take long to confirm that Nick Bowen was registered at the hotel, spent two nights there, and disappeared without bothering to check out. They had a credit card imprint on file, but after running the number through the American Express system, the card proved to be invalid. Eva asks to see the manager in order to settle Nick's bill, and once she's sitting in the office, handing him her own newly validated card to cover the delinquent fees, she begins to cry, breaking down in earnest for the first time since her husband went missing. Mr. Lloyd Sharkey is discomfited by this outpouring of feminine anguish, but with the smooth and unctuous manner of a veteran service professional, he offers Mrs. Bowen whatever assistance he can provide her. Several minutes later, Eva is back on the tenth floor, talking to the Mexican chambermaid responsible for cleaning room 1046. The woman informs her that the DO NOT DISTURB sign was hanging on the doorknob outside Nick's room for the entire length of his stay and she never saw him. Ten minutes after that, Eva is downstairs in the kitchen talking to Leroy Washington, the room-service waiter who served Nick some of his meals. He recognizes Eva's husband from the photo and adds that Mr. Bowen was a generous tipper, although he didn't say much and seemed 'preoccupied' by something. Eva asks if Nick was alone or with a woman. Alone, says Washington. Unless there was a lady hiding in the bathroom or the closet, he continues, but the meals were always for one person, and as far as he could tell, only one side of the bed was ever slept in.

Now that she's paid his hotel bill, and now that she's nearly certain he hasn't run off with another woman, Eva begins to feel like a wife again, a full-fledged wife battling to find her husband and save her marriage. No more information comes from the interviews she conducts with other members of the Hyatt Regency staff. She can't begin to guess where Nick might have gone after leaving the hotel, and yet she feels encouraged, as if knowing he was here, in the same place where she is now, can be construed as a sign that he isn't far away – even if it's no more than a suggestive overlap, a spatial congruency that means nothing.

Once she steps out onto the street, however, the hopelessness of her situation comes crashing down on her again. For the fact remains that Nick left without a word – left her, left his job, left everything in New York behind him – and the only explanation she can think of now is that he's cracking up, in the throes of some violent nervous collapse. Has living with her made him that miserable? Is she the one who's driven him to take such a drastic step, who's pushed him to the point of desperation? Yes, she tells herself, she's probably done that to him. And to make matters worse, he's penniless. A miserable, half-mad soul wandering around a strange city without a penny in his pocket. And that's her fault too, she tells herself, the whole wretched business is her fault.

That same morning, as Eva begins her futile rounds of inquiry, going in and out of restaurants and shops in downtown Kansas City, Rosa Leightman flies home to New York.

She unlocks the door of her apartment in Chelsea at one o'clock, and the first thing she sees is Eva's note lying on the threshold. Caught off guard, perplexed by the urgent tone of the message, she drops her bag without bothering to unpack and immediately calls the first of the two numbers listed at the bottom of the note. No one answers at the Barrow Street apartment, but she leaves a message on the machine, explaining that she's been out of town and can now be reached at her home number. Then she calls Eva's office. The secretary tells her that Mrs. Bowen is away on business, but she's due to call in later that afternoon, and when she does, the message will be passed on to her. Rosa is mystified. She has met Nick Bowen only once and knows nothing about him. The conversation in his office went extremely well, she thought, and even though she sensed that he was attracted to her (she could see it in his eyes, feel it in the way he kept looking at her), his manner was reserved and gentlemanly, even a trifle distant. A man more lost than aggressive, she remembers, with an unmistakable tinge of sadness hovering about him. Married, she now realizes, and therefore out of bounds, disqualified from consideration. But touching somehow, a sympathetic sort with kind instincts.

She unpacks her bag and looks through her mail before listening to the messages on her answering machine. It's close to two by then, and the first thing that comes on is Bowen's voice, declaring his love for her and asking her to join him in Kansas City. Rosa stands stock-still, listening in awed confusion. She is so rattled by what Nick is saying to her that she has to back up the tape to the end of the message two more times before she can be certain she's written down Ed Victory's number correctly – notwithstanding the diminuendo of evenly descending figures, which makes the number all but impossible to forget. She is tempted to stop the answering machine and call Kansas City right away, but then decides to spool through the fourteen other messages to see if Nick has called again. He has. On Friday, and again on Sunday. 'I hope you weren't scared off by what I said the other day,' the second message begins, 'but I meant every word of it. I can't get rid of you. You're in my thoughts all the time, and while you seem to be telling me you aren't interested – what else can your silence mean? – I'd appreciate it if you'd give me a call. If nothing else, we can talk about your grandmother's book. Use Ed's number, the one I gave you before: 816-765-4321. By the way, those numbers aren't random. Ed asked for them on purpose. He says they're a metaphor – of what I don't know. I think he wants me to figure it out for myself.' The last message is the shortest of the three, and by then Nick has all but given up on her. 'It's me,' he says, 'giving it one last try. Please call, even if it's only to tell me you don't want to talk.'

Rosa dials Ed Victory's number, but no one picks up on the other end, and after letting the phone ring more than a dozen times, she concludes that it's an old device, with no answering machine attached to it. Without taking the time to examine what she feels (she doesn't know what she feels), Rosa hangs up the phone convinced that she has a moral obligation to contact Bowen – and that it must be done as quickly as possible. She thinks of sending a telegram, but when she calls directory assistance in Kansas City and asks for Ed's address, the operator tells her his number is unlisted, which means she isn't allowed to give out that information. Rosa then tries Eva's office again, hoping that Nick's wife has called in by now, but the secretary tells her there's been no news. As it happens, Eva is so swept up in her Kansas City drama that she will forget to call her office for several days, and by the time she does contact the secretary, Rosa herself will be gone, on her way to Kansas City by Greyhound bus. Why does she go? Because, over the course of those several days, she has called Ed Victory close to a hundred times, and no one has answered the phone. Because, in the absence of any further communication from Nick, she has talked herself into believing that he's in trouble – perhaps serious, life-threatening trouble. Because she is young and adventurous and currently unemployed (in between jobs as a freelance illustrator) and perhaps – one can only speculate about this – because she is enamored with the idea that a man she barely knows has openly confessed that he can't stop thinking about her, that she has made a man fall in love with her at first sight.

Backing up to the previous Wednesday, to the afternoon when Bowen climbed the steps of Ed's boardinghouse and was offered the job of helper in the Bureau of Historical Preservation, I then resumed the chronicle of my latter-day Flitcraft. . . .

Ed buttons up his trousers, stubs out his half-smoked Pall Mall, and leads Nick down the stairs. They walk out into the chill of the early spring afternoon and keep on going for nine or ten blocks, turning left, turning right, slowly wending their way through a network of dilapidated streets until they come to an abandoned stockyard near the river, the liquid boundary that separates the Missouri side of the city from the Kansas side. They continue walking until the water is directly in front of them, with no more buildings in sight and nothing else ahead but half a dozen sets of train tracks, which all run parallel to one another and no longer seem to be in service, given the oxidized condition of the rails and the numerous broken and splintered ties heaped about the surrounding gravel and dirt. A strong wind is blowing off the river as the two men step over the first set of rails, and Nick can't help thinking about the wind that was blowing through the streets of New York on Monday night, just before the gargoyle fell from the building and nearly crushed him to death. Wheezing from the exertion of their long walk, Ed suddenly stops as they cross the third set of rails and points to the ground. A weatherworn, unpainted square of wood is embedded in the gravel, a kind of hatch or trapdoor, and it blends in so unobtrusively with the environment that Nick doubts he would have spotted it on his own. Please be kind enough to lift that thing off the ground and put it to the side, Ed asks him. I'd do it myself, but I've grown so portly these days, I don't think I can bend down anymore without falling over.

Nick carries out his new employer's request, and a moment later the two men are climbing down an iron ladder affixed to a cement wall. They reach the bottom about twelve feet below the surface. Aided by the light shining through the open hatch above, Nick sees that they're in a narrow passageway, facing a bare plywood door. No handle or knob is visible, but there's a padlock on the right side at about chest level. Ed takes a key from his pocket and inserts it into the plug at the bottom of the casing. Once the spring mechanism is released and the padlock is in his hand, he flicks away the latch with his thumb and slides the freed end of the shackle back through the eye of the hasp. It's a smooth and practiced gesture, Nick realizes, surely the product of countless visits to this dank, subterranean hideout over the years. Ed gives the door a little push, and as it swings open on its hinges Nick peers into the darkness before him, unable to see a thing. Ed gently nudges him aside, steps across the threshold, and an instant later Nick hears the flick of a light switch, then another, then a third, and perhaps even a fourth. In a stuttering succession of flashes and buzzing oscillations, several banks of overhead fluorescent lights gradually come on, and Nick finds himself looking into a large storeroom, a windowless enclosure that measures approximately fifty by thirty feet. In precise rows running the length of the floor, gray metal bookshelves fill the entire space, each one extending all the way to the ceiling, which is somewhere between nine and ten feet high. Bowen has the impression that he's entered the stacks of some secret library, a collection of forbidden books that no one but the initiated can be trusted to read.

The Bureau of Historical Preservation, Ed says, with a

small wave of the hand. Take a look. Don't touch anything, but look as long as you like.

The circumstances are so bizarre, so remote from anything Nick was expecting, he can't even begin to guess what's in store for him. He walks down the first aisle and discovers that the shelves are crammed with telephone books. Hundreds of telephone books, thousands of telephone books, arranged alphabetically by city and set out in chronological order. He happens to be in the row that contains Baltimore and Boston. Checking the dates on the spines of the directories, he sees that the earliest Baltimore book is from 1927. There are several gaps after that, but beginning with 1946 the collection is complete until the present year, 1982. The first Boston book is even older, dating from 1919, but again there are a number of missing volumes until 1946, when all years begin to be accounted for. On the strength of this scant evidence, Nick surmises that Ed started the collection in 1946, the year after the end of World War II, which also happens to be the year that Bowen himself was born. Thirty-six years devoted to a vast and apparently meaningless undertaking, which tallies exactly with the span of his own life.

Atlanta, Buffalo, Cincinnati, Chicago, Detroit, Houston, Kansas City, Los Angeles, Miami, Minneapolis, the five boroughs of New York, Philadelphia, St. Louis, San Francisco, Seattle – every American metropolis is on hand, along with dozens of smaller cities, rural counties in Alabama, suburban towns in Connecticut, and unincorporated territories in Maine. But America isn't the end of it. Four of the twenty-four double-backed rows of towering metal bookcases are given over to cities and towns in foreign countries. These archives aren't as thorough or exhaustive as their domestic counterparts, but in addition to Canada and Mexico, most nations from western and eastern Europe are represented: London, Madrid, Stockholm, Paris, Munich, Prague, Budapest. To his astonishment, Nick sees that Ed has even managed to acquire a Warsaw phone directory from 1937/38: *Spis Abonentów Warszawskiej Sieci TELEFONÓW*. As Nick fights the temptation to pull it off the shelf, it occurs to him that nearly every Jewish person listed in that book is long dead – murdered before Ed's collection was ever started.

The tour lasts for ten or fifteen minutes, and everywhere Nick goes, Ed trails after him with a little grin on his face, relishing his visitor's bafflement. When they come to the final row of shelves at the southern end of the room, Ed finally says: The man is mystified. He's asking himself, What the hell is going on?

That's one way of putting it, Nick answers.

Any thoughts – or just out and out confusion?

I'm not sure, but I have the impression it's not just a game for you. I think I understand that much. You're not someone who collects for the sake of collecting. Bottle caps, cigarette wrappers, hotel ashtrays, glass figurines of elephants. People spend their time looking for all kinds of junk. But these phone books aren't junk. They mean something to you.

This room contains the world, Ed replies. Or at least a part of it. The names of the living and the dead. The Bureau of Historical Preservation is a house of memory, but it's also a shrine to the present. By bringing those two things together in one place, I prove to myself that mankind isn't finished.

I don't think I follow.

I saw the end of all things, Lightning Man. I went down into the bowels of hell, and I saw the end. You return from a trip like that, and no matter how long you go on living, a part of you will always be dead.

When did this happen?

April 1945. My unit was in Germany, and we were the ones who liberated Dachau. Thirty thousand breathing skeletons. You've seen the pictures, but the pictures don't tell you what it was like. You have to go there and smell it for yourself; you have to be there and touch it with your own hands. Human beings did it to human beings, and they did it with a clear conscience. That was the end of mankind, Mr. Good Shoes. God turned his eyes away from us and left the world forever. And I was there to witness it.

How long were you in the camp?

Two months. I was a cook, so I worked kitchen detail. My job was to feed the survivors. I'm sure you've read the stories about how some of them couldn't stop eating. The starved ones. They'd thought about food for so long, they couldn't help it. They ate until their stomachs burst, and they died. Hundreds of them. On the second day, a woman came up to me with a baby in her arms. She'd lost her mind, this woman, I could see it, I could see it in the way her eyes kept dancing around in their sockets, and so thin, so malnourished, I couldn't understand how she managed to stay on her feet. She didn't ask for any food, but she wanted me to give the baby some milk. I was happy to oblige, but when she handed me the baby, I saw that it was dead, that it had been dead for days. Its face was shriveled up and black, blacker than my own face, a tiny thing that weighed almost nothing, just shriveled skin and dried pus and weightless bones. The woman kept begging for milk, and so I poured some onto the baby's lips. I didn't know what else to do. I poured the milk onto the dead baby's lips, and then the woman took back her child – so happy, so happy that she began to hum, almost to sing, really, to sing in this cooing, joyful sort of way. I don't know if I've ever seen anyone happier than she was at that moment, walking off with her dead baby in her arms, singing because she'd finally been able to give it some milk. I stood there watching her as she left. She staggered along for about five yards, and then her knees buckled, and before I could run over there and catch her, she fell down dead in the mud. That was the thing that started it for me. When I saw that woman die, I knew I was going to have to do something. I couldn't just go home after the war and forget about it. I had to keep that place in my head, to go on thinking about it every day for the rest of my life.

Nick still doesn't follow. He can grasp the enormity of what Ed lived through, sympathize with the anguish and horror that continue to haunt him, but how those feelings found expression in the mad enterprise of collecting telephone books eludes his understanding. He can imagine a hundred other ways to translate the experience of the death camp into an enduring lifelong action, but not this strange underground archive filled with the names of people from around the world. But who is he to judge another man's passion? Bowen needs work, he enjoys Ed's company, and he has no qualms about spending the next weeks or months helping him to reorganize the storage system of the books, useless as that job might be. The two men come to terms on the matter of wages, hours, and so on, and then shake hands to seal the contract. But Nick is still in the embarrassing position of having to ask for an advance on future earnings. He needs clothes and a place to live, and the sixty-odd dollars in his billfold are not enough to cover those expenses. His new boss, however, is one step ahead of him. There's a Goodwill Mission not one mile from where we're standing, he says, and Nick can stock up on new duds for just a few dollars that afternoon. Nothing fancy, of course, but working for him will require work clothes, not expensive business suits. Besides, he already has one of those, and if he ever feels like stepping out on the town, all he has to do is climb back into it.

That problem solved, Ed immediately solves the housing problem as well. There's a one-room apartment on the premises, he informs Nick, and if Bowen isn't spooked by the thought of spending his nights underground, he's welcome to stay there free of charge. Beckoning Nick to follow him, Ed waddles down one of the center stacks, moving gingerly on his sore and swollen ankles until he reaches the gray cinder-block wall at the western limit of the room. I often stay here myself, he says, reaching into his pocket and pulling out his keys. It's a cozy place.

A metal door is fitted into the wall flush with the surface, and since it's the same shade of gray as the wall itself, Nick never even noticed it when he walked past the spot a few minutes earlier. Like the wooden entrance door at the other end of the room, this one has no knob or handle, and it opens inward with a soft push from Ed's hand. Yes, Nick says politely when he steps inside, it's a cozy place, although he finds the room rather dismal, as bare and sparsely furnished as Ed's lodgings at the boardinghouse. But all the rudiments are there – except for a window, of course, a prospect to look out on. Bed, table and chair, refrigerator, hot plate, flush toilet, a cupboard filled with canned goods. Not so terrible, really, and in the end what choice does Nick have but to accept Ed's offer? Ed seems pleased by Bowen's willingness to stay there, and as he locks the door and the two men turn around to head for the ladder that will take them aboveground again, he tells Nick that he started building the room twenty years ago. Back in the fall of 'sixty-two, he says, in the middle of the Cuban missile crisis. I thought they were going to drop the big one on us, and I figured I'd need a place to hide out in. You know, a whatchamacallit.

A fallout shelter.

Right. So I broke through the wall and added on that little room. The crisis was over before I finished, but you never know, do you? Those maniacs who run the world are capable of anything.

Nick feels a slight flush of alarm when he hears Ed talk like this. Not that he doesn't share his opinion about the rulers of the world, but he wonders now if he hasn't joined forces with an unhinged person, a destabilized and/or demented crank. It's certainly possible, he tells himself, but Ed Victory is the man fate has delivered to him, and if he means to abide by the principles of the falling gargoyle, then he must carry on and pursue the direction he's taken – for better or worse. Otherwise, his departure from New York becomes a hollow, childish gesture. If he can't accept what's happening, accept it and actively embrace it, he should admit defeat and call his wife to tell her he's coming home.

In the end, these anxieties prove groundless. The days go by, and as the two men work together in the crypt below the railroad tracks, lugging telephone books back and forth across the room in wooden apple boxes mounted on roller skates, Nick discovers that Ed is nothing less than a stalwart character, a man of his word. He never asks his helper to explain himself or tell his story, and Nick grows to admire that discretion, especially in someone as garrulous as Ed, whose very being emanates curiosity about the world. Ed's manners are so refined, in fact, that he never even asks Nick his name. At one point, Bowen mentions to his boss that he can call him Bill, but understanding that the name is an invention, Ed rarely bothers, preferring to address his employee as *Lightning Man*, *New York*, and *Mr. Good Shoes*. Nick is perfectly satisfied with the arrangement. Dressed in the various outfits acquired from the Goodwill Mission store (flannel shirts, jeans and khaki pants, white tube socks, and frayed basketball sneakers), he wonders about the men who originally owned the clothes he's now wearing. Castoffs can come from one of two sources, and they're given away for one of two reasons. A person loses interest in a garment and donates it to charity, or else a person dies, and his heirs dispose of his goods for a meager tax deduction. Nick warms to the idea of walking around in a dead man's clothes. Now that he has ceased to exist, it seems fitting to don the wardrobe of a man who has likewise ceased to exist – as if that double negation made the erasure of his past more thorough, more permanent.

But Bowen nevertheless has to stay on his guard. He and Ed take frequent breaks while they work, and each time they interrupt their labors Ed enjoys passing the time in conversation, often punctuating his remarks with a swig from a can of beer. Nick learns about Wilhamena, Ed's first wife, who vanished one morning in 1953 with a liquor salesman from

Detroit, and about Rochelle, Wilhamena's successor, who bore him three daughters and then died of heart trouble in 1969. Bowen finds Ed an engaging raconteur, but he is careful to refrain from asking him any pointed questions – so as not to open the way to be asked any questions about himself. They have established a silent pact about not probing into each other's secrets, and much as Nick would like to know if Victory is Ed's real name, for example, or if he owns the underground space that houses the Bureau of Historical Preservation or has simply appropriated it without being caught by the authorities, he says nothing about these matters and contents himself with listening to what Ed offers of his own free will. More dangerous are the moments when Nick almost gives himself away, and each time that happens, he warns himself to keep a more careful watch over what he says. One afternoon, when Ed is talking about his experiences as a soldier in World War II, he brings up the name of a young private who joined his regiment in late 'forty-four, John Trause. Just eighteen years old, Ed says, but the quickest, brightest lad he ever ran into. He's a famous writer now, he continues, and no wonder when you think about how sharp that boy's mind was. That's when Bowen makes a near catastrophic slip. I know him, he says, and when Ed looks up and asks how John's doing these days, Nick immediately covers his tracks by clarifying the statement. Not personally, he says. I mean his books, I've read his books, and there the subject is dropped and they move on to other things. But the truth is that Nick works with John and is the editor responsible for his backlist. Not one month ago, in fact, he finished working on a set of newly commissioned covers for the paperback editions of Trause's novels. He has known him for years, and the principal reason why he applied for the job at the company he works for (or did work for until a few days ago) was that John Trause's novels were published there.

Nick starts working for Ed on Thursday morning, and the

task of rearranging the telephone books is so daunting, so colossal in terms of the poundage to be dealt with – the bulk and heft of countless thousand-page volumes to be taken off the shelves, carted to other areas of the room, and lifted onto new shelves – that progress is slow, much slower than they anticipated it would be. They decide to work straight through the weekend, and by Wednesday of the following week (the same day Eva walks into a photocopy store to design the poster that will broadcast the news of her missing husband, which also happens to be the day Rosa Leightman returns to New York and listens to Bowen's lovelorn messages on her answering machine), Nick's growing concern over Ed's health finally blossoms into full-scale distress. The ex-cabbie is sixty-seven years old and at least sixty-seven pounds overweight. He smokes three packs of unfiltered cigarettes a day and has trouble walking, trouble breathing, and trouble mounting in every one of his cholesterol-packed arteries. Already the victim of two heart attacks, he is in no shape to do the work that he and Nick are trying to accomplish. Even going up and down the ladder every day requires an enormous effort of concentration and will, taxing his strength to such a point that he can barely breathe when he comes to the top or bottom of his climb. Nick has been aware of this from the beginning and has continually encouraged Ed to sit down and rest, assuring him that he's capable of handling the job himself, but Ed is a stubborn fellow, a man with a vision, and now that his dream of reorganizing his telephone-book museum is at last under way, he ignores Bowen's advice and jumps in to help at every opportunity. On Wednesday morning, things finally take a darker turn. Bowen returns from a trip to the other end of the room with his empty apple box in tow and finds Ed sitting on the floor leaning against one of the bookcases. His eyes are shut, and his right hand is pressed tightly over his heart.

Chest pains, Nick says, leaping to the obvious conclusion. How bad?

Just give me a minute, Ed says. I'll be all right.

But Nick refuses to accept that as an answer and insists on accompanying Ed to the emergency room of the nearest medical facility. After putting up a short token protest, Ed agrees to go.

More than an hour ticks by before the two of them are sitting in the backseat of a taxi on their way to Saint Anselm's Charity Hospital. First, there is the arduous business of pushing Ed's broad, voluminous body up the ladder and getting him outside; then, there is the equally desperate challenge of hunting down a cab in this grim and forsaken part of the city. Nick runs for twenty minutes before he can find a functioning pay phone, and when he finally gets hold of the Red and White Cab Company (Ed's former employer), it takes another fifteen minutes before the car shows up. Nick instructs the driver to head for the railroad tracks near the river. They retrieve the languishing Ed, who is sprawled out among the cinders in considerable pain (but still conscious, still in sufficient command of himself to crack a couple of jokes as they help him into the cab), and set off for the hospital.

This medical emergency accounts for Rosa Leightman's failure to reach Ed by telephone later that day. The man known as Victory, but whose driver's license and Medicare card show his name to be Johnson, has suffered his third heart attack. By the time Rosa calls him from her New York apartment, he is already confined to the intensive care unit at Saint Anselm's, and, based on the cardiovascular data written on the chart at the foot of his bed, he will not be returning to his boardinghouse anytime soon. From that Wednesday until she leaves for Kansas City on Saturday morning, Rosa goes on calling him at all hours of the night and day, but not once is anyone there to hear the telephone ring.

In the cab on the way to the hospital, Ed is already thinking ahead, preparing himself for what promises to be bad news, even as he pretends not to be worried. I'm a fat man, he tells Nick, and fat men never die. It's a law of nature. The world can punch us, but we don't feel a thing. That's why we have all this padding – to protect us from moments like this.

Nick tells Ed to stop talking. Save your strength, he says, and as Ed struggles to ride out the pain that's burning in his chest and down his left arm and up into his jaw, his thoughts turn to the Bureau of Historical Preservation. I'm probably going to have to spend some time in the hospital, he says, and it grieves me to think about interrupting the work we've started. Nick assures him that he's willing to carry on alone, and Ed, moved by his helper's loyalty, shuts his eyes to block the tears that are spontaneously gathering in them and calls him a good man. Then, because he's too weak to do it himself, Ed asks Bowen to stick his hand into his trouser pockets and pull out his wallet and key ring. Nick extracts the two items from Ed's pants, and a moment later Ed is telling him to open the wallet and remove the cash inside it. Just leave me twenty bucks, he says, but take the rest for yourself – an advance on services rendered. That's when Nick learns that Ed's real name is Johnson, but he quickly decides that this discovery is of little importance and makes no comment. Instead, he counts out the money, which comes to more than six hundred dollars, and puts the bundle into the right front pocket of his own pants. After that, in a near breathless litany, fighting to talk through the pain, Ed informs him of the use of each key on the ring: the front door of the boardinghouse, the door of his room upstairs, his box at the local post office, the padlock on the wooden door at the Bureau, and the door of the underground apartment. As Bowen slips his own key to the apartment onto the ring, Ed tells him that he's expecting a big shipment of European phone books this week, so Nick should remember to check in at the post office on Friday. A long silence ensues after that remark, as Ed withdraws into himself and battles to catch his breath again, but just before they reach the hospital, he opens his eyes and tells Nick that he's welcome to stay in his room at the boardinghouse while he's gone. Nick thinks about it for a moment and then turns down the offer. That's very kind of you, he says, but there's no need to change anything. I'm happy living in my hole.

He hangs around the hospital for several hours, wanting to make sure that Ed is out of danger before he leaves. Triple bypass surgery has been scheduled for the next morning, and when Nick walks out of Saint Anselm's at three o'clock, he's confident that when he returns to visit the following afternoon, Ed will be on his way to a full recovery. Or so the cardiologist has led him to believe. But nothing is certain in the realm of medical practice, least of all when it's a question of knives cutting through the flesh of diseased bodies, and when Edward M. Johnson, better known as Ed Victory, expires on the operating table Thursday morning, that same cardiologist who offered Nick such a promising diagnosis can do no more than admit he was wrong.

By then, Nick is no longer in a position to talk to the doctor and ask him why his friend didn't make it. Less than an hour after he returns to the underground archive on Wednesday, Bowen commits one of the great blunders of his life, and because he assumes Ed will live – and goes on assuming that even after his boss is dead – he has no idea how gigantic the calamity he has made for himself truly is.

Both the key ring and the cash that Ed gave him are in the right front pocket of his pants when he climbs down the ladder to the entranceway of the Bureau. After Nick undoes the padlock on the wooden door, he puts the keys into the left pocket of the aged, hand-me-down khakis bought at the Goodwill Mission store. As it happens, there's a large hole in that pocket, and the keys slide straight through it, travel down Nick's legs, and land at his feet. He bends over and picks them up, but instead of putting them back into the right pocket, he keeps them in his hand, carries them over to the place where he intends to begin working, and sets them on a shelf in front of a row of telephone books – so as not to have them bulging in his pants and digging into his leg as he goes about his chores of lifting and carting, of squatting down and standing up. The air underground is especially clammy that day. Nick works for half an hour, hoping the exercise will warm him up, but the chill settles ever more deeply into his bones, and eventually he decides to withdraw to the apartment at the back of the room, which is equipped with a portable electric heater. He remembers the keys, returns to the spot where he left the ring, and again takes hold of it in his hand. Instead of going straight to the apartment, however, he starts thinking about the Warsaw phone book from 1937/38 that caught his attention the first time he visited the Bureau with Ed. He walks to the other end of the room to look for it, wanting to take it into the apartment with him and study during his break. Again, he puts the keys down on a shelf, but this time, absorbed in his search for the book, he forgets to take them with him after the volume is located. Under normal circumstances, this wouldn't have caused a problem. He would have needed the keys to open the door of the apartment, and once he realized his mistake, he would have gone back to fetch them. But that morning, in the frenzy that followed Ed's sudden collapse, the door was left open, and as Nick walks toward that door now, already flipping through the pages of the Warsaw phone book and thinking about some of the gruesome stories Ed told him about 1945, he is distracted enough not to pay attention to what he is doing. If he thinks about the keys at all, he will take it for granted that he's put them in his right pocket, and so he walks straight into the room, turns on the overhead light, and kicks the door shut behind him – thereby locking himself in. Ed has installed a self-locking door, and once a person enters that room, he can't get out again unless he uses a key to unlock the door from the inside.

Because he imagines the key is in his pocket, Nick still

isn't aware of what he has done. He switches on the electric heater, sits down on the bed, and begins reading the Warsaw phone book more carefully, giving its browned and brittle pages his full attention. An hour goes by, and when Nick feels warm enough to return to work, he finally realizes his mistake. His first response is to laugh, but as the sickening truth of what he has done to himself gradually sinks in, he stops laughing and spends the next two hours in a frantic attempt to find a way out of there.

This is a hydrogen-bomb shelter, not an ordinary room, and the double-insulated walls are four feet thick, the concrete floor extends thirty-six inches below him, and even the ceiling, which Bowen thinks will be the most vulnerable spot, is constructed of a plaster and cement combination so solid as to be impregnable. There are air vents running along the tops of all four walls, but after Bowen manages to detach one of the grates from its tight metal housing, he understands that the opening is too narrow for a man to crawl through, even a smallish man like himself.

Aboveground, in the brightness of the afternoon sun, Nick's wife is gluing pictures of his face to every wall and lamppost in downtown Kansas City, and the following day, when the residents of the greater metropolitan area climb out of bed and repair to their kitchens to down their breakfast coffee, they will stumble across that same picture on page seven of the morning paper: HAVE YOU SEEN THIS MAN?

Exhausted by his efforts, Bowen sits down on the bed and calmly tries to reassess the situation. In spite of everything, he decides there's no need to panic. The refrigerator and cupboards are stocked with food, there are abundant supplies of water and beer on hand, and if worse came to worst, he could manage to hold out for two weeks in relative comfort. But it won't be that long, he tells himself, not even half that long. Ed will be out of the hospital in just a few days, and once he's mobile enough to climb down the ladder again, he'll come to the Bureau and set him free.

With no other option available to him, Bowen settles in to wait out his solitary confinement, hoping to discover enough patience and fortitude to bear up to his absurd predicament. He passes the time reading the manuscript of *Oracle Night* and perusing the contents of the Warsaw telephone book. He thinks and dreams and does a thousand push-ups a day. He makes plans for the future. He struggles not to think about the past. Although he doesn't believe in God, he tells himself that God is testing him – and that he mustn't fail to accept his misfortune with grace and equanimity of spirit.

When Rosa Leightman's bus arrives in Kansas City on Sunday night, Nick has been in the room for five days. Deliverance is at hand, he tells himself, Ed will be coming anytime now, and ten minutes after he thinks that thought, the bulb in the overhead light burns out, and Nick finds himself sitting alone in the darkness, staring at the glowing orange coils of the electric heater.

The doctors had told me my recovery depended on keeping regular hours and getting a sufficient amount of sleep every night. Working until three-thirty in the morning was hardly an intelligent move, but I'd been too absorbed in the blue notebook to keep track of the time, and when I crawled into bed beside Grace at quarter to four, I understood that I would probably have to pay a price for departing from my regimen. Another nosebleed, perhaps, or a new attack of the wobbles, or a prolonged high-intensity headache – something that promised to rattle my system and make the next day more difficult than most. When I opened my eyes at nine-thirty, however, I felt no worse than I usually did when I woke up in the morning. Maybe rest wasn't the cure, I said to myself, but work. Maybe writing was the medicine that would make me completely well again.

After Grace's bout with the heaves on Sunday, I had assumed she would take Monday off, but when I rolled over to my left to see if she was still asleep, I discovered that her side of the bed was empty. I looked for her in the bathroom, but she wasn't there. When I went into the kitchen, I found a note lying on the table. *I'm feeling much better,* it said, *so I've gone to work. Thanks for being so nice to me last night. You're the darling of darlings, Sid, Blue Team through and through.* Then, after signing her name, she had added a P.S. at the bottom of the page. *I almost forgot. We're out of Scotch tape, and I want to wrap my father's birthday present tonight so it gets to him in time. Could you pick up a roll today when you go out on your walk?*

I knew it was just a small point, but that request seemed to symbolize everything that was good about Grace. She worked as a graphic designer for a major New York publishing house, and if there was one thing her department was well supplied with, it was Scotch tape. Nearly every white-collar worker in America steals from the office. Hordes of wage earners routinely pocket pens, pencils, envelopes, paper clips, and rubber bands, and few of them feel the vaguest twinge of conscience over these acts of petty larceny. But Grace wasn't one of those people. It had nothing to do with a fear of being caught: it simply had never crossed her mind to take something that didn't belong to her. Not out of respect for the law, not because of some priggish rectitude, not because her religious training as a child had taught her to tremble at the words of the Ten Commandments, but because the idea of theft was alien to her sense of who she was, a betrayal of all her instincts about how she wanted to live her life. She might not have supported the concept, but Grace was a permanent, dyed-in-the-wool member of the Blue Team, and it touched me that she had bothered to bring up the subject again in her note. It was another way of telling me she was sorry about her little outburst in the cab on Saturday night, a discreet and altogether characteristic form of apology. Gracie in a nutshell.

I swallowed the four pills I took every morning at breakfast, drank some coffee, ate a couple of pieces of toast, and then walked down to the end of the hall and opened the door of my workroom. I figured I would continue with the story until lunchtime. At that point, I would go out and pay another visit to Chang's store – not only to look for Grace's Scotch tape, but to buy whatever Portuguese notebooks were still in stock. It didn't matter to me that they weren't blue. Black, red, and brown would serve just as well, and I wanted to have as many of them on hand as possible. Not for the present, perhaps, but to build up a supply for future projects, and the longer I put off going back to Chang's store, the greater the chances were that they'd be gone.

Until then, writing in the blue notebook had given me nothing but pleasure, a soaring, manic sense of fulfillment. Words had rushed out of me as though I were taking dictation, transcribing sentences from a voice that spoke in the crystalline language of dreams, nightmares, and unfettered thoughts. On the morning of September 20, however, two days after the day in question, that voice suddenly went silent. I opened the notebook, and when I glanced down at the page in front of me, I realized that I was lost, that I didn't know what I was doing anymore. I had put Bowen into the room. I had locked the door and turned out the light, and now I didn't have the faintest idea of how to get him out of there. Dozens of solutions sprang to mind, but they all seemed trite, mechanical, dull. Trapping Nick in the underground bomb shelter was a compelling idea to me – both terrifying and mysterious, beyond all rational explanation – and I didn't want to let go of it. But once I'd pushed the story in that direction, I had diverged from the original premise of the exercise. My hero was no longer walking the same path that Flitcraft had followed. Hammett ends his parable with a neat comic twist, and although it has a certain air of inevitability to it, I found his conclusion a little too pat for my taste. After wandering around for a couple of years, Flitcraft winds up in Spokane and marries a woman who is nearly the double of his first wife. As Sam Spade puts it to

Brigid O'Shaughnessy: 'I don't think he even knew he had settled back naturally into the same groove he had jumped out of in Tacoma. But that's the part of it I always liked. He adjusted himself to beams falling, and then no more of them fell, and he adjusted himself to them not falling.' Cute, symmetrical, and ironic – but not strong enough for the kind of story I was interested in telling. I sat at my desk for more than an hour with the pen in my hand, but I didn't write a word. Perhaps that was what John had been referring to when he spoke of the 'cruelty' of the Portuguese notebooks. You flew along in them for a while, borne away by a feeling of your own power, a mental Superman speeding through a bright blue sky with your cape flapping behind you, and then, without any warning, you came crashing down to earth. After so much excitement and wishful thinking (even, I confess, to the point of imagining I might be able to turn the story into a novel, which would have put me in a position to earn some money and begin pulling my weight in the household again), I felt disgusted, ashamed that I had allowed three dozen hastily written pages to delude me into thinking I had suddenly turned things around for myself. All I had accomplished was to back myself into a corner. Maybe there was a way out, but for the time being I couldn't see one. The only thing I could see that morning was my hapless little man – sitting in the darkness of his underground room, waiting for someone to rescue him.

The weather was warm that day, with temperatures in the low 60s, but the clouds had returned, and when I left the apartment at eleven-thirty, rain seemed imminent. I didn't bother to go back upstairs for an umbrella, however. Another trip up and down the three flights would have taken too much out of me, so I decided to risk it, banking on the chance that the rain would hold off until after I returned.

I moved down Court Street at a slow pace, starting to sag a little from the effects of my late-night work session, feeling some of the old dizziness and discombobulation. It took me over fifteen minutes to reach the block between Carroll and President. The shoe-repair shop was open, just as it had been on Saturday morning, as was the bodega two doors down, but the store in between them was empty. Just forty-eight hours earlier, Chang's business had been in full operation, with a handsomely decorated front window and an over-flowing stock of stationery goods inside, but now, to my absolute astonishment, everything was gone. A padlocked gate stretched across the façade, and when I peered through the diamond-shaped openings, I saw that a small handwritten sign had been mounted on the window: STORE FOR RENT. 858-1143.

I was so puzzled, I just stood there for a while staring into the vacant room. Had business been so bad that Chang had impulsively decided to pack it in? Had he dismantled his shop in a crazy fit of sorrow and defeat, carting away his entire inventory over the course of a single weekend? It didn't seem possible. For a moment or two, I wondered if I hadn't imagined my visit to the Paper Palace on Saturday morning, or if the time sequence hadn't been scrambled in my head, meaning that I was remembering something that had happened much earlier – not two days ago, but two weeks or two months ago. I went into the bodega and talked to the man behind the counter. Mercifully, he was just as befuddled as I was. Chang's store had been there on Saturday, he said, and it was still there when he went home at seven o'clock. 'It musta happened that night,' he continued, 'or maybe yesterday. I got Sunday off. Talk to Ramón – he's the Sunday guy. When I got here this morning, the place was cleaned out. You want weird, my friend, that's weird. Just like some magician dude waves his magic wand, and poof, the Chinaman is gone.'

I bought the Scotch tape somewhere else and then walked down to Landolfi's to buy a pack of cigarettes (Pall Malls, in honor of the late Ed Victory) and some newspapers to read at lunch. Half a block from the candy store was a place called

Rita's, the small, noisy coffee shop where I had whiled away most of the summer. I hadn't been there in almost a month, and I found it gratifying that the waitress and the counterman both greeted me warmly when I walked in. Out of sorts as I was that day, it felt good to know that I hadn't been forgotten. I ordered my usual grilled cheese sandwich and settled in with the papers. The *Times* first, then the *Daily News* for the sports (the Mets had lost both ends of a Sunday doubleheader to the Cardinals), and finally a look at *Newsday*. I was an old hand at wasting time by then, and with my work at a standstill and nothing urgent calling me back to the apartment, I was in no rush to leave, especially now that the rain had started and I had been too lazy to climb the stairs to fetch an umbrella before going out.

If I hadn't lingered in Rita's for so long, ordering a second sandwich and a third cup of coffee, I never would have seen the article printed at the bottom of page thirty-seven in *Newsday*. Just the night before, I had written several paragraphs about Ed Victory's experiences in Dachau. Although Ed was a fictional character, the story he told about giving milk to the dead baby was true. I borrowed it from a book I'd once read about the Second World War,[8] and with Ed's

---

8. *The Lid Lifts* by Patrick Gordon-Walker (London, 1945). More recently, the same story was retold by Douglas Botting in *From the Ruins of the Reich: Germany 1945–1949* (New York: Crown Publishers, 1985), p. 43.

Just for the record, I should also mention that I happen to own a copy of a 1937/38 Warsaw telephone book. It was given to me by a journalist friend who went to Poland to cover the Solidarity movement in 1981. He apparently found it in a flea market somewhere, and knowing that my paternal grandparents had both been born in Warsaw, he gave it to me as a present after he returned to New York. I called it my *book of ghosts*. At the bottom of page 220, I found a married couple whose address was given as Wejnerta 19 – Janina and Stefan Orlowscy. That was the Polish spelling of my family's name, and although I wasn't sure if these people were related to me or not, I felt there was a good chance that they were.

words still ringing in my ears ('That was the end of mankind'), I came across this clumsily written news item about another dead baby, another dispatch from the bowels of hell. I can quote the article verbatim because I have it in front of me now. I tore it out of the paper that afternoon twenty years ago and have been carrying it around in my wallet ever since.

BORN IN A TOILET,
BABY DISCARDED

High on crack, a 22-year-old reputed prostitute gave birth over a toilet in a Bronx SRO, then dumped her dead baby in an outdoor garbage bin, police said yesterday.

The woman, police said, had been having sex with a john about 1 a.m. yesterday when she left the room they were sharing at 450 Cyrus Pl. and walked into a bathroom to smoke crack. Sitting over a toilet, the woman 'feels the water break, feels something come out,' Sgt. Michael Ryan said.

But police said the woman – wasted on crack – apparently was not aware she had given birth.

Twenty minutes later, the woman noticed the dead baby in the bowl, wrapped her in a towel, and dropped her in a garbage bin. She then returned to her customer and resumed having sex, Ryan said. A dispute over payment soon broke out, however, and police said the woman stabbed her customer in the chest about 1:15 a.m.

Police said the woman, identified as Kisha White, fled to her apartment on 188th Street. Later, White returned to the Dumpster and recovered her baby. A neighbor, however, saw her return and called the police.

When I finished reading the article for the first time, I said to myself: *This is the worst story I have ever read*. It was hard enough to absorb the information about the baby, but when I came to the stabbing incident in the fourth paragraph, I understood that I was reading a story about the end of mankind, that that room in the Bronx was the precise spot on earth where human life had lost its meaning. I paused for a few moments, trying to catch my breath, trying to stop myself from trembling, and then I read the article again. This time, my eyes filled with tears. The tears were so sudden, so unexpected, that I immediately covered my face with my hands to make sure no one saw them. If the coffee shop hadn't been crowded with customers, I probably would have collapsed in a fit of real sobbing. I didn't go that far, but it took every bit of strength in me to hold myself back.

I walked home in the rain. Once I had peeled off my wet clothes and changed into something dry, I went into my workroom, sat down at my desk, and opened the blue notebook. Not to the story I had been writing earlier, but to the last page, the final verso opposite the inside back cover. The article had churned up so much in me, I felt I had to write some kind of response to it, to tackle the misery it had provoked head on. I kept at it for about an hour, writing backward in the notebook, beginning with page ninety-six, then turning to page ninety-five, and so on. When I finished my little harangue, I closed the notebook, stood up from my desk, and walked down the hall to the kitchen. I poured myself a glass of orange juice, and as I put the carton back into the refrigerator, I happened to glance over at the telephone, which sat on a little table in the corner of the room. To my surprise, the light was flashing on the answering machine. There hadn't been any messages when I'd returned from my lunch at Rita's, and now there were two. Strange. Insignificant, perhaps, but strange. For the fact was, I hadn't heard the phone ring. Had I been so caught up in what I was doing that I hadn't noticed the sound? Possibly. But if that were so, then it was the first time it had ever happened to me. Our phone had a particularly loud bell, and the noise always carried down the hall to my workroom – even when the door was shut.

The first message was from Grace. She was rushing to meet a deadline and wouldn't be able to get out of the office until seven-thirty or eight o'clock. If I got hungry, she said, I should start dinner without her, and she would heat up the leftovers when she came home.

The second message was from my agent, Mary Sklarr. It seemed that someone had just called her from Los Angeles, asking if I was interested in writing another screenplay, and she wanted me to call her back so she could fill me in on the details.[9] I called, but it took a while before she got down to business. Like everyone else who was close to me, Mary began the conversation by asking about my health. They'd all thought they had lost me, and even though I'd been home from the hospital for four months now, they still couldn't believe I was alive, that they hadn't buried me in some graveyard back at the beginning of the year.

'Tip-top,' I said. 'A few lulls and droops every now and then, but basically good. Better and better every week.'

---

9. Four years earlier, I had adapted one of the stories from my first book, *Tabula Rasa*, for a young director named Vincent Frank. It was a small, low-budget film about a musician who recovers from a long illness and slowly puts his life together again (a prophetic story, as it turned out), and when the film was released in June 1980, it did fairly well. *Tabula Rasa* played in just a few art houses around the country, but it was perceived as a critical success, and – as Mary was fond of reminding me – it helped bring my name to the attention of a so-called wider public. Sales of my books began to improve somewhat, it's true, and when I turned in my next novel nine months later, *A Short Dictionary of Human Emotions*, she negotiated a contract with Holst & McDermott worth twice the amount I'd been given for my previous book. That advance, along with the modest sum I'd earned from the screenplay, allowed me to quit my high school teaching job, which had been my bread-and-butter work for the past seven years. Until then, I had been one of those obscure and driven writers who wrote between five and seven in the morning, who wrote at night and on weekends, who never went anywhere on his summer vacation in order to sit at home in a sweltering Brooklyn

'There's a rumor going around that you've started writing something. True or false?'

'Who told you that?'

'John Trause. He called this morning, and your name happened to come up.'

'It's true. But I don't know where I'm going with it yet. It could be nothing.'

'Let's hope not. I told the movie people you've started a new novel and probably wouldn't be interested.'

'But I am interested. Very interested. Especially if there's real money involved.'

'Fifty thousand dollars.'

'Good lord. With fifty thousand dollars, Grace and I would be out of the woods.'

'It's a dumb project, Sid. Not your kind of thing at all. Science fiction.'

'Ah. I see what you mean. Not exactly my line of work, is it? But are we talking about fictitious science or scientific fiction?'

---

apartment and make up for lost time. Now, a year and a half after my marriage to Grace, I found myself in the luxurious position of being an independent, self-employed scribbler. We were hardly what could be called well off, but if I continued to produce work at a steady pace, our combined incomes would keep us floating along with our heads above water. Following the release of *Tabula Rasa*, a few offers came in to write more films, but the projects hadn't interested me, and I'd turned them down to push on with my novel. When Holst & McDermott brought out the book in February 1982, however, I wasn't aware that it had been published. I had already been in the hospital for five weeks by then, and I wasn't aware of anything – not even that the doctors thought I would be dead within a matter of days.

Tabula Rasa had been a union production, and in order to be given credit for my screenplay I had been obliged to join the Writers Guild. Membership entailed sending in quarterly dues and turning over a small percentage of your earnings to them, but among the things they gave you in return was a decent health insurance policy. If not for that insurance, my illness would have landed me in debtor's prison. Most of the costs were covered, but as with all medical plans,

'Is there a difference?'

'I don't know.'

'They're planning a remake of *The Time Machine*.'

'H. G. Wells?'

'Exactly. To be directed by Bobby Hunter.'

'The guy who makes those big-budget action movies? What does he know about me?'

'He's a fan. Apparently, he's read all your books and loved the movie of *Tabula Rasa*.'

'I suppose I should be flattered. But I still don't get it. Why me? I mean, why me for this?'

'Don't worry, Sid. I'll call back and tell them no.'

'Give me a couple of days to think about it first. I'll read the book and see what happens. You never know. Maybe I'll come up with an interesting idea.'

'Okay, you're the boss. I'll tell them you're considering it. No promises, but you want to mull it over before you decide.'

---

there were countless other issues to be reckoned with: deductibles, extra charges for experimental treatments, arcane percentages and sliding-scale calculations for various medicines and disposable implements, a staggering range of bills that had put me in the hole to the tune of thirty-six thousand dollars. That was the burden Grace and I had been saddled with, and the more my strength returned, the more I worried about how to get us out from under this debt. Grace's father had offered to help, but the judge wasn't a rich man, and with Grace's two younger sisters still in college, we couldn't bring ourselves to accept. Instead, we sent in a small amount every month, trying to chip away at the mountain slowly, but at the rate we were going, we would still be at it when we were senior citizens. Grace worked in publishing, which meant her salary was meager at best, and I had earned nothing now for close to a year. A few microscopic royalties and foreign advances, but that was the extent of it. That explains why I returned Mary's call immediately after I listened to her message. I hadn't given any thought to writing more screenplays, but if the price was right for this one, I had no intention of turning down the job.

'I'm pretty sure there's a copy of the book in the apartment. An old paperback I bought in junior high school. I'll start reading it now and call you back in a day or two.'

The paperback had sold for thirty-five cents in 1961, and it included two of Wells's early novels, *The Time Machine* and *War of the Worlds. The Time Machine* was under a hundred pages, and it didn't take me much more than an hour to finish it. I found it thoroughly disappointing – a bad, awkwardly written piece of work, social criticism disguising itself as adventure yarn and heavy-handed on both counts. It didn't seem possible that anyone would want to do a straight adaptation of the book. That version had already been done, and if this Bobby Hunter character was as familiar with my work as he claimed to be, then it must have meant that he wanted me to take the story somewhere else, to leap out of the book and find a way of doing something fresh with the material. If not, why had he asked me? There were hundreds of professional screenwriters with more experience than I had. Any one of them could have translated Wells's novel into an acceptable script – which, I imagined, would have wound up looking similar to the Rod Taylor–Yvette Mimieux film I'd seen as a boy, with more dazzling special effects.

If there was anything that grabbed me about the book, it was the underlying conceit, the notion of time travel itself. Yet Wells had somehow managed to get that wrong too, I felt. He sends his hero into the future, but the more I thought about it, the more certain I became that most of us would prefer to visit the past. Trause's story about his brother-in-law and the 3-D viewer was a good example of how powerfully the dead keep their hold on us. If given the choice of going forward or backward, I for one wouldn't have hesitated. I would much rather have found myself among the no-longer-living than the unborn. With so many historical enigmas to be solved, how not to feel curious about what the world had looked like in, say, the Athens of Socrates or the Virginia of Thomas Jefferson? Or, like Trause's brother-in-law, how to resist the urge to reencounter the people you had lost? To see your mother and father on the day they met, for example, or to talk to your grandparents when they were young children. Would anyone turn down that opportunity in exchange for a glimpse of an unknown and incomprehensible future? Lemuel Flagg had seen the future in *Oracle Night*, and it had destroyed him. We don't want to know when we will die or when the people we love will betray us. But we're hungry to know the dead before they were dead, to acquaint ourselves with the dead as living beings.

I understood that Wells needed to send his man forward in time in order to make his point about the injustices of the English class system, which could be exaggerated to cataclysmic levels if placed in the future, but even granting him the right to do that, there was another, more serious problem with the book. If a man living in London at the end of the nineteenth century could invent a time machine, then it stood to reason that other people in the future would be able to do the same thing. If not on their own, then with the time traveler's help. And if people from future generations could travel back and forth across the years and centuries, then both the past and the future would be filled with people who did not belong to the time they were visiting. In the end, all times would be tainted, thronged with interlopers and tourists from other ages, and once people from the future began to influence events in the past and people from the past began to influence events in the future, the nature of time would change. Instead of being a continuous progression of discrete moments inching forward in one direction only, it would crumble into a vast, synchronistic blur. Simply put, as soon as one person began to travel in time, time as we know it would be destroyed.

Still, fifty thousand dollars was a lot of money, and I wasn't going to let a few logical flaws stand in my way. I put down the book and started pacing around the apartment, walking in and out of rooms, scanning the titles of the books on the shelves, parting the curtains and looking through the window at the wet street below, accomplishing nothing for several hours. At seven o'clock, I went into the kitchen to prepare a meal that would be ready for Grace when she returned from Manhattan. A mushroom omelet, a green salad, boiled potatoes, and broccoli. My culinary skills were limited, but I had once worked as a short-order cook, and I had a certain talent for whipping up spare and simple dinners. The first job was to peel the potatoes, and as I started slicing away the skins over a brown paper bag, the plot of the story finally came to me. It was just a beginning, with many rough edges and a host of particulars to be added later, but I felt pleased with it. Not because I felt it was good, but because I thought it might work for Bobby Hunter – whose opinion was the only one that mattered.

There would be two time travelers, I decided, a man from the past and a woman from the future. The action would cut back and forth between them until they embark on their journeys, and then, about a third of the way into the film, they would meet up in the present. I didn't know what to call them yet, so for the time being I referred to them as Jack and Jill.

Jack is similar to the hero in Wells's book – but American, not British. It's 1895, and he lives on a ranch in Texas, the twenty-eight-year-old son of a deceased cattle baron. Independently wealthy, with no interest in running his father's business, he leaves the operation of the ranch to his mother and older sister and devotes himself to scientific research and experimentation. After two years of unrelenting work and failure, he manages to build a time machine. He takes off on his first voyage. Not thousands of years into the future as the Wellsian character does, but just sixty-eight years ahead, climbing out of his glittering contraption on a cool and sunny day in late November 1963.

Jill belongs to the world of the mid-twenty-second century. Time travel has been mastered by then, but it is practiced only rarely, and severe restrictions have been placed on its use. Understanding its potential for disruption and disaster, the government allows each person only one journey in his or her lifetime. Not for the pleasure of visiting other moments in history, but as an initiation rite into adulthood. It happens when you reach the age of twenty. A celebration is held in your honor, and that same night you're sent into the past to travel around the world for one year and observe your ancestors. You begin two hundred years before your birth, roughly seven generations back, and then gradually work your way home to the present. The purpose of the trip is to teach you humility and compassion, tolerance for your fellow men. Out of the hundreds of forebears you encounter on the voyage, the entire gamut of human possibilities will be played out before you, every number in the genetic lottery will turn up. The traveler will understand that he has come from an immense cauldron of contradictions and that among his antecedents are beggars and fools, saints and heroes, cripples and beauties, gentle souls and violent criminals, altruists and thieves. To be exposed to so many lives in such a short span of time is to gain a new understanding of yourself and your place in the world. You see yourself as part of something greater than yourself, and you see yourself as a distinct individual, an unprecedented being with your own irreplaceable future. You understand, finally, that you alone are responsible for making yourself who you are.

Certain rules are in force for the length of the journey. You must not reveal your true identity; you must not interfere with anyone's actions; you must not allow anyone to enter your machine. To break any one of these rules is to suffer banishment from your own time and live in exile for the rest of your days.

Jill's story begins on the morning of her twentieth birth-

106

day. Once the party is over, she says good-bye to her parents and friends and straps herself into her government-issued time machine. She is carrying a long list of names with her, a dossier of the ancestors she will meet on her journey. The dial on the control panel is set to November 20, 1963, exactly two hundred years before her birth. She studies the papers one last time, shoves them into her pocket, and starts up the engine of the machine. Ten seconds later, with her friends and family waving their tearful farewells, the machine vanishes into thin air, and Jill is on her way.

Jack's machine has come to a stop in a meadow on the outskirts of Dallas. It's November 27, five days after Kennedy's assassination, and Oswald is already dead, gunned down by Jack Ruby in a basement passageway of City Hall. Within six hours of his arrival, Jack has read enough newspapers and listened to enough radio and TV broadcasts to understand that he has arrived in the midst of a national tragedy. He has lived through a presidential assassination himself (Garfield, in 1881), and he has painful memories of the trauma and chaos it produced. He ponders the dilemma for a couple of days, wondering if he has a moral right to alter the facts of history, and in the end he concludes that he does. He will take action for the good of his country; he will do everything in his power to save Kennedy's life. He returns to his time machine in the meadow, sets the dial of the chronometer to November 20, and travels back nine days into the past. When he emerges from the cockpit of his vessel, he finds himself standing not ten feet from another time machine – a sleek, twenty-second-century version of his own. Jill steps out, a bit woozy and disheveled. When she sees Jack standing there, looking at her in utter stupefaction, she reaches into her pocket and pulls out her list of names. Excuse me, sir, she says, but I wonder if you happen to know where I could find a man named Lee Harvey Oswald.

I hadn't worked out many details after that. I knew Jack and Jill would have to fall in love (this was Hollywood, after all), and I knew Jack would ultimately persuade her to help him stop Oswald from murdering Kennedy – even at the risk of turning her into an outlaw, of making it impossible for her to return to her own time. They would ambush Oswald on the morning of the twenty-second just as he is entering the Texas School Book Depository with his rifle, tie him up, and hold him hostage for several hours. And yet, for all their efforts, nothing would change. Kennedy would still be shot and killed, and American history would not be altered by a single comma. Oswald, the self-proclaimed patsy, had been telling the truth. Whether he had fired at the president or not, he was not the only gunman involved in the conspiracy.

Because Jill can't go home now, and because Jack loves her and can't bear the thought of leaving her behind, he chooses to stay with her in 1963. In the final scene of the movie, they destroy their time machines and bury them in the meadow. Then, with the sun rising before them, they walk off into the morning of November twenty-third, two young people who have renounced their pasts, preparing to face the future together.

It was pure rubbish, of course, fantasy drek of the lowest order, but it felt like a possible movie to me, and that was all I was hoping to accomplish: to deliver something that would fit the formula they wanted. It wasn't prostitution so much as a financial arrangement, and I didn't have any second thoughts about working for hire to scare up a pot of some much-needed cash. It had been a rocky day for me, beginning with my failure to advance the story I was working on, then the jolt of discovering Chang's store had gone out of business, and then the horrifying newspaper article I had read at lunch. If nothing else, thinking about *The Time Machine* had served as a painless distraction, and when Grace walked through the door at eight-thirty, I was in relatively good spirits. The table was set, a bottle of white wine was chilling in the refrigerator, and the omelet was ready to be poured into the pan. She was a little surprised that I had waited for her, I think, but she didn't make any comment about it. She looked worn-out, with dark circles under her eyes and a certain heaviness in her movements. After I helped her out of her coat, I immediately led her into the kitchen and sat her down at the table. 'Eat,' I said. 'You must be starved.' I put some bread and a plate of salad in front of her and then walked over to the stove to begin fixing the omelet.

She complimented me on the food, but otherwise she didn't say much during the meal. I was glad to see that her appetite had returned, but at the same time she seemed to be somewhere else, less present than usual. When I told her about going out on my Scotch tape errand and the mysterious closing of Chang's store, she barely seemed to be listening. I was tempted to tell her about the screenplay offer, but it didn't feel like the right moment. Maybe after dinner, I thought, and then, just as I stood up and was about to start clearing the table, she looked over at me and said, 'I think I'm pregnant, Sid.'

She'd blurted out the news so unexpectedly, I didn't know what else to do but sit back down in my chair.

'It's been almost six weeks since my last period. You know how regular I am. And all that throwing up yesterday. What else can it mean?'

'You don't sound too happy about it,' I finally said.

'I don't know what I feel. We've always talked about having kids, but this seems like the worst possible moment.'

'Not necessarily. If the test comes back positive, we'll figure out something. That's what everyone else does. We're not stupid, Grace. We'll find a way.'

'The apartment's too small, we don't have any money, and I'd have to stop working for three or four months. If you were all the way back, none of that would matter. But you're still not there.'

'I got you pregnant, didn't I? Who says I'm not there? Ain't nothing wrong with my plumbing, anyway.'

Grace smiled. 'So you vote yes.'

'Of course I do.'

'That makes one yes and one no. Where do we go from there?'

'You can't be serious.'

'What do you mean?'

'An abortion. You're not thinking of getting rid of it, are you?'

'I don't know. It's a horrible idea, but it might be best to put off having kids for a while.'

'Married people don't kill their babies. Not when they love each other.'

'That's an awful thing to say, Sidney. I don't like it.'

'Last night you said, "Just go on loving me, and everything will take care of itself." That's what I'm trying to do. To love you and take care of you.'

'This isn't about love. It's about trying to figure out what's best for both of us.'

'You already know, don't you?'

'Know what?'

'That you're pregnant. You don't think you might be pregnant. You've already found out that you are. When did you have the test?'

For the first time since I'd known her, Grace turned away from me when she spoke – unable to look at me, addressing her words to the wall. I'd caught her out in a lie, and the humiliation was almost too much for her to bear. 'Saturday morning,' she said. Her voice was nearly inaudible, scarcely louder than a whisper.

'Why didn't you tell me then?'

'I couldn't.'

'Couldn't?'

'I was too shaken up. I didn't want to accept it, and I needed time to digest the news. I'm sorry, Sid. I'm really sorry.'

We went on talking for another two hours, and in the end I wore down her resistance, hammering away at her until she gave in and promised to keep the child. It was probably the worst struggle we'd ever been through together. From every practical vantage, she was right to hesitate about the pregnancy, but the very rationality of her doubts seemed to touch off some morbid, irrational fear in me, and I kept on assaulting her with wildly emotional arguments that made little sense. When it came to the money end of things, I mentioned both the screenplay and the story I'd been outlining in the blue notebook, neglecting to add that the first project was no more than a tentative query, the faintest promise of future work, and that the second project had already stalled. If neither one of them panned out, I said, I would apply for a teaching post in every creative writing department in America, and if nothing turned up there, I would go back to teaching high school history, knowing full well that I still didn't have the physical stamina to hold down a regular job. In other words, I lied to her. My only object was to talk her out of aborting the child, and I was willing to indulge in any sort of dishonesty to plead my case. The question was why. Even as I bombarded her with my endless justifications and brutally efficient rhetoric, demolishing each one of her quiet, perfectly reasonable statements, I wondered why I was battling so hard. At bottom, I wasn't at all certain that I was ready to become a father, and I knew Grace was right to contend that the timing was off, that we shouldn't start thinking about children until I was fully recovered. Months went by before I understood what I was actually up to that night. It wasn't about having a baby – it was about me. Ever since I'd met her, I had lived in mortal fear that I would lose Grace. I had lost her once before our marriage, and after falling ill and turning into a semi-invalid, I had gradually succumbed to a kind of terminal hopelessness, a secret conviction that she would be better off without me. Having a child together would erase that anxiety and prevent her from wanting to

111

decamp. Conversely, for her to argue against the baby was a sign that she wanted out, that she was already slipping away from me. That explains why I became so worked up that night, I think, and I defended myself as ruthlessly as any shyster lawyer, even going so low as to take that dreadful newspaper clipping out of my wallet and insist that she read it. BORN IN A TOILET, BABY DISCARDED. When she came to the end of the article, Grace looked up at me with tears in her eyes and said, 'It isn't fair, Sidney. What does this . . . this nightmare have to do with us? You talk to me about dead babies in Dachau, about couples who can't have children, and now you show me this. What's wrong with you? I'm only trying to hold our life together in the best way I can. Don't you understand that?'

The next morning, I woke up early and made breakfast for the two of us, carrying a tray into the bedroom at seven o'clock, one minute before the alarm was set to go off. I parked the tray on top of the bureau, switched off the alarm, and then sat down on the bed next to Grace. The moment she opened her eyes, I put my arms around her and began kissing her cheek, her neck, and her shoulder, pressing my head against her and apologizing for the idiotic things I'd said the night before. I told her she was free to do what she wanted, that it was up to her and I would stand behind any decision she made. Beautiful Grace, who never looked puffy or bleary in the morning, who always emerged from sleep with the alacrity of a boot-camp soldier or a young child, rising up from deepest oblivion to full alertness in a matter of seconds, wrapped her arms around me and hugged me back, not saying a word, but emitting a series of small purring sounds from the bottom of her throat that told me I was forgiven, that the disagreement was already behind us.

I served her the breakfast while she remained in bed. Orange juice first, then a cup of coffee with some milk in it, followed by a pair of two-and-a-half-minute eggs and a slice of toast. Her appetite was good, with no signs of queasiness or morning sickness, and as I drank my own coffee and ate my own piece of toast, I thought she had never looked more splendid than she did at that moment. My wife is a luminous being, I said to myself, and may lightning strike me dead if I ever forget how lucky I am to be sitting next to her now.

'I was having the strangest dream,' Grace said. 'One of those nutty, mixed-up marathons where one thing keeps changing into another. But very clear – more real than real, if you know what I mean.'

'Can you remember it?'

'Most of it, I think, but it's already starting to fade. I can't see the beginning anymore, but somewhere along the line, you and I were with my parents. We were looking for a new place to live.'

'A bigger apartment, I suppose.'

'No, not an apartment. A house. We were driving around some city. Not New York or Charlottesville, but somewhere else, a place I'd never been to before. And my father said we should check out an address on Bluebird Avenue. Where do you suppose I dug up that one? Bluebird Avenue.'

'I don't know. But it's a nice name.'

'That's just what you said in the dream. You said it was a nice name.'

'Are you sure the dream is over? Maybe we're still asleep, and we're having the dream together.'

'Don't be silly. We were riding in my parents' car. You were with me in the backseat, and you said to my mother, "That's a nice name."'

'And then?'

'We pulled up in front of an old house. It was a huge place – a mansion, really – and then the four of us went inside and started looking around. All the rooms were empty, with no furniture in them, but they were enormous, like museum galleries or basketball courts, and we could hear our steps echoing against the walls. Then my parents decided to go upstairs to have a look at the second floor, but I wanted to go down to the basement. At first, you didn't want to go, but I took your hand and sort of dragged you along with me. It turned out to be pretty much like the ground floor – one empty room after another – but right in the middle of the last room there was a trapdoor. I yanked it open and saw that there was a ladder leading to a lower level. I started climbing down, and this time you followed right after me. You were just as curious as I was by then, and it was like we were having an adventure. You know, two kids exploring a strange house, both of us a little scared, but enjoying ourselves at the same time.'

'How long was the ladder?'

'I don't know. Ten or twelve feet. Something like that.'

'Ten or twelve feet . . . And then?'

'We found ourselves in a room. Smaller than the ones upstairs, with a much lower ceiling. The whole place was filled with bookshelves. Metal ones, painted gray, like the ones they use in libraries. We started looking at the titles of the books, and it turned out they'd all been written by you, Sid. Hundreds and hundreds of books, and every spine had your name on it: Sidney Orr.'

'Scary.'

'No, not at all. I felt very proud of you. After we'd looked at the books for a while, I started walking around again, and eventually I found a door. I opened it, and inside there was this perfect little bedroom. Very plush, with soft Persian rugs and comfortable chairs, paintings on the walls, incense burning on the table, and a bed with silk pillows and a red satin comforter. I called you over, and the minute you stepped inside, I threw my arms around you and started kissing you on the mouth. I was completely hot. All sexed up and raring to go.'

'And me?'

'You had the biggest hard-on of your life.'

'Keep this up, Grace, and you'll give me an even bigger one now.'

'We took off our clothes and started rolling around on the bed, all sweaty and hungry for each other. It was delicious. We both came once, and then, without pausing for breath, we started in again, going at each other like two animals.'

'It sounds like a porno movie.'

'It was wild. I don't know how long we kept at it, but at some point we heard my parents' car drive away. It didn't bother us. We'll catch up with them later, we said, and then we started screwing again. After we were done, we both collapsed. I dozed off for a while, and when I woke up you were standing naked by the door, pulling on the handle, looking a little desperate. "What's wrong," I asked, and you said, "It looks like we're locked in."'

'This is the strangest thing I've ever heard.'

'It's just a dream, Sid. All dreams are strange.'

'I haven't been talking in my sleep, have I?'

'What do you mean?'

'I know you never go into my workroom. But if you did, and if you happened to open the blue notebook I bought on Saturday, you'd see that the story I've been writing is similar to your dream. The ladder that goes down to an underground room, the library bookcases, the little bedroom at the back. My hero is locked in that room right now, and I don't know how to get him out.'

'Weird.'

'It's more than weird. It's chilling.'

'The funny thing is, that's where the dream ended. You had that scared look on your face, but before I could do anything to help you, I woke up. And there you were on the bed with your arms around me, hugging me in the same way you did in the dream. It was a wonderful thing. It felt like the dream was still going on, even after I'd woken up.'

'So you don't know what happens to us after we're locked in the room.'

'I didn't get that far. But we would have found a way out. People can't die in their dreams, you know. Even if the door

115

was locked, something would have happened to get us out. That's how it works. As long as you're dreaming, there's always a way out.'

After Grace left for Manhattan, I sat down at my typewriter and worked on the film treatment for Bobby Hunter. I tried to boil the synopsis down to four pages, but I wound up writing six. Certain matters needed more clarification, I realized, and I didn't want there to be any holes in the story. For one thing, if the initiation journey was fraught with so many dangers and the potential for such harsh punishment, why would anyone want to risk traveling into the past? I decided to make the journey optional, something one does by choice, not compulsion. For another thing, how do the people in the twenty-second century know when the traveler has broken the rules? I invented a special branch of the national police to take care of that. Time-travel agents sit in libraries poring over books, magazines, and newspapers, and when a young traveler interferes with someone's actions in the past, the words in the books change. The name Lee Harvey Oswald, for example, would suddenly disappear from every work on the Kennedy assassination. Imagining that scene, I understood that those alterations could be turned into a striking visual effect: hundreds of words scrambling around and rearranging themselves on printed pages, moving back and forth like tiny, maddened bugs.

When I finished typing, I read over the treatment once, corrected a few typos, and then walked down the hall to the kitchen and rang up the Sklarr Agency. Mary was busy on another call, but I told her assistant I would be turning up at the office in an hour or two to drop off the manuscript. 'That was fast,' she said.

'Yeah, I guess so,' I answered, 'but you know how it is, Angela. When you travel in time, you don't have a second to lose.'

Angela laughed at my feeble remark. 'All right,' she said,

'I'll tell Mary you're on your way. But there's no big rush, you know. You could put it in the mail and save yourself the trip.'

'Don't trust the mail, ma'am,' I said, lapsing into my Oklahoma cowboy twang. 'Never did and never will.'

After we hung up, I lifted the receiver off the hook again and dialed Trause's number. Mary's office was on Fifth Avenue between 12th and 13th Streets, not far from where John lived, and it occurred to me that he might be interested in getting together for lunch. I also wanted to know how his leg was doing. We hadn't talked since Saturday night, and it was time to check up on him and get the latest report.

'Nothing new,' he said. 'It's no worse than it was, but no better. The doctor prescribed an anti-inflammatory drug, and when I took the first pill yesterday, I had a bad reaction. Upchucking, spinning head, the works. I'm still feeling a bit drained from all that.'

'I'm leaving for Manhattan in a little while to see Mary Sklarr, and I thought I'd stop by to see you afterward. Maybe have lunch or something, but it doesn't sound like a good moment.'

'Why don't you come tomorrow? I'm bound to be okay by then. At least I fucking well better be.'

I left the apartment at eleven-thirty and walked over to Bergen Street, where I caught the F train to Manhattan. There were several mysterious glitches along the way – a lengthy pause in a tunnel, a blackout in the car that lasted for four stops, an unusually slow traverse from the York Street station to the other side of the river – and by the time I made it to Mary's office, she had already gone out to lunch. I left the treatment with Angela, the chubby, chain-smoking answerer of phones and sender of packages, who surprised me by standing up from her desk and kissing me good-bye – an Italian doubleheader, one peck on each cheek. 'Too bad you're married,' she whispered. 'You and I could have made some beautiful music together, Sid.'

Angela was always horsing around like that, and after three years of diligent practice, we'd worked out a fairly polished routine. Trying to keep up my end of the game, I gave her the answer she was looking for. 'Nothing's forever,' I said. 'Just hang in there, angelic one, and sooner or later I'm bound to be free.'

There was no point in returning to Brooklyn right away, so I decided to take my afternoon walk in the Village, then round off the excursion with a bite to eat somewhere before taking the subway home. I headed west from Fifth Avenue, strolling along 12th Street with its pretty brownstones and small, neatly tended trees, and by the time I'd passed the New School and was approaching Sixth Avenue, I was already lost in thought. Bowen was still trapped in the room, and with the unsettling contents of Grace's dream still echoing in my head, several new ideas had occurred to me about the story. I lost track of where I was after that, and for the next thirty or forty minutes I wandered around the streets like a blind man, more in that underground room in Kansas City than in Manhattan, taking only the scantest notice of the things around me. It wasn't until I found myself on Hudson Street, gliding past the front window of the White Horse Tavern, that my feet finally stopped moving. I had built up an appetite, I discovered, and once I became aware of that fact, the focus of my attention shifted from my head to my stomach. I was ready to sit down and eat lunch.[10]

---

10. I hadn't made any serious progress, but I understood that I could improve Bowen's condition somewhat without having to alter the central thrust of the narrative. The overhead light has burned out, but it no longer seemed necessary to keep Nick in total darkness. There could be other sources of illumination in Ed's well-equipped fallout shelter. Matches and candles, for instance, a flashlight, a table lamp – something to prevent Nick from feeling he's been buried alive. That would push any man over the edge of sanity, and the last thing I wanted was to turn Bowen's predicament into a study of terror and madness. I had left Hammett behind, but

118

I had been to the White Horse many times in the past, but not for several years now, and the instant I opened the door, I was happy to see that nothing had changed. It was the same woody, smoke-filled watering hole it had always been, with the same scarred tables and wobbly chairs, the same sawdust on the floor, the same big clock on the northern wall. All the tables were occupied, but there were a couple of spots open at the bar. I slid onto one of the stools and ordered a hamburger and a glass of beer. I rarely drank during the day, but being in the White Horse had put me in a nostalgic mood (remembering all the hours I'd spent there in my late teens and early twenties), and I decided to have one for old times' sake. It was only after I'd settled this business with the bartender that I looked over at the man sitting to my right. I had seen him from behind when I'd entered the tavern, a thin fellow in a brown sweater hunched over a drink, and something about his posture had set off a little signal in my head. Concerning what I didn't know. Recognition, perhaps. Or perhaps something more obscure: a memory of another man in a brown sweater who'd been sitting in that same position years earlier, a lilliputian fragment from the ancient past. This man had his head down and was looking into his glass, which was half filled with Scotch or bourbon. I could only see his profile, which was partially blocked by his left wrist and hand, but there was no question that the face belonged to a person I'd thought I would never see again. M. R. Chang.

that didn't mean I intended to replace the Flitcraft story with a new version of 'The Premature Burial.' Give Nick light, then, and allow him a shred of hope. And even after the matches and candles have been used up, even after the batteries in the flashlight have lost their power, he can open the refrigerator door and cast some light into the room with the small bulb that burns inside the white enameled box.

More significant, there was the question of Grace's dream. Listening to her talk that morning, I had been too shaken by the resemblances to the story I was writing to grasp how many differences there were as well. Her room was a sanctuary to be shared by

'Mr. Chang,' I said. 'How are you?'

Chang turned at the mention of his name, looking down-cast and perhaps a little drunk. At first, he didn't seem to remember who I was, but then his face gradually bright-ened. 'Ah,' he said. 'Mr. Sidney. Mr. Sidney O. Nice fellow.'

'I went back to your store yesterday,' I said, 'but every-thing was gone. What happened?'

'Big trouble,' Chang replied, shaking his head and taking a sip of his drink, apparently on the verge of tears. 'Landlord raise rent on me. I tell him I have lease, but he laugh and say he seize goods with city marshal if cash not in his fist Monday morning. So I pack up my store Saturday night and leave. All Mafia men in that neighborhood. They shoot you dead if you don't play ball.'

'You should hire a lawyer and take him to court.'

'No lawyer. Too much money. I look for new place tomor-row. Maybe Queens or Manhattan. No more Brooklyn. Paper Palace a flop. Big American dream a flop.'

I shouldn't have let myself succumb to pity, but when Chang offered to buy me a drink, I didn't have the heart to turn him down. Ingesting Scotch at one-thirty in the after-noon was not on my list of prescribed medical therapies. Even worse, now that Chang and I had become friends and were deep in conversation, I felt compelled to return the favor and order a second round. That made one glass of beer and two double Scotches in approximately an hour. Not

---

two people, a small erotic paradise. My room was a bleak cell, inhabited by one man, whose only ambition is to escape. But what if I managed to get Rosa Leightman in there with him? Nick has already fallen for her, and if they're trapped in the room together for any length of time, perhaps she would begin to reciprocate his feel-ings. Rosa was the physical and spiritual double of Grace, and there-fore she would have the same sexual appetites as Grace – the same recklessness, the same lack of inhibition. Nick and Rosa could spend their time together reading passages out loud from *Oracle Night*, baring their souls to each other, making love. As long as there was

enough to achieve full intoxication, but I was swimming pleasantly by then, and with my usual reserve growing progressively weaker as time wore on, I asked Chang a number of personal questions about his life in China and how he had come to America – something I never would have done if I hadn't been drinking. Much of what he said confused me. His ability to express himself in English slowly deteriorated as his intake of alcohol increased, but in the flow of stories I heard about his childhood in Beijing, the Cultural Revolution, and his perilous escape from the country by way of Hong Kong, one stood out in particular, no doubt because he told it early in the conversation.

'My father was math teacher,' he said, 'employed by Beijing Number Eleven Middle School. When the Cultural Revolution comes, they call him member of the Black Gang, reactionary bourgeois person. One day the Red Guard students order the Black Gang to take all books out from library not written by Chairman Mao. They hit them with belts to make them do this. These are bad books, they say. They spread capitalism and revisionist ideas, and they must be burned. My father and the other Black Gang teachers carry books out to the sports ground. The Red Guards shout at them and beat them to make them do this. They carry heavy load after heavy load, and then they have a big mountain of books. The Red Guards set them on fire, and my father begins to weep. They hit him with their belts because of this.

---

enough food to sustain them, why would they ever want to leave?

That was the little fantasy I carried around with me through the streets of the Village. Even as I played it out in my mind, however, I knew it was deeply flawed. Grace had aroused me with her erotic dream, but in spite of the temptations it seemed to offer, it was just another dead end. If Rosa can get into the room, then Nick can get out, and once that opportunity is presented to him, he wouldn't hesitate to leave. But the point is that he can't leave. I had given him some light, but he was still locked inside that grim chamber, and without the proper tools to dig his way out, he was eventually going to die in there.

Then the fire gets big and hot, and the Red Guards push the Black Gang right to the edge of the fire. They make them lower their heads and bend forward. They say they are being tried by the flames of the Great Cultural Revolution. It is a hot day in August, terrible sun. My father has blisters on his face and arms, cuts and bruises all over his back. At home, my mother cries when she sees him. My father cries. We all cry, Mr. Sidney. The next week, my father is arrested, and we are all sent to the countryside to work as farmers. That is when I learn to hate my country, my China. From that day, I begin to dream of America. I get my big American dream in China, but there is no dream in America. This country is bad too. Everywhere the same. All people bad and rotten. All countries bad and rotten.'[11]

After I finished my second Cutty Sark, I shook Chang's hand and told him it was time for me to go. It was two-thirty, I said, and I had to get back to Cobble Hill to do some pre-dinner shopping. Chang looked disappointed. I didn't know what he was expecting from me, but perhaps he thought I was prepared to accompany him on an all-day bender.

'No problem,' he finally said. 'I drive you home.'

'You have a car?'

---

11. When Chang told this story to me twenty years ago, I was certain he was telling the truth. There was too much conviction in his voice for me to doubt his sincerity. Several months ago, however, while preparing for another project, I read a number of works on China during the period of the Cultural Revolution. In one of them, I came across an account of the same incident by Liu Yan, who was a student at the Beijing Number Eleven Middle School at the time of the book burning and witnessed the event. No teacher named Chang is mentioned. A female language teacher is referred to, Yu Changjiang, who broke down and wept at the sight of the burning books. 'Her tears provoked the Red Guards to give her a few extra lashes, and the belts left ugly scars on her skin.' (*China's Cultural Revolution, 1966–1969*, edited by Michael Schoenhals; Armonk, New York: M. E. Sharpe, 1996.)

I'm not saying this proves Chang was lying to me, but it does cast

'Of course. Everyone have car. Not you?'

'No. You don't really need one in New York.'

'Come, Mr. Sid. You cheer me up and make me happy again. Now I drive you home.'

'No thanks. A man in your condition shouldn't drive. You're too potted.'

'Potted?'

'You've had too much to drink.'

'Nonsense. M. R. Chang sober as a judge.'

I smiled when I heard that old American phrase, and seeing that I was amused, Chang suddenly burst out laughing. It was the same staccato eruption I'd heard in his store on Saturday. *Ha-ha-ha. Ha-ha-ha. Ha-ha-ha.* It was a disconcerting sort of gaiety, I found, dry and soulless somehow, without the vibrant, lilting quality one usually hears when people laugh. To prove his point, Chang hopped off the bar stool and began striding back and forth across the room, demonstrating his ability to keep his balance and walk a straight line. In all fairness, I had to admit that he passed the test. His movements were steady and unforced, and he seemed to be in complete control of himself. Understanding that there was no stopping this man, that his determination

---

some suspicion over his story. Possibly, there were two teachers who wept, and Liu Yan didn't notice the other one. But it should be pointed out that the book burning was a highly publicized event in Beijing at the time and, in Liu Yan's words, 'caused a major stir all over the city.' Chang would have known about it, even if his father hadn't been there. Perhaps he told this infamous story in order to impress me. I can't say. On the other hand, his version was extremely vivid – more vivid than most secondhand accounts – which leads me to wonder if Chang wasn't present at the book burning himself. And if he was, that must have meant he'd been there as a member of the Red Guard. Otherwise, he would have told me that he'd been a student at the school – which he never did. It is even possible (this is pure speculation) that he himself was the person who lashed the weeping teacher.

to drive me home had become a passionate, single-minded cause, I reluctantly gave in and accepted his offer.

The car was parked around the corner on Perry Street, a spanking-new red Pontiac with whitewall tires and a retractable sun roof. I told Chang I thought it looked like a fresh Jersey tomato, but I didn't ask how a self-proclaimed American flop had managed to acquire such a costly machine. With evident pride, he unlocked my door first and ushered me into the passenger's seat. Then, patting the hood as he walked around the front of the car, he stepped up onto the curb and unlocked the other door. Once he'd settled in behind the wheel, he turned to me and grinned. 'Solid merchandise,' he said.

'Yes,' I replied. 'Very impressive.'

'Make yourself comfortable, Mr. Sid. Reclining seats. Go all the way back.' He leaned over and showed me where to push the button, and sure enough, the seat began propelling itself backward, coming to rest at a forty-five-degree angle. 'Like that,' Chang said. 'Always better to ride in comfort.'

I couldn't disagree with him, and in my slightly tipsy state I found it pleasant to be in something other than a vertical position. Chang started up the engine of the car, and I closed my eyes for a moment, trying to imagine what Grace would want for dinner that evening and what food I should buy when I got back to Brooklyn. That turned out to be a mistake. Instead of opening my eyes again to see where Chang was going, I promptly fell asleep – just like any other drunk on a midday binge.

I didn't wake up until the car stopped and Chang turned off the engine. Assuming I was back in Cobble Hill, I was about to thank him for the lift and open the door when I realized I was somewhere else: a crowded commercial street in an unfamiliar neighborhood, no doubt far from where I lived. When I sat up to have a better look, I saw that most of the signs were in Chinese.

'Where are we?' I asked.

'Flushing,' Chang said. 'Chinatown Number Two.'

'Why did you bring me here?'

'Driving in car, I have better idea. Nice little club on next block, good place to relax. You look tired out, Mr. Sid. I take you there, you feel better.'

'What are you talking about? It's quarter past three, and I have to get home.'

'Just half an hour. Do you a world of good, I promise. Then I drive you home. Okay?'

'I'd rather not. Just point me to the nearest subway, and I'll go home myself.'

'Please. This very important to me. Maybe a business opportunity, and I need advice from a smart man. You very smart, Mr. Sid. I can trust you.'

'I have no idea what you're talking about. First you want me to relax. Then you want me to give you advice. Which is it?'

'Both things. All things together. You see place, you relax, and then you tell me what you think. Very simple.'

'Half an hour?'

'No skin off nose. Everything on me, free of charge. Then I drive you to Cobble Hill, Brooklyn. Deal?'

The afternoon was turning stranger by the minute, but I allowed myself to be talked into going with him. I can't really explain why. Curiosity, maybe, but it also could have been just the opposite – a feeling of total indifference. Chang had begun to get on my nerves, and I couldn't take his incessant pleading anymore, especially not while cooped up in that ridiculous car of his. If another half hour of my time would satisfy him, I figured it was worth it to play along. So I climbed out of the Pontiac and followed him down the densely thronged avenue, breathing in the pungent fumes and acrid smells of the fish stores and vegetable stands that lined the block. At the first corner, we turned left, walked for about a hundred feet, and then turned left again, entering a narrow alley with a small cinder-block structure at the end of it, a tiny one-story house with no windows and a flat roof. It was a classic setup for a mugging, but I didn't feel the least bit threatened. Chang was in too jolly a mood, and with his usual intensity of purpose, he seemed hell-bent on reaching our destination.

When we came to the yellow cinder-block house, Chang pressed his finger against the doorbell. A few seconds later, the door opened a crack and a Chinese man in his sixties poked out his head. He nodded in recognition when he saw Chang, they exchanged a few sentences in Mandarin, and then he let us in. The so-called club of relaxation turned out to be a small sweatshop. Twenty Chinese women sat at tables with sewing machines, stitching together brightly colored dresses made of cheap, synthetic materials. Not one of them looked up at us when we entered, and Chang rushed past them as quickly as he could, acting as if they weren't there. We kept on walking, threading our way around the tables until we came to a door at the back of the room. The old man opened it for us, and Chang and I stepped into a space that was so black, so dark in comparison to the fluorescent-lit workshop behind us, that at first I couldn't see a thing.

Once my eyes had adjusted a little, I noticed some dim low-wattage lamps glowing in various places around the room. Each one had been fitted with a bulb of a different color – red, yellow, purple, blue – and for a moment I thought about the Portuguese notebooks in Chang's bankrupt store. I wondered if the ones I'd seen on Saturday were still available and, if they were, whether he'd be willing to sell them to me. I made a mental note to ask him about it before we left.

By and by, he led me to a tall chair or stool, something made of leather or imitation leather that swiveled on its base and had a nice cushiony feel to it. I sat down, and he sat down next to me, and I realized that we were at some kind of bar – a lacquered, oval-shaped bar that occupied the center of the room. Things were becoming clearer to me now. I could make out several people sitting across from us, a couple of men in suits and ties, an Asian man in what looked like a Hawaiian shirt, and two or three women, none of whom seemed to be wearing any clothes. Ah, I said to myself, so that's what this place is. A sex club. Oddly enough, it was only then that I noticed the music playing in the background – a soft, rumbling piece that wafted in from some invisible sound system. I strained to pick out the song, but I couldn't identify it. Some Musak version of an old rock-and-roll number – maybe the Beatles, I thought, but maybe not.

'Well, Mr. Sid,' Chang said, 'what do you think?'

Before I could answer him, a bartender appeared in front of us and asked for our orders. It might have been the old man who had opened the door earlier, but I wasn't certain. It could have been his brother, or perhaps some other relative with a stake in the enterprise. Chang leaned over and whispered in my ear. 'No alcohol,' he said. 'Fake beer, 7-Up, Coke. Too risky to sell booze in place like this. No liquor license.' Now that I'd been informed of the possibilities, I opted for a Coke. Chang did the same.

'Brand-new place,' the ex-stationer continued. 'Just open on Saturday. They still iron out the kinks, but I see large potential here. They ask if I want to invest as minority partner.'

'It's a brothel,' I said. 'Are you sure you want to get mixed up in an illegal business?'

'Not brothel. Relaxation club with naked women. Help the workingman feel better.'

'I'm not going to split hairs with you. If you're so keen on it, go ahead. But I thought you were broke.'

'Money never a problem. I borrow. If profit from investment stay ahead of interest on loan, everything okay.'

'If.'

'Very little if. They find gorgeous girls to work here. Miss Universe, Marilyn Monroe, Playmate of Month. Only the hottest, most sexy women. No man can resist. Look, I show you.'

'No thanks. I'm a married man. I have everything I need at home.'

'Every man say that. But the dick always win out over duty. I prove it to you now.'

Before I could stop him, Chang wheeled around in his chair and made a beckoning gesture with his hand. I looked over in that direction myself and saw five or six cocktail booths lining the wall, something I had managed to miss when I first entered the room. Naked women sat at three of them, apparently waiting for customers, but the others had been curtained off, presumably because the women who occupied those spots were busy at work. One of the women rose from her seat and came walking toward us. 'This one the best,' Chang said, 'the most beautiful of all. They call her the African Princess.'

A tall black woman emerged from the darkness. She was wearing a pearl-and-rhinestone choker, knee-high white boots, and a white G-string. Her hair was done up in elaborate cornrow braids, ornamented with bangles at the ends that tinkled like wind chimes when she moved. Her walk was graceful, languorous, erect – a regal sort of bearing that no doubt explained why she was called the Princess. By the time she was within six feet of the bar, I understood that Chang had not been exaggerating. She was a stunningly beautiful woman – perhaps the most beautiful woman I had ever seen. And all of twenty, perhaps twenty-two years old. Her skin looked so smooth and inviting, I found it almost impossible to resist touching it.

'Say hello to my friend,' Chang instructed her. 'I settle up with you later.'

She turned to me and smiled, exposing a set of astonishing white teeth. 'Bonjour, chéri,' she said. 'Tu parles français?'

'No, I'm sorry. I only speak English.'

'My name is Martine,' she said, with a heavy Creole accent.

'I'm Sidney,' I answered, and then, trying to make a stab at conversation, I asked her which country in Africa she came from.

She laughed. 'Pas d'Afrique! Haïti.' She pronounced the last word in three syllables, *Ha-ee-tee*. 'A bad place,' she said. 'Duvalier is very méchant. It is nicer here.'

I nodded, having no idea what to say next. I wanted to get up and leave before I got myself into trouble, but I couldn't move. The girl was too much, and I couldn't stop looking at her.

'Tu veux danser avec moi?' she said. 'You dance with me?'

'I don't know. Maybe. I'm not a very good dancer.'

'Something else?'

'I don't know. Well, maybe one thing . . . if it isn't too much to ask.'

'One thing?'

'I was wondering. . . . Would you mind terribly if I touched you?'

'Touched me? Of course. That is easy. Touch me anywhere you like.'

I reached out my hand and ran it down the length of her bare arm. 'You are very timide,' she said. 'Do you not see my breasts? Mes seins sont très jolis, n'est-ce pas?'

I was sober enough to realize that I was traveling down the road to perdition, but I didn't let that stop me. I cupped her small round breasts in my two hands and held them there for some time – long enough to feel her nipples harden.

'Ah, that is better,' she said. 'Now you let me touch you, okay?'

I didn't say yes, but neither did I say no. I assumed she had something innocent in mind – a pat on the cheek, a finger traced across my lips, a playful squeeze of the hand. Nothing to compare with what she actually did, in any case, which was to press herself against me, slide her elegant hand down into my jeans, and take hold of the erection that had been growing in there for the past two minutes. When she felt how stiff I was, she smiled. 'I think we are ready to dance,' she said. 'You come with me now, okay?'

To his credit, Chang didn't laugh at this sad little spectacle of male weakness. He had proved his point, and rather than gloat over his triumph, he merely winked at me as I walked off with Martine to her booth.

The whole transaction seemed to last no longer than the time it takes to fill a bathtub. She closed the curtain around the booth and immediately unbuckled my pants. Then she dropped to her knees and put her right hand around my penis, and after a few gentle strokes, followed by some timely licks of the tongue, she put it in her mouth. Her head began to move, and as I listened to the tinkling of her braids and looked down at her extraordinary bare back, I felt a rush of warmth rising up through my legs and into my groin. I wanted to prolong the experience and savor it for a little while, but I couldn't. Martine's mouth was a deadly instrument, and like any aroused teenage boy, I came almost at once.

Regret set in within a matter of seconds. By the time I'd pulled up my jeans and fastened my belt, regret had turned into shame and remorse. The only thing I wanted was to get out of there as quickly as I could. I asked Martine how much I owed her, but she waved me off and said my friend had already taken care of it. She kissed me when I said good-bye, an amiable little peck on the cheek, and then I parted the curtain and went back to the bar to look for Chang. He wasn't there. Perhaps he'd found a woman for himself and was already with her in another booth, testing the professional qualifications of one of his future employees. I didn't bother to stick around to find out. I walked around the bar once, just to make sure I hadn't missed him, and then I found the door that led to the dress factory and started out for home.

The next morning, Wednesday, I served Grace breakfast in

bed again. There was no talk about dreams this time, and neither one of us mentioned the pregnancy or what she was planning to do about it. The issue was still up in the air, but after my disgraceful behavior in Queens the day before, I felt too embarrassed to broach the subject. In the span of thirty-six short hours, I had gone from being a self-righteous defender of moral certainties to an abject, guilt-ridden husband.

Nevertheless, I tried to keep up a good front, and even though she was unusually quiet that morning, I don't think Grace suspected anything was wrong. I insisted on walking her to the subway, holding her hand for the entire four blocks to the Bergen Street station, and for most of the way we talked about ordinary matters: a jacket she was designing for a book on nineteenth-century French photography, the film treatment I had handed in the day before and the money I hoped would come from it, what we would have for dinner that night. On the last block, however, Grace abruptly changed the tone of the conversation. She gripped my hand tightly and said: 'We trust each other, don't we, Sid?'

'Of course we do. We wouldn't be able to live together if we didn't. The whole idea of marriage is based on trust.'

'People can go through rough times, can't they? But that doesn't mean things can't work out in the end.'

'This isn't a rough time, Grace. We've been through that already, and we're beginning to pull ourselves together again.'

'I'm glad you said that.'

'I'm glad you're glad. But why?'

'Because that's what I think too. No matter what happens with the baby, everything between us is going to be fine. We're going to make it.'

'We've already made it. We're cruising down Easy Street, kid, and that's where we're going to stay.'

Grace stopped walking, put her hand on the back of my

neck, and pulled my face toward her for a kiss. 'You're the best, Sidney,' she said, and then she kissed me once more for good measure. 'No matter what happens, don't ever forget that.'

I didn't understand what she was talking about, but before I could ask her what she meant, she disentangled herself from my arms and started running toward the subway. I stood where I was on the sidewalk, watching her cover the last ten yards. Then she came to the top step, grabbed hold of the railing, and disappeared down the stairs.

Back at the apartment, I kept myself busy for the next hour, killing time until the Sklarr Agency opened at nine-thirty. I washed the breakfast dishes, made the bed, tidied up the living room, and then I went back into the kitchen and called Mary. The ostensible reason was to make sure Angela had remembered to give her my pages, but knowing that she had, I was actually calling to find out what Mary thought of them. 'Good job,' she said, sounding neither greatly excited nor terribly disappointed. The fact that I had written the outline so quickly, however, had enabled her to pull off a high-speed communications miracle, and that had her gushing with excitement. In those days before fax machines, e-mails, and express letters, she had sent the treatment to California by private courier, which meant that my work had already traveled across the country on last night's red-eye. 'I had to get a contract off to another client in LA,' Mary said, 'so I hired the courier service to come by the office at three o'clock. I read your treatment right after lunch, and half an hour later the guy shows up for the contract. "This one's also going to LA," I said, "so you might as well take it too." So I handed him your manuscript, and off it went, just like that. It should be on Hunter's desk in about three hours.'

'Great,' I said. 'But what about the idea? Do you think it has a chance?'

'I only read it once. I didn't have time to study it, but it seemed fine to me, Sid. Very interesting, nicely worked out. But you never know with those Hollywood people. My guess is it's too complicated for them.'

'So I shouldn't get my hopes up.'

'I wouldn't say that. Just don't count on it, that's all.'

'I won't. But the money would be nice, wouldn't it?'

'Well, I do have some good news for you on that front. I was just going to call you, in fact, but you beat me to it. A Portuguese publisher has made an offer on your last two novels.'

'Portugal?'

'Self-Portrait was published in Spain while you were in the hospital. You know that, I told you. The reviews were very good. Now the Portuguese are interested.'

'That's nice. I suppose they're offering something like three hundred dollars.'

'Four hundred for each book. But I can easily get them up to five.'

'Go for it, Mary. After you deduct the agents' fees and foreign taxes, I'll wind up with about forty cents.'

'True. But at least you'll be published in Portugal. What's wrong with that?'

'Nothing. Pessoa is one of my favorite writers. They've kicked out Salazar and have a decent government now. The Lisbon earthquake inspired Voltaire to write *Candide*. And Portugal helped get thousands of Jews out of Europe during the war. It's a terrific country. I've never been there, of course, but that's where I live now, whether I like it or not. Portugal is perfect. The way things have been going these past few days, it had to be Portugal.'

'What are you talking about?'

'It's a long story. I'll tell you about it some other time.'

I made it to Trause's apartment on the dot of one. As I rang the bell, it occurred to me that I should have stopped off somewhere in the neighborhood and bought take-out

133

lunches for the two of us, but I had forgotten about Madame Dumas, the woman from Martinique who managed the household. The meal was already prepared, and it was served to us in John's den on the second floor, the same room where we had eaten our Chinese dinner on Saturday night. I should note that Madame Dumas was not on duty that day. It was her daughter, Régine, who opened the door and led me upstairs to *Monsieur John*. I remembered that Trause had called her 'nice to look at,' and now that I'd seen her myself, I was forced to admit that I, too, found her remarkably attractive – a tall, well-proportioned young woman with glowing ebony skin and keen, watchful eyes. No G-string, of course, no bare breasts or white leather boots, but this was the second twenty-year-old French-speaking black woman I had met in two days, and I found the repetition jarring, almost intolerable. Why couldn't Régine Dumas have been a short, homely girl with a bad complexion and a hump on her back? She wasn't the heart-stopping beauty that Martine of Haiti was, perhaps, but she was a fetching creature in her own right, and when she opened the door and smiled at me in her friendly, self-assured way, I felt it as a reproof, a mocking rejoinder from my own troubled conscience. I had been doing everything in my power not to think about what had happened the day before, to forget my sorry peccadillo and put it behind me, but there was no escape from what I had done. Martine had come to life again in the form of Régine Dumas. She was everywhere now, even in my friend's Barrow Street apartment, half a world away from that shabby cinder-block building in Queens.

As opposed to his unkempt appearance on Saturday night, John looked presentable this time. His hair was combed, his whiskers were gone, and he was wearing a freshly laundered shirt and clean socks. But he was still immobilized on the sofa, his left leg propped up on a mountain of pillows and blankets, and he seemed to be in considerable pain – as bad as the other night, if not worse. The clean-shaven look had thrown me. When Régine brought the lunch upstairs on a tray (turkey sandwiches, salads, sparkling water), I did everything I could not to look at her. That meant focusing my attention on John, and when I studied his features more carefully, I saw that he was exhausted, with a sunken, hollowed-out look in his eyes and a disturbing pallor to his skin. He left the sofa twice while I was there, and both times he reached for his crutch before maneuvering himself into a standing position. From the look on his face when his left foot touched the ground, the slightest pressure on the vein must have been unbearable.

I asked him when he was supposed to get better, but John didn't want to talk about it. I kept after him, however, and eventually he admitted that he hadn't told us everything on Saturday night. He hadn't wanted to alarm Grace, he said, but the truth was that there were two clots in his leg, not one. The first was in a superficial vein. It had nearly dissolved by now and posed no threat, even though it was causing most of what John referred to as his 'discomfort.' The second was lodged in a deep interior vein, and that was the one the doctor was worried about. Massive doses of blood thinner had been prescribed, and John was scheduled to have a scan at Saint Vincent's on Friday. If the results were less than satisfactory, the doctor was planning to admit him to the hospital and keep him there until the clot disappeared. Deep-vein thrombosis could be fatal, John said. If the clot broke loose, it could travel through his bloodstream and wind up in a lung, causing a pulmonary embolism and almost certain death. 'It's like walking around with a little bomb in my leg,' he said. 'If I shake it around too much, it could blow me up.' Then he added, 'Not a word to Gracie. This is strictly between you and me. Got it? Not a single goddamn word.'

Not long after that, we started talking about his son. I can't remember what led us into that pit of despair and self-recrimination, but Trause's anguish was palpable, and whatever concerns he had about his leg were nothing compared to the hopelessness he felt about Jacob. 'I've lost him,' he said. 'After the stunt he's just pulled, I'll never believe another word he says to me.'

Until the latest crisis, Jacob had been an undergraduate at SUNY Buffalo. John was acquainted with several members of the English Department there (one of them, Charles Rothstein, had published a long study of his novels), and after Jacob's disastrous, near-failing record in high school, he had pulled some strings in order to get the boy accepted. The first semester had gone reasonably well, and Jacob had managed to pass all his courses, but by the end of the second term his grades had fallen off so badly that he was put on academic probation. He needed to maintain a B average to avoid suspension, but in the fall semester of his sophomore year he cut more classes than he attended, did little or no work, and was summarily booted out for the next term. He went back to his mother in East Hampton, where she was living with her third husband (in the same house where Jacob had grown up with his much-despised stepfather, an art dealer named Ralph Singleton), and found a part-time job at a local bakery. He also formed a rock band with three of his high school friends, but there were so many tensions and squabbles among them that the group broke up after six months. He told his father he had no use for college and didn't want to go back, but John managed to talk him into it by offering certain financial incentives: a comfortable allowance, a new guitar if he kept his grades up in the first semester, a Volkswagen minibus if he finished the year with a B average. The kid went for it, and in late August he'd gone back to Buffalo to play at being a student again – with green hair, a row of safety pins dangling from his left ear, and a long black overcoat. The punk era was in full bloom then, and Jacob had joined the ever-expanding club of snarling, middle-class renegades. He was hip, he lived on the edge, and he didn't take crap from anyone.

Jacob had enrolled for the semester, John said, but a week later, without having attended a single class, he returned to the registrar's office and dropped out of school. The tuition was returned to him, and instead of sending the check to his father (who had provided him with the money in the first place), he cashed it in at the nearest bank, put the three thousand dollars in his pocket, and headed south to New York. At last word, he was living somewhere in the East Village. If the rumors circulating about him were correct, he was deep into heroin – and had been for the past four months.

'Who told you this?' I asked. 'How do you know it's true?'

'Eleanor called me yesterday morning. She'd been trying to get hold of Jacob about something, and his roommate answered the phone. Ex-roommate, I should say. He told her Jacob had left school two weeks ago.'

'And the heroin?'

'He told her about that too. There's no reason for him to lie about a thing like that. According to Eleanor, he sounded very concerned. It's not that I'm surprised, Sid. I've always suspected he was taking drugs. I just didn't know it was this bad.'

'What are you going to do about it?'

'I don't know. You're the one who used to work with kids. What would you do?'

'You're asking the wrong person. All my students were poor. Black teenagers from tumbledown neighborhoods and broken families. A lot of them took drugs, but their problems have nothing to do with Jacob's.'

'Eleanor thinks we should go out looking for him. But I can't move. I'm stuck on this couch with my leg.'

'I'll do it if you like. It's not as if I'm very busy these days.'

'No, no, I don't want you getting involved. It's not your problem. Eleanor and her husband will do it. At least that's what she said. With her, you never know if she means it or not.'

'What's her new husband like?'

'I don't know. I've never met him. The funny thing is, I can't even remember his name. I've been lying here trying to think of it, but I keep drawing blanks. Don something, I think, but I'm not sure.'

'And what's the plan once they find Jacob?'

'Get him into a drug rehab program.'

'Those things aren't cheap. Who's going to pay for it?'

'Me, of course. Eleanor's rolling in money these days, but she's so fucking tight, I wouldn't even bother to ask her. The kid chisels three thousand bucks out of me, and now I have to cough up another bundle to get him clean. If you want to know the truth, I feel like wringing his neck. You're lucky you don't have any children, Sid. They're nice when they're small, but after that they break your heart and make you miserable. Five feet, that's the maximum. They shouldn't be allowed to grow any taller than that.'

After John's last comment, I couldn't hold back from telling him my news. 'I might not be childless much longer,' I said. 'It's not clear what we're going to do about it yet, but for the moment Grace is pregnant. She had the test on Saturday.'

I didn't know what I was expecting John to say, but even after his bitter pronouncements on the agonies of fatherhood, I figured he'd manage to come out with some kind of perfunctory congratulations. Or at least wish me luck and warn me to do a better job than he'd done. Something, in any case, some little word of acknowledgment. But John didn't make a sound. For a moment he looked stricken, as if he'd just been told about the death of someone he loved, and then he turned his face away from me, abruptly swiveling his head on the pillow and looking straight into the back of the sofa.

'Poor Grace,' he muttered.

'Why do you say that?'

John slowly turned back toward me, but he stopped midway, his head aligned with the sofa, and when he talked he kept his gaze fixed on the ceiling. 'It's just that she's been through so much,' he said. 'She's not as strong as you think she is. She needs a rest.'

'She'll do exactly what she wants to do. The decision is in her hands.'

'I've known her much longer than you have. A baby is the last thing she needs right now.'

'If she goes through with it, I was thinking of asking you to be the godfather. But I don't suppose you'd be interested. Not from what you're saying now.'

'Just don't lose her, Sidney. That's all I'm asking you. If things fall apart, it would be a catastrophe for her.'

'They're not going to fall apart. And I'm not going to lose her. But even if I did, what business is it of yours?'

'Grace is my business. She's always been my business.'

'You're not her father. You might think you are sometimes, but you're not. Grace can handle herself. If she decides to have the baby, I'm not going to stop her. The truth is, I'll be glad. Having a child with her would be about the best thing that ever happened to me.'

That was the closest John and I had ever come to an out-and-out argument. It was an upsetting moment for me, and as my last words hung defiantly in the air, I wondered if the conversation wasn't about to take an even nastier turn. Fortunately, we both backed off before the flare-up developed any further, realizing that we were about to goad each other into saying things we would later regret – and which could never be expunged from memory, no matter how many apologies we made after our tempers had calmed down.

Very wisely, John picked that moment to pay a visit to the bathroom. As I watched him go through the arduous manipulations of hauling himself off the sofa and then hobble across the room, all the hostility suddenly drained out of me. He was living under extreme duress. His leg was killing him, he was grappling with the awful news about his son, and how could I not forgive him for having spoken a few harsh words? In the context of Jacob's betrayal and possible drug addiction, Grace was the adored good child, the one who had never let him down, and perhaps that was the reason why John had been so adamant in coming to her defense, butting into matters that finally didn't concern him. He was angry at his son, yes, but that anger was also laden with a substantial dose of guilt. John knew he had more or less abdicated his responsibilities as a father. Divorced from Eleanor when Jacob was one and a half, he had allowed her to remove the child from New York when she settled in East Hampton with her second husband in 1966. After that, John had seen little of the boy: an occasional weekend together in the city, a few trips to New England and the Southwest during summer vacations. Hardly what one could call an actively involved parent, and then, after Tina's death, he had disappeared from Jacob's life for four years, seeing him only once or twice from age twelve to sixteen. Now, at twenty, his son had turned into a full-blown mess, and whether it was his fault or not, John blamed himself for the disaster.

He was gone from the room for ten or fifteen minutes. When he returned, I helped him onto the sofa again, and the first thing he said to me had nothing to do with what we'd been talking about earlier. The conflict seemed to be over – swept away during his trip down the hall and apparently forgotten.

'How's Flitcraft?' he asked. 'Making any progress?'

'Yes and no,' I said. 'I wrote up a storm for a couple of days, but then I got stuck.'

'And now you're having second thoughts about the blue notebook.'

'Maybe. I'm not sure I know what I think anymore.'

'You were so revved up the other night, you sounded like a demented alchemist. The first man to turn lead into gold.'

'Well, it was quite an experience. The first time I used the notebook, Grace tells me I wasn't there anymore.'

'What do you mean?'

'That I disappeared. I know it sounds ridiculous, but she knocked on my door while I was writing, and when I didn't answer she poked her head into the room. She swears she didn't see me.'

'You must have been somewhere else in the apartment. In the bathroom, maybe.'

'I know. That's what Grace says too. But I don't remember going to the bathroom. I don't remember anything but sitting at my desk and writing.'

'You might not remember it, but that doesn't mean it didn't happen. One tends to get a little absentminded when the words are flowing. Not true?'

'True. Of course true. But then something similar happened on Monday. I was in my room writing, and I didn't hear the phone ring. When I got up from my desk and went into the kitchen, there were two messages on the machine.'

'So?'

'I didn't hear the ring. I always hear the phone when it rings.'

'You were distracted, lost in what you were doing.'

'Maybe. But I don't think so. Something strange happened, and I don't understand it.'

'Call your doctor, Sid, and set up an appointment to have your head examined.'

'I know. It's all in my head. I'm not saying it isn't, but ever since I bought that notebook, everything's gone out of whack. I can't tell if I'm the one who's using the notebook or if the notebook's been using me. Does that make any sense?'

'A little. But not much.'

'All right, let me put it another way. Have you ever heard of a writer named Sylvia Maxwell? An American novelist from the twenties.'

'I've read some books by Sylvia Monroe. She published a bunch of novels in the twenties and thirties. But not Maxwell.'

141

'Did she ever write a book called *Oracle Night*?'

'No, not that I know of. But I think she wrote something with the word *night* in the title. *Havana Night*, maybe. Or *London Night*, I can't remember. It shouldn't be hard to find out. Just go to the library and look her up.'

Little by little, we veered away from the blue notebook and started discussing more practical matters. Money, for one thing, and how I was hoping to solve my financial problems by writing a film script for Bobby Hunter. I told John about the treatment, giving him a quick summary of the plot I'd cooked up for my version of *The Time Machine*, but he didn't offer much of a response. *Clever*, I think he said, or some equally mild compliment, and I suddenly felt stupid, embarrassed, as though Trause looked on me as some tawdry hack trying to peddle my wares to the highest bidder. But I was wrong to interpret his muffled reaction as disapproval. He understood what a tight spot we were in, and it turned out that he was thinking, trying to come up with a plan to help me.

'I know it's idiotic,' I said, 'but if they go for the idea, we'll be solvent again. If they don't, we're still in the red. I hate to count on such flimsy prospects, but it's the only trick I have up my sleeve.'

'Maybe not,' John said. 'If this *Time Machine* thing doesn't work, maybe you could write another screenplay. You're good at it. If you got Mary to push hard enough, I'm sure you'd find someone willing to fork over a nice chunk of cash.'

'It doesn't work that way. They come to you; you don't go to them. Unless you have an original idea, of course. But I don't.'

'That's what I'm talking about. Maybe I have an idea for you.'

'A movie idea? I thought you were against writing for the movies.'

'A couple of weeks ago, I found a box with some of my old

stuff in it. Early stories, a half-finished novel, two or three plays. Ancient material, written when I was still in my teens and twenties. None of it was ever published. Thankfully, I should add, but in reading over the stories, I found one that wasn't half terrible. I still wouldn't want to publish it, but if I gave it to you, you might be able to rethink it as a film. Maybe my name will help. If you tell a film producer you're adapting an unpublished story by John Trause, it might have some appeal. I don't know. But even if they don't give a shit about me, there's a strong visual component to the story. I think the images would lend themselves to film in a pretty natural way.'

'Of course your name would help. It would make a huge difference.'

'Well, read the story and let me know what you think. It's just a first draft – very rough – so don't judge the prose too harshly. And remember, I was hardly more than a kid when I wrote it. Much younger than you are now.'

'What's it about?'

'It's an odd piece, not at all like my other work, so you might be a little surprised at first. I guess I'd call it a political parable. It's set in an imaginary country in the eighteen thirties, but it's really about the early nineteen fifties. McCarthy, HUAC, the Red Scare – all the sinister things that were going on then. The idea is that governments always need enemies, even when they're not at war. If you don't have a real enemy, you make one up and spread the word. It scares the population, and when the people are scared, they tend not to step out of line.'

'What about the country? Is it a stand-in for America or something else?'

'It's part North America, part South America, but with a completely different history from either one. Way back, all the European powers had set up colonies in the New World. The colonies evolved into independent states, and then, little by little, after hundreds of years of wars and skirmishes, they gradually merge into an enormous confederation. The question is: What happens after the empire is established? What enemy do you invent to make people scared enough to hold the confederation together?'

'And what's the answer?'

'You pretend you're about to be invaded by barbarians. The confederation has already pushed these people off their lands, but now you spread the rumor that an army of anti-confederationist soldiers has crossed into the primitive territories and is stirring up a rebellion among the people there. It isn't true. The soldiers are working for the government. They're part of the conspiracy.'

'Who tells the story?'

'A man sent to investigate the rumors. He works for a branch of the government that isn't in on the plot, and he winds up being arrested and tried for treason. To make matters more complicated, the officer in charge of the false army has run off with the narrator's wife.'

'Deceit and corruption at every turn.'

'Exactly. A man ruined by his own innocence.'

'Does it have a title?'

'"The Empire of Bones." It's not very long. Forty-five or fifty pages – but there's enough to squeeze a film out of it, I think. You decide. If you want to use it, I give you my blessing. If you don't like it, then chuck it in the garbage, and we'll forget all about it.'

I left Trause's apartment feeling overwhelmed, tongue-tied with gratitude, and not even the small torment of having to say good-bye to Régine downstairs could diminish my happiness. The manuscript was in a side pocket of my sport coat, tucked away in a manila envelope, and I kept my hand on it as I walked to the subway, itching to open it up and start reading. John had always been behind me and my work, but I knew this gift had as much to do with Grace as it did with me. I was the half-destroyed cripple responsible for

144

taking care of her, and if there was anything he could do to help us get back on our feet, he was willing to do it – even to the extent of donating an unpublished manuscript to the cause. There was only the slimmest chance that anything would come of his idea, but whether I could turn his story into a film or not, the important thing was his readiness to go beyond the normal bounds of friendship and involve himself in our affairs. Selflessly, without any thought of profiting from what he'd done.

It was already past five o'clock when I made it to the West Fourth Street station. Rush hour was in full swing, and as I descended the two flights of stairs to the downtown F platform, gripping the banister tightly so as not to stumble, I despaired of finding a seat on the train. There would be a crush of passengers traveling back to Brooklyn. That meant I would have to read John's story standing up, and since that would be immensely difficult, I prepared myself to fight for a little extra space if I had to. When the doors of the train opened, I ignored subway etiquette and slipped in past the jostle of disembarking passengers, entering the car before anyone else on the platform, but it didn't do me any good. A mob came pouring in behind me. I was pushed to the center of the car, and by the time the doors closed and the train left the station, I was crammed in among so many people that my arms were pinned to my sides, with no room to reach into my pocket and take out the envelope. It was all I could do not to crash into my fellow riders as we rocked and lurched our way through the tunnel. At one point, I managed to get my hand up far enough to hook my fingers onto one of the overhead bars, but that was the extent of the movement possible for me under the circumstances. Few passengers got off at the succeeding stops, and for every one who did, two others shouldered themselves in to take that person's place. Hundreds were left standing on the platforms to wait for the next train, and from the beginning of the ride to the end, I didn't have a single chance to look at the story. When we pulled into the Bergen Street station, I tried to get my hand back onto the envelope, but I was bumped from behind, squeezed from both left and right, and as I pivoted around the center pole to get ready to exit the car, the train suddenly stopped, the doors opened, and I was pushed out onto the platform before I could check to see if the envelope was still there. It wasn't. The surge of the departing crowd carried me along with it for six or seven feet, and by the time I spun around to elbow my way back into the car, the doors had already closed and the subway was moving again. I pounded my fist against a passing window, but the conductor paid no attention to me. The F glided out of the station, and a few seconds later it was gone.

I had been guilty of similar lapses of concentration since coming home from the hospital, but none was worse or more wrenching than this one. Instead of keeping the envelope in my hand, I had foolishly shoved the thing into a pocket that was too small to hold it, and now John's manuscript was lying on the floor of a subway car headed for Coney Island, no doubt trampled and smudged by half the shoes and sneakers in the borough of Brooklyn. It was an unforgivable mistake. John had entrusted me with the only copy of an unpublished story, and given the academic interest in his work, the manuscript alone was probably worth hundreds of dollars, perhaps thousands. What was I going to tell him when he asked me what I thought of it? He had said I should toss it in the garbage if I didn't like it, but that was merely a hyperbolic way of denigrating his own work, a joke. Of course he would want the manuscript back – whether I liked it or not. I had no idea how to make amends. If someone had done to me what I'd just done to Trause, I think I would have been angry enough to want to strangle him.

Demoralizing as that loss was, it was only the beginning of what turned out to be a long and difficult night. When I returned home and walked up the three flights of stairs to the apartment, I discovered that the door was open – not

146

simply ajar, but flung back on its hinges and standing flush against the wall. My first thought was that Grace had come home early, perhaps carrying an armful of bundles and grocery bags, and had forgotten to shut the door behind her. One look at the living room, however, and I understood that Grace had nothing to do with it. Someone had broken into the apartment, most likely by climbing up the fire escape and jimmying the kitchen window. Books were strewn about the floor, our small black-and-white TV was gone, and a photograph of Grace, which had always stood on the mantel, had been torn up into little pieces and scattered onto the sofa. It was a remarkably vicious gesture, I felt, almost a personal attack. When I went over to the bookcase to inspect the damage, I saw that only the most valuable books were missing: signed copies of novels by Trause and a number of other writer friends, along with half a dozen first editions that had been given to me as presents over the years. Hawthorne, Dickens, Henry James, Fitzgerald, Wallace Stevens, Emerson. Whoever had robbed us was no ordinary thief. He knew something about literature, and he had zeroed in on the few treasures we owned.

My study appeared to be untouched, but the bedroom had been systematically and thoroughly ransacked. Every drawer had been pulled out of the bureau, the mattress had been overturned, and the Bram van Velde lithograph that Grace had bought at the Galerie Maeght in Paris in the early seventies was missing from its place on the wall above our bed. When I sifted through the contents of the bureau drawers, I discovered that Grace's jewelry box was also missing. She didn't own much, but a pair of moonstone earrings she'd inherited from her grandmother had been in that box, along with a charm bracelet from her childhood and a silver necklace I'd given to her on her last birthday. Now some stranger had walked off with these things, and it felt as cruel and pointless to me as a rape, a savage plundering of our little world.

We had no theft or home insurance, and I was disinclined to call the police to report the break-in. Burglars were never caught, and I saw no reason to pursue what struck me as a hopeless case, but before I made that decision I had to find out if anyone else in the building had been robbed. There were three other apartments in the brownstone – one above us and two below – and I began by going downstairs to the ground floor and talking to Mrs. Caramello, who shared the superintendent duties with her husband, a retired barber who spent most of his time watching television and betting on football games. Their place hadn't been touched, but Mrs. Caramello was sufficiently distressed by my news to call out to Mr. Caramello, who came shuffling to the door in his slippers and merely sighed when he was told what had happened. 'Probably one of them goddamn junkies,' he said. 'Gotta get bars on your windows, Sid. Ain't no other way to keep the trash from crawling in.'

The other two tenants had also been spared. It seemed that everyone had bars on their back windows but us, and therefore we'd been the logical target – trusting dumbbells who hadn't bothered to take the proper precautions. They all felt sorry for us, but the implicit message was that we'd deserved what we'd got.

I went back into the apartment, even more horrified now that I could survey the mess in a calmer state of mind. One by one, details I had overlooked earlier suddenly jumped out at me, further aggravating the effect of the intrusion. A standing lamp to the left of the sofa had been tipped over and broken, a flower vase lay smashed on the rug, and even our pathetic, nineteen-dollar toaster had vanished from its spot on the kitchen counter. I called Grace at her office, wanting to prepare her for the shock, but no one answered, which seemed to imply that she had already left and was on her way home. Not knowing what else to do with myself, I began straightening up the apartment. It must have been about six-thirty at that point, and even though I was expecting Grace to walk through the door at any moment, I worked steadily for over an hour, sweeping up debris, returning the books to the shelves, righting the mattress and putting it back on the bed, sliding the drawers back into the bureau. At first, I was glad to be making so much progress while Grace was still gone. The more effectively I could put the place in order, the less disconcerting it would be for her when she walked into the apartment. But then I finished what I had set out to do, and she still hadn't come home. It was seven-forty-five by then, long past the time when a subway breakdown could have accounted for her failure to reach Brooklyn. It was true that she sometimes worked late, but she always called to let me know when she would be leaving the office, and there was no message from her on the answering machine. I called her number at Holst & McDermott again, just to make sure, but again no one picked up. She wasn't at work, and she hadn't come home, and all of a sudden the break-in seemed to be of no importance, a minor irritation from the distant past. Grace was missing, and by the time eight o'clock rolled around, I had already worked myself into a feverish, all-out panic.

I made a number of calls – to friends, co-workers, even to her cousin Lily in Connecticut – but only the last person I talked to had any information to give me. Greg Fitzgerald was head of the art department at Holst & McDermott, and according to him, Grace had called the office just after nine that morning to tell him she couldn't make it to work that day. She was very sorry, but something urgent had come up that required her immediate attention. She didn't say what the something was, but when Greg asked her if she was all right, Grace had apparently hesitated before answering. 'I think so,' she'd finally said, and Greg, who had known her for years and was extremely fond of her (a gay man half in love with his prettiest female colleague), had found the response puzzling. 'Not like her' was the phrase he used, I think, but when he heard the mounting alarm in my voice, he tried to reassure me by adding that Grace had ended the conversation by telling him she would be back in the office tomorrow morning. 'Don't worry, Sidney,' Greg continued. 'When Grace says she's going to do something, she does it. I've been working with her for five years, and she hasn't let me down once.'

I sat up all night waiting for her, half out of my mind with dread and confusion. Before talking to Fitzgerald, I had convinced myself that Grace had been harmed in some violent way – mugged, molested, knocked down by a speeding truck or cab, a victim of one of the countless brutalities that can befall a woman alone on the streets of New York. That seemed unlikely now, but if she wasn't dead or in physical danger, what had happened to her, and why hadn't she called to tell me where she was? I kept going over the conversation we'd had that morning on our walk to the subway, trying to make sense of her curiously emotional statements about trust, remembering the kisses she'd given me and how, without warning, she'd broken free of my arms and started running along the sidewalk, not even bothering to turn around and wave good-bye before disappearing down the stairs. It was the behavior of someone who had come to an abrupt and impulsive decision, whose mind had been made up about something but who was still full of doubts and uncertainties, so shaky in her resolve that she hadn't dared to pause for a single backward glance, fearing that one more look at me might destroy her determination to do whatever it was she was planning to do. I understood that much, I felt, but beyond that point I knew nothing. Grace had become a blank to me, and every thought I had about her that night quickly turned into a story, a gruesome little drama that played on my deepest anxieties about our future – which rapidly seemed to be turning into no future at all.

She came home a few minutes past seven, roughly two hours after I had resigned myself to the fact that I would never see her again. She was wearing different clothes from the ones she'd had on the previous morning, and she looked fresh and beautiful, with bright red lipstick, elegantly made-up eyes, and a hint of rouge on her cheeks. I was sitting on the sofa in the living room, and when I saw her walk in I was so taken aback that I couldn't speak, was literally unable to get any words out of my mouth. Grace smiled at me – calmly, resplendently, in full possession of herself – and then walked over to where I was sitting and kissed me on the lips.

'I know I've put you through hell,' she said, 'but it had to be this way. It won't ever happen again, Sidney. I promise.'

She sat down next to me and kissed me again, but I couldn't bring myself to put my arms around her. 'You have to tell me where you were,' I said, startled by the anger and bitterness in my voice. 'No more silence, Grace. You have to talk.'

'I can't,' she said.

'Yes you can. You have to.'

'Yesterday morning, you said you trusted me. Go on trusting me, Sid. That's all I ask.'

'When people say that, it means they're hiding something. Always. It's like a mathematical law, Grace. What is it? What are you holding back from me?'

'Nothing. I just needed to be alone yesterday, that's all. I needed time to think.'

'Fine. Go ahead and think. But don't torture me by not calling to tell me where you are.'

'I wanted to, but then I couldn't. I don't know why. It was like I had to pretend I didn't know you anymore. Just for a little while. It was a rotten thing to do, but it helped me, it really did.'

'Where did you spend the night?'

'It wasn't like that, believe me. I was alone. I checked into a room at the Gramercy Park Hotel.'

'What floor? What was the number of the room?'

'Please, Sid, don't do that. It's not right.'

'I could call them and find out, couldn't I?'

151

'Of course you could. But that would mean you didn't believe me. And then we'd be in trouble. But we're not in trouble. That's the whole point. We're good, and the fact that I'm here now proves it.'

'I suppose you were thinking about the baby. . . .'

'Among other things, yes.'

'Any new thoughts?'

'I'm still on the fence. I'm still not sure which way to jump.'

'I spent a few hours with John yesterday, and he thinks you should have an abortion. He was very insistent about it.'

Grace looked both surprised and upset. 'John? But he doesn't know I'm pregnant.'

'I told him.'

'Oh, Sidney. You shouldn't have done that.'

'Why not? He's our friend, isn't he? Why shouldn't he know?'

She hesitated for several seconds before answering my question. 'Because it's our secret,' she finally said, 'and we haven't decided what we're going to do about it. I haven't even told my parents. If John talks to my father, things could get awfully complicated.'

'He won't. He's too worried about you to do that.'

'Worried?'

'Yes, worried. In the same way I'm worried. You haven't been yourself, Grace. Anyone who loves you is bound to be worried.'

She was becoming slightly less evasive as the conversation continued, and I meant to go on prodding her until the full story came out, until I understood what had driven her to run off on her mysterious twenty-four-hour fugue. So much was at stake, I felt, and if she didn't come clean and tell me the truth, how was I going to be able to trust her anymore? Trust was the one thing she demanded of me, and yet ever since she'd broken down in the cab on Saturday night, it had become impossible not to feel that something was

152

wrong, that Grace was slowly crumbling under the pressure of a burden she refused to share with me. For a little while, the pregnancy had seemed to account for it, but I was no longer certain about that now. It was something else, something in addition to the baby, and before I started tormenting myself with thoughts about other men and clandestine affairs and sinister betrayals, I needed her to tell me what was going on. Unfortunately, the conversation was suddenly interrupted at that point, and I was no longer in a position to pursue my line of thought. It happened just after I told Grace how worried I was about her. I took hold of her hand, and as I pulled her toward me to kiss her on the cheek, she finally noticed that the standing lamp wasn't where it was supposed to be, that the area to the left of the sofa was vacant. I had to tell her about the burglary, and just like that the entire mood shifted, and instead of talking to her about one thing, I had no choice but to talk to her about another.

At first, Grace seemed to take the news calmly. I showed her the gap in the bookshelf where the first editions had been, pointed to the end table on which the portable TV had stood, then led her into the kitchen and informed her that we would have to buy a new toaster. Grace opened the drawers below the counter (which I had neglected to do) and discovered that our best set of silverware, which had been given to us by her parents as a first-anniversary present, was also missing. That was when anger took hold of her. She kicked the bottom drawer with her right foot and started to curse. Grace seldom used four-letter words, but for a minute or two that morning she was beside herself, and she let go with a barrage of invective that surpassed anything I'd heard from her lips before. Then we went into the bedroom, and her anger spilled over into tears. Her lower lip started to tremble when I told her about the jewelry box, but when she saw that the lithograph was gone as well, she sat down on the bed and started to cry. I did my best to comfort her, promising to look for another van Velde as soon as possible, but I knew that nothing could

153

ever replace the one she'd bought as a twenty-year-old on her first trip to Paris: a swooping configuration of variegated, glowing blues, punctuated by a roundish blank in the center and a broken streak of red. I had been living with it for several years by then, and I had never grown tired of looking at it. It was one of those works that kept giving you something, that never seemed to use itself up.[12]

It took her about fifteen or twenty minutes to pull herself together, and then she went into the bathroom to wash away the streaked mascara and reassemble her face. I waited for her in the bedroom, thinking we would be able to go on with our conversation there, but when she returned it was only to announce that she was running late and had to go to work. I tried to talk her out of it, but she wouldn't relent. She'd promised Greg she would be there this morning, she said, and after he'd been nice enough to give her yesterday off, she didn't want to take further advantage of his friendship. A promise was a promise, she said, to which I answered that we still had things to talk about. Maybe we did, she replied, but they could wait until she came home from work. As if to

---

12. Grace had been a student at the Rhode Island School of Design, off on a junior-year-abroad program in Paris. Trause was the one who had written to her about van Velde, whom he had met once or twice in the fifties and who was known, he said, to be Samuel Beckett's favorite artist. (He included Beckett's dialogue with Georges Duthuit about van Velde in his letter. *My case is that van Velde is . . . the first to admit that to be an artist is to fail, as no other dare fail, that failure is his world.*) Van Velde's paintings were rare and expensive, but his graphic works from the sixties and early seventies were quite affordable at the time, and Grace had bought the piece in installments with her own money, skimping on food and other necessities in order to stay within the allowance sent each month by her father. The lithograph was an important part of her youth, an emblem of her growing passion for art as well as a sign of independence – a bridge between the last days of her girlhood and her first days as an adult – and it meant more to her than any other object she owned.

prove her good intentions, she sat down on the bed before leaving, threw her arms around me, and hugged me tightly for what felt like a long time. 'Don't worry about me,' she said. 'I'm really okay now. Yesterday did me a lot of good.'

I took my morning pills, returned to the bedroom, and slept until the middle of the afternoon. I didn't have any plans for the day, and the sole business on my agenda was to pass the time as quietly as possible until Grace returned home. She had promised to go on talking to me that evening, and if a promise was a promise, then I meant to hold her to it and do what I could to pull the truth from her. I wasn't terribly optimistic, but whether I failed or not, I wasn't going to get anywhere unless I buckled down and made an effort.

The sky was bright and clear that afternoon, but the temperature had dropped down into the 40s, and for the first time since the day in question, I could feel a touch of winter in the air, a foretaste of things to come. Once again, my normal sleep pattern had been disrupted, and I was in worse shape than usual – unsteady in my movements, at a loss for breath, tottering precariously with each step I took. It was as though I had regressed to some earlier stage of my recovery and was back in the period of swirling colors and fractured, unstable perceptions. I felt exceedingly vulnerable, as though the very air were a threat, as though an unexpected gust of wind could blow right through me and leave my body scattered in pieces on the ground.

I bought a new toaster in an appliance store on Court Street, and that simple transaction used up nearly all my physical resources. By the time I'd chosen one we could afford and had dug the money out of my wallet and handed it to the woman behind the counter, I was trembling and felt close to tears. She asked if anything was wrong. I said no, but my answer must have been unconvincing, for the next thing I knew she was asking me if I wanted to sit down and drink a glass of water. She was a fat woman in her early sixties with the faint trace of a mustache on her upper lip, and the shop she presided over was a dim and dusty hole-in-the-wall, a run-down family business with nearly half the shelves denuded of stock. Generous as her offer was, I didn't want to stay there another minute. I thanked her and moved on, staggering toward the exit and then leaning against the door to shove it open with my shoulder. I stood on the sidewalk for a few moments after that, gulping down deep drafts of the chilly air as I waited for the spell to pass. In retrospect, I realized it must have looked as if I'd been on the verge of blacking out.

I bought a slice of pizza and a large Coke at Vinny's two doors down, and by the time I stood up and left I was feeling a little better. It was about three-thirty then, and Grace wouldn't be home until six at the earliest. I didn't have it in me to trudge around the neighborhood and shop for groceries, and I knew I wasn't up to preparing dinner. Eating out was an indulgence for us then, but I figured we could order in some take-out food from the Siam Garden, a Thai restaurant that had just opened up near Atlantic Avenue. I knew that Grace would understand. Whatever difficulties we might have been having, she was concerned enough about my health not to hold that kind of thing against me.

Once I'd polished off the last of my pizza, I decided to walk over to the Clinton Street branch of the public library to see if they had any books by the novelist Trause had mentioned the day before, Sylvia Monroe. Two titles were listed in the card catalogue, *Night in Madrid* and *Autumn Ceremony*, but neither one had been checked out in over ten years. I skimmed them both, sitting at one of the long wooden tables in the reading room, and quickly discovered that Sylvia Monroe had nothing in common with Sylvia Maxwell. Monroe's books were conventional mystery stories, written in the style of Agatha Christie, and as I read through the arch, wittily contrived prose of the two novels, I felt increasingly disappointed, angry with myself for having assumed there could be a similarity between the two Sylvia M.s. At the very least, I thought maybe I'd read a book by Sylvia Monroe as a boy and had since forgotten about it, only to dredge up an unconscious memory of her in the person of Sylvia Maxwell, the pretend author of the pretend *Oracle Night*. But it seemed I'd plucked Maxwell out of thin air and *Oracle Night* was an original story, with no connection to any novel other than itself. I probably should have felt relieved, but I didn't.

When I returned to the apartment at five-thirty, there was a message from Grace on the answering machine. Bluntly and quietly, in a series of simple, forthright sentences, she dismantled the architecture of unhappiness that had been growing up around us for the past several days. She was calling from her office, she said, and had to talk in a low voice, 'but if you can hear me, Sid,' she began, 'there are four things I want you to know. First, I haven't stopped thinking about you since I left the house this morning. Second, I've decided to have the baby, and we're never going to use the word *abortion* again. Third, don't bother to make dinner. I'm leaving the office at five sharp, and from there I'm going down to Balducci's to buy some nice ready-made stuff that we can heat up in the oven. If the subway doesn't break down, I should be home by six-twenty, six-thirty. Fourth, make sure Mr. Johnson's ready for action. I'm going to attack you the minute I walk in the door, my love, so be prepared. Miss Virginia's achin' to get naked with her man.'

Miss Virginia was one of my pet names for her, but I hadn't used it since the first or second year of our marriage, and certainly not since my return from the hospital. Grace was evoking early good times with that phrase, and it moved me to know that she remembered it, since it had generally been reserved for moments of postcoital decompression: Grace rising from the bed after we had finished making love and strolling across the floor on the way to the bathroom, immodest, languid, happy in the nakedness of her body, and sometimes (it was coming back to me now), I would jokingly call her *Miss Nude Virginia*, which always made her laugh, and then, inevitably, she would stop to strike a comic cheesecake pose, which in turn would always get a laugh from me. In effect, *Miss Virginia* was shorthand for *Miss Nude Virginia*, and whenever I called her Miss Virginia in public, it was always a secret communication about our sex life, a reference to the bare skin under her clothes, an homage to her beautiful, much-adored body. Now, immediately after announcing that she wasn't going to end the pregnancy, she had reanimated the mythic personage of Miss Virginia, and by juxtaposing the one statement against the other, she was telling me that she was mine again, mine as before and yet mine in a different way as well, subtly announcing (as only Grace could) that she was prepared to enter the next phase of our marriage, that a new era of our life together was about to begin.

I called off the showdown I had been planning for that evening and didn't ask her a single question about her absence on Wednesday night. We did all the things she had warned me about on the answering machine, wrestling each other to the floor the moment she entered the apartment, then dragging our half-dressed bodies toward the bedroom, which we never quite managed to reach. Later on, after we had slipped into our bathrobes, we warmed the food in the oven and sat down to a late dinner. I showed her the new wide-slotted, bagel-compatible toaster I had bought that afternoon, and although that led to some sad talk about the robbery, it was cut short when my nose suddenly started to bleed, gushing out onto the apricot pastry that Grace had just put in front of me for dessert. She stood behind me at the sink as I tilted my head back and waited for the flow to stop, her arms wrapped around me, kissing my shoulder and my neck, all the while suggesting funny names for us to give the baby. If it was a girl, we decided, we would call her Goldie Orr. If it was a boy, we would name him after one of Kierkegaard's books, Ira Orr. We were stupidly happy that night, and I couldn't remember a time when Grace had been more giddy or effusive in her affections toward me. When the blood finally stopped flowing from my nose, she turned me around and washed my face with a damp cloth, looking steadily into my eyes as she dabbed my mouth and chin until all traces of the spill had vanished. 'We'll clean up the kitchen in the morning,' she said. Then, without adding another word, she took me by the hand and led me toward the bedroom.

I slept late the next morning, and when I finally rolled out of bed at ten-thirty, Grace was long gone. I went into the kitchen to take my pills and start a pot of coffee, and then slowly cleaned up the mess we had walked away from the night before. Ten minutes after I had put the last dish in the cupboard, Mary Sklarr called with bad news. Bobby Hunter's people had read my treatment, and they'd decided to pass on it.

'I'm sorry,' Mary said, 'but I'm not going to pretend I'm shocked.'

'It's all right,' I said, feeling less chagrined than I thought I would. 'The idea was a piece of shit. I'm glad they don't want it.'

'They said your plot was too cerebral.'

'I'm surprised they know what the word means.'

'I'm happy you're not upset. It wouldn't be worth it.'

'I wanted the money, that's all. A case of pure greed. I wasn't even very professional about it, was I? You're not supposed to write anything without a contract. It's the first rule of the business.'

'Well, they *were* pretty amazed. The sheer speed of it. They're not used to that kind of gung ho approach. They like to have lots of discussions with lawyers and agents first. It makes them feel as if they're doing something important.'

'I still don't understand why they thought of me.'

'Somebody there likes your work. Maybe Bobby Hunter,

maybe the kid who works in the mailroom. Who knows? In any case, they're going to send you a check. As an act of goodwill. You wrote the pages without a contract, but they want to reimburse you for your time.'

'A check?'

'Just a token.'

'How much of a token?'

'A thousand dollars.'

'Well, at least that's something. It's the first money I've earned in a long time.'

'You're forgetting Portugal.'

'Ah, Portugal. How could I forget Portugal?'

'Any news on the novel you might or might not be writing?'

'Not much. There could be one piece to salvage from it, but I'm not sure. A novel within the novel. I keep thinking about it, so maybe that's a good sign.'

'Give me fifty pages, and I'll get you a contract, Sid.'

'I've never been paid for a book I haven't finished. What if I can't write page fifty-one?'

'These are desperate times, my friend. If you need money, I'll try to get you money. That's my job.'

'Let me think about it.'

'You think, and I'll wait. When you're ready to call, I'll be here.'

After we hung up, I went into the bedroom to fetch my coat from the closet. Now that the *Time Machine* business was officially dead, I had to start thinking about a new plan, and I figured a walk in the cool air might do me some good. Just as I was about to leave the apartment, however, the phone rang again. I was tempted not to answer it, but then I changed my mind and picked up on the fourth ring, hoping it would be Grace. It turned out to be Trause, probably the last person on earth I wanted to talk to just then. I still hadn't told him about losing the story, and as I prepared myself to blurt out the confession I'd been putting off for the past two days, I was so wrapped up in my own thoughts that I had trouble following him. Eleanor and her husband had found Jacob, he said. They'd already checked him into a drug clinic – a place called Smithers on the Upper East Side.

'Did you hear me?' John asked. 'They've put him in a twenty-eight-day program. That probably won't be enough, but at least it's a start.'

'Oh,' I said, in a faint voice. 'When did they find him?'

'Wednesday night, not long after you left. They had to do a lot of finagling to get him in there. Fortunately, Don knows someone who knows someone, and they managed to cut through the red tape.'

'Don?'

'Eleanor's husband.'

'Of course. Eleanor's husband.'

'Are you all right, Sid? You sound completely out of it.'

'No, no, I'm okay. Don. Eleanor's new husband.'

'The reason I called is to ask a favor. I hope you don't mind.'

'I don't mind. Whatever it is. Just ask and I'll do it.'

'Tomorrow's Saturday, and they have visiting hours at the clinic from noon to five. I was wondering if you'd go up there for me and check in on him. You don't have to stay long. Eleanor and Don can't make it. They've gone back to Long Island, and they've already done enough as it is. I just want to know if he's all right. They don't lock the doors there. It's a voluntary program, and I want to make sure he hasn't changed his mind. After all we've been through, it would be a pity if he decided to run away.'

'Don't you think you should go yourself? You're his father, after all. I barely know the kid.'

'He won't talk to me anymore. And whenever he forgets he's not supposed to talk to me, he feeds me nothing but lies. If I thought it would do any good, I'd hobble up there on my crutch and see him. But it won't.'

'And what makes you think he'll talk to me?'

'He likes you. Don't ask me why, but he thinks you're a

161

cool person. That's an exact quote. "Sid's a cool person."
Maybe because you look so young, I don't know. Maybe
because you once talked to him about a rock band he's interested in.'

'The Bean Spasms, a punk group from Chicago. One night
an old friend played a couple of their songs for me. Not very
good. I think they're gone by now.'

'At least you knew who they were.'

'That was the longest conversation I've ever had with
Jacob. It lasted about four minutes.'

'Well, four minutes isn't bad. If you can get four minutes
out of him tomorrow, that would be an accomplishment.'

'Don't you think it would be better if I took Grace along
with me? She's known him a lot longer than I have.'

'Out of the question.'

'What do you mean?'

'Jacob despises her. He can't stand to be in the same room
with her.'

'No one despises Grace. You'd have to be unhinged to feel
that way.'

'Not according to my son.'

'She's never breathed a word to me about this.'

'It goes all the way back to when they first met. Grace was
thirteen, and Jacob was three. Eleanor and I had just gone
through our divorce, and Bill Tebbetts invited me down to
his country place in Virginia to spend a couple of weeks
with his family. It was summer, and I took Jacob with me.
He seemed to get along with the other Tebbetts kids, but
every time Grace walked into the room, he'd punch her or
throw things at her. One time, he picked up a toy truck and
smashed her on the knee with it. The poor kid was bleeding
all over the place. We rushed her to a doctor, and it took ten
stitches to sew up the wound.'

'I know that scar. Grace told me about it once, but she
didn't mention Jacob. She just said it was some little boy,
and that was all.'

'He seemed to hate her right from the start, from the first moment he laid eyes on her.'

'He probably sensed that you liked her too much, so she became a rival. Three-year-olds are pretty irrational creatures. They don't know many words, and when they're angry, the only way they can talk is with their fists.'

'Maybe. But he kept it up, even after he got older. The worst time was in Portugal, about two years after Tina died. I'd just bought my little house on the northern coast, and Eleanor sent him over to stay with me for a month. He was fourteen, and he knew as many words as I did. Grace happened to be there when he showed up. She was out of college then and about to start working for Holst & McDermott in September. In July, she came to Europe to look at paintings – Amsterdam first, then Paris, and then Madrid. After that, she took the train to Portugal. I hadn't seen her in over two years, and we had a lot of catching up to do, but when Jacob got there he didn't want her around. He muttered insults at her under his breath, pretended not to hear her when she asked him questions, and once or twice even managed to spill food on her. I kept warning him to stop. One more nasty move, I said, and I'd ship him back to his mother and stepfather in America. And then he crossed the line, and I put him on a plane and sent him home.'

'What did he do?'

'He spat in her face.'

'Good God.'

'The three of us were in the kitchen, chopping vegetables for dinner. Grace made some innocuous remark about something – I can't even remember what it was – and Jacob took offense. He walked over to her waving a knife in his hand and called her a stupid bitch, and Grace finally lost her temper. That's when he spat at her. Looking back on it now, I suppose it's lucky he didn't take the knife and stab her in the chest.'

'And this is the person you want me to talk to tomorrow?

What he deserves is a swift kick in the ass.'

'If I went up there myself, I'm afraid that's what would happen. It'll be a lot better for everyone if you go there for me.'

'Has anything happened since Portugal?'

'I've kept them apart. They haven't crossed paths in years, and as far as I'm concerned, the world will be a safer place if they never see each other again.'[13]

Grace didn't have to go to work the next morning, and she was still asleep when I left the apartment. After talking to Trause on Friday, I had decided not to tell her about the promise I'd made to go to Smithers that afternoon. That would have forced me to mention Jacob, and I didn't want to run the risk of stirring up bad memories for her. We had lived through a difficult stretch of days, and I was loath to talk about anything that could cause the slightest agitation – and perhaps destroy the fragile balance we'd managed to find again in the past forty-eight hours. I left a note on the kitchen table, telling her I was going into Manhattan to visit some bookstores and would be home by six at the latest. One more lie, added to all the other little lies we had told each other in the past week. But my intention wasn't to deceive

---

13. The conversation ended with my agreeing to visit Jacob – alone. I was willing to do John that small service, but I was appalled by what he'd said about the boy's animosity toward Grace. Even if there was some cause for envy on his part (the neglected son cast off in favor of the beloved 'goddaughter'), I felt no sympathy for him – only disgust and contempt. I would go to the clinic for his father's sake, but I wasn't looking forward to the time I would have to spend in his company.

As far as I could remember, I had met him only twice before. Knowing nothing about his history with Grace, it had never occurred to me to question why she hadn't been with us on those occasions. The first was a Friday-night outing to Shea Stadium to see a game between the Mets and the Cincinnati Reds. Trause had been given tickets by someone who owned a season box, and because he

her. I simply wanted to protect her from more unpleasantness, to keep the space we shared as small and private as possible, without having to entangle ourselves in painful matters from the past.

The rehab facility was housed in a large mansion that had once belonged to the Broadway producer Billy Rose. I didn't know how or when the place had been turned into Smithers, but it was a solid example of old New York architecture, a limestone palace from an age when wealth had flaunted itself with diamonds, top hats, and white gloves. How odd that it should have been inhabited now by the bottom dogs of society, an endlessly evolving population of drug addicts, alcoholics, and ex-criminals. It had become a way station for the lost, and when the door buzzed open and I went inside, I noted that a certain shabbiness had begun to set in. The bones of the building were still intact (the huge entrance hall with the black-and-white tile floor, the curving staircase with the mahogany banister), but the flesh looked sad and dirty, dilapidated after years of strain and overwork.

I asked for Jacob at the front desk, announcing myself as a family friend. The woman in charge seemed suspicious of me, and I had to empty my pockets to prove I wasn't trying to smuggle in drugs or weapons. Even though I passed the test,

---

knew I was a fan, he'd invited me to go along with him. That was in May 1979, just a few months after I'd fallen in love with Grace, and John and I had met for the first time only a couple of weeks earlier. Jacob was about to turn seventeen then, and he and one of his classmates rounded out the foursome. From the moment we entered the stadium, it was clear that neither boy had any interest in baseball. They sat through the first three innings with bored and sullen expressions on their faces, and then they stood up and left, supposedly to buy some hot dogs and 'wander around for a while,' as Jacob put it. They didn't return until the bottom of the seventh – giggling, glassy-eyed, and in far better spirits than before. It wasn't difficult to guess what they'd been up to. I was still teaching then, and I'd seen enough kids high on pot to recognize the symptoms. John was wrapped up in the game and seemed not to notice, and I didn't

I felt certain that she was going to turn me away, but before I could begin arguing my case, Jacob happened to appear in the front hall, walking with three or four other residents toward the dining room for lunch. He looked taller than the last time I had seen him, but with his black clothes and green hair and excessively thin body, there was something grotesque and clownish about him, as if he were a ghostly Punchinello on his way to perform a dance for the Duke of Death. I called out his name, and when he turned and saw me, he looked shocked – not happy or unhappy, simply shocked. 'Sid,' he muttered, 'what are you doing here?' He separated from the group and walked over to where I was standing, which prompted the woman behind the desk to ask a superfluous question: 'You know this man?' 'Yeah,' Jacob said. 'I know him. He's a friend of my father's.' That statement was enough to get me in. The woman pushed a clipboard at me, and once I'd printed my name on the sheet for visitors, I accompanied Jacob down a long hallway into the dining room.

'No one told me you were coming,' he said. 'I suppose the old man put you up to it, huh?'

'Not really. I happened to be in the neighborhood, and I thought I'd stop by and see how you were doing.'

Jacob grunted, not even bothering to comment on how

---

bother to mention it to him. I scarcely knew him at the time, and I figured that what happened between him and his son was none of my business. Beyond saying hello and good-bye to each other, I don't think Jacob and I exchanged more than eight or ten words the whole night.

The next time I saw him was about six months later. He was in the middle of his senior year and in danger of flunking all his courses, and John had called up with a last-minute invitation to spend an evening shooting pool. He and Jacob were barely on speaking terms then, and I think he wanted me to come along to serve as a buffer, a neutral third party to prevent war from breaking out between them in a public place. That was the night Jacob and I talked about the Bean Spasms and I acquired my reputation as a cool person. He struck me as an exceedingly bright and hostile kid, determined to screw up his

thoroughly he disbelieved me. It was a transparent fib, but I'd said it in order to keep John out of the discussion, thinking I'd get more out of Jacob if I avoided talking about his family. We continued in silence for a few moments and then, unexpectedly, he put his hand on my shoulder. 'I heard you were real sick,' he said.

'I was. I seem to be getting better now.'

'They thought you were going to die, didn't they?'

'So I'm told. But I fooled them and walked out of there about four months ago.'

'That means you're immortal, Sid. You're not going to croak until you're a hundred and ten.'

The dining hall was a large sunny room with sliding glass doors that led out to a small garden, where some of the residents and their families had gone to smoke and drink coffee. The food was served cafeteria-style, and after Jacob and I loaded up our trays with meat loaf, mashed potatoes, and salad, we began looking for an empty table. There must have been fifty or sixty people in the room, and we had to circle around for a couple of minutes before we found one. The delay seemed to irritate him, as if it were a personal affront. When we finally sat down, I asked him how things were going, and he launched into a recitation of bitter grievances,

---

life in every way he could. If I detected any shadow of hope, it was in his determination to beat his father at pool. I was a lousy player and quickly fell behind in every game, but John knew what he was doing, and somewhere along the line he must have taught his son how to play. It brought out the competitiveness in both of them, and the mere fact that Jacob was concentrating on something struck me as an encouraging sign. I didn't know then that John had been an expert pool hustler in the army. If he'd wanted to, he could have run the table and wiped Jacob out, but he didn't do that. He pretended to be trying, and in the end he let the boy win. Under the circumstances, it was probably the right thing to do. Not that it did them any good in the long run, but at least Jacob cracked a smile when they finished and walked over to his father and shook his hand. For all I knew, it could have been the last time that ever happened.

nervously jiggling his left leg as he spoke.

'This place is for shit,' he said. 'All we do is go to meetings and talk about ourselves. I mean, how boring is that? As if I want to listen to these fuckups pour out their dumb stories about how rotten their childhoods were and how they stumbled off the true path and fell into the grip of Satan.'

'What happens when it's your turn? Do you get up and speak?'

'I have to. If I don't say anything, they point their fingers at me and start calling me a coward. So I make up something that sounds like what everyone else says, and then I start to cry. It always gets them. I'm a pretty good actor, you know. I tell them what a crud I am, and then I break down and can't go on anymore, and everyone's happy.'

'Why scam them? You're just wasting your time here if you do that.'

'Because I'm not an addict, that's why. I've fooled around with junk a little bit, but it's not a serious thing for me. I can take it or leave it.'

'That's what my college roommate used to say. And then one night he wound up dead from an overdose.'

'Yeah, well, he was probably stupid. I know what I'm doing, and I ain't gonna die from no overdose. I'm not hooked on the stuff. My mother thinks I am, but she doesn't know shit.'

'Then why did you agree to come here?'

'Because she said she'd cut me off if I didn't. I've already pissed off your pal, the almighty Sir John, and I don't want Lady Eleanor getting any stupid ideas about stopping my allowance.'

'You could always get a job.'

'Yeah, I could, but I don't want to. I've got other plans, and I need a little more time to work them out.'

'So you're just sitting here, waiting for the twenty-eight days to end.'

'It wouldn't be so bad if they didn't keep us busy all the

time. When we're not wearing out our asses at those goddamn meetings, they make us study these terrible books.
You've never read such garbage in all your life.'

'What books?'

'The AA manual, the twelve-step program, all that horseshit.'

'It might be horseshit, but it's helped a lot of people.'

'It's for cretins, Sid. All that crap about trusting in a higher power. It's like some baby-talk religion. Give yourself up
to the higher power, and you'll be saved. You'd have to be a
moron to swallow that stuff. There is no higher power. Take
a good look at the world, and tell me where he is. I don't see
him. There's just you and me and everyone else. A bunch of
poor fucks doing what we can to stay alive.'

We had been together for only a few minutes, and already
I felt drained, depleted by the boy's vapid, cynical talk. I
wanted to get out of there as quickly as I could, but for
form's sake I decided to wait until the meal was over.
Trause's pale and emaciated son appeared to have little
appetite for the Smithers cuisine. He picked at his mashed
potatoes for a while, sampled one taste of the meat loaf, and
then put down his fork. A moment later, he rose from his
seat and asked me if I wanted dessert. I shook my head, and
he marched off to the food line again. When he returned, he
was carrying two cups of chocolate pudding, which he set
before him and ate one after the other, showing considerably
more interest in the sweets than he had in the main course.
With no drugs around, sugar was the only substitute available, and he devoured the puddings with the relish of a
small child, scooping every morsel out of each cup.
Somewhere between the first and second helping, a man
stopped by the table to say hello to him. He looked to be in
his mid-thirties, with a rough pockmarked face and his hair
pulled back in a short ponytail. Jacob introduced him as
Freddy, and with the warmth and earnestness of a true
rehab veteran, the older man extended his hand to me and

said it was a pleasure to meet one of Jake's friends.

'Sid's a famous novelist,' Jacob announced, apropos of nothing. 'He's published about fifty books.'

'Don't listen to what he says,' I told Freddy. 'He tends to exaggerate.'

'Yeah, I know,' Freddy answered. 'This one's a real hell-raiser. Gotta keep a close eye on him. Right, kid?'

Jacob looked down at the table, and then Freddy patted him on the head and walked off. As Jacob dug into his second chocolate pudding, he informed me that Freddy was his group leader and not such a bad guy, all things considered.

'He used to steal things,' he said. 'You know, a professional shoplifter. But he had a smart gimmick, so he never got caught. Instead of going into stores with a big overcoat on, the way most of them do it, he'd dress up as a priest. No one ever suspected him of anything. Father Freddy, the man of God. One time, though, he got himself into a weird jam. He was somewhere in midtown, about to go in and rob a drugstore, when there was this big traffic accident. A guy crossing the street was hit by one of the cars. Someone dragged him onto the sidewalk, right where Freddy was standing. There was blood all over the place, the guy was unconscious, and it looked like he was going to die. A crowd gathers around him, and suddenly a woman spots Freddy in his priest's costume and asks him to say the last rites. Father Freddy is fucked. He doesn't know the words to any of the prayers, but if he runs away, they'll know he's a fake and arrest him for impersonating a priest. So he bends down over the guy, puts his hands together to make it look like he's praying, and mumbles some solemn bullshit he once heard in a movie. Then he stands up, makes the sign of the cross, and splits. Pretty funny, huh?'

'It sounds like you're getting quite an education at those meetings.'

'That's nothing. I mean, Freddy was just a junkie trying to support his habit. A lot of the other people around here have done some pretty crazy shit. See that black guy sitting at the corner table, the big one in the blue sweatshirt? Jerome. He spent twelve years in Attica for murder. And that blond girl at the next table with her mother? Sally. She grew up on Park Avenue and comes from one of the richest families in New York. Yesterday, she told us she's been turning tricks on Tenth Avenue over by the Lincoln Tunnel, fucking guys in cars at twenty dollars a pop. And that Hispanic guy on the other side of the room, the one in the yellow shirt? Alfonso. He went to jail for raping his ten-year-old daughter. I'm telling you, Sid, compared to most of these characters, I'm just a nice middle-class boy.'

The puddings seemed to have energized him a bit, and when we carried our dirty trays into the kitchen, he moved with a certain spring in his step, unlike the shuffling somnambulist I'd spotted in the front hall before lunch. All in all, I'd guess I was with him for thirty or thirty-five minutes – long enough to feel I'd discharged my duty to John. As we walked out of the dining hall, Jacob asked me if I'd like to go upstairs and see his room. There was going to be a big group meeting at one-thirty, he said, and family members and guests were invited to attend. I was welcome to come along if I wanted to, and in the meantime we could hang out in his room on the fourth floor. There was something pathetic about the way he'd latched on to me, about how reluctant he seemed to let me go. We were barely even acquaintances, and yet he must have been lonely enough in that place to think of me as a friend, even though he knew I'd come as a secret agent on behalf of his father. I tried to feel some pity for him, but I couldn't. He was the person who had spat in my wife's face, and even though the incident had happened six years before, I couldn't bring myself to forgive him for that. I looked at my watch and told him I was supposed to meet someone on Second Avenue in ten minutes. I saw a flash of disappointment in his eyes, and then, almost immediately, his face hardened into a mask of indifference. 'No big deal, man,' he said. 'If you gotta go, you gotta go.'

'I'll try to come back next week,' I said, knowing full well that I wouldn't.

'Whatever you like, Sid. It's your call.'

He gave me a condescending pat on the shoulder, and before I could shake his hand good-bye, he turned on his heels and started walking toward the stairs. I stood in the hall for a few moments, waiting to see if he'd look back over his shoulder for a farewell nod, but he didn't. He kept on mounting the staircase, and when he rounded the curve and disappeared from sight, I went over to the woman at the front desk and signed myself out.

It was a little past one o'clock. I rarely went to the Upper East Side, and since the weather had improved in the past hour, rapidly warming to the point where my jacket now felt like an encumbrance, I turned my daily walk into an excuse to prowl around the neighborhood. It was going to be hard to tell John how depressing the visit had been for me, and instead of calling him right away, I decided to put it off until I returned to Brooklyn. I couldn't do it from the apartment (at least not if Grace was home), but there was an ancient telephone booth in the back corner of Landolfi's, complete with a closable accordion door, and I figured I would have enough privacy to do it from there.

Twenty minutes after leaving Smithers, I was on Lexington Avenue in the low 90s, moving along among a small crowd of pedestrians and thinking about heading home. Someone knocked into me, accidentally grazing my left shoulder as he walked by, and as I turned to see who it was, something remarkable happened, something so outside the realm of probability that at first I took it for a hallucination. Directly across the avenue, at a perfect ninety-degree angle from where I was standing, I saw a small shop with a sign above the door that read PAPER PALACE. Was it possible that Chang had managed to relocate his business? It struck me as incredible, and yet given the speed with which this man conducted his affairs – closing up his store in one night, rushing around town in his red car, investing in dubious enterprises, borrowing money, spending money – why should I have doubted it? Chang seemed to live in a blur of accelerated motion, as if the clocks of the world ticked more slowly for him than they did for everyone else. A minute must have felt like an hour to him, and with so much extra time at his disposal, why couldn't he have pulled off the move to Lexington Avenue in the days since I'd last seen him?

On the other hand, it also could have been a coincidence. Paper Palace was hardly an original name for a stationery store, and there easily could have been more than one of them in the city. I crossed the street to find out, more and more certain that this Manhattan version was owned by someone other than Chang. The display in the window proved to be different from the one that had caught my attention in Brooklyn the previous Saturday. There were no paper towers to suggest the New York skyline, but the replacement was even more imaginative than the old one, I felt, even more clever. A tiny doll-sized statue of a man sat at a small table with a miniature typewriter on it. His hands were on the keys, a sheet of paper had been rolled into the cylinder, and if you pressed your face against the window and looked very closely, you could read the words that had been typed on the page: *It was the best of times, it was the worst of times, it was the age of wisdom, it was the age of foolishness, it was the epoch of belief, it was the epoch of incredulity, it was the season of Light, it was the season of Darkness, it was the spring of hope, it was the winter of despair, we had everything before us, we had nothing before us . . .*

I opened the door and went in, and as I crossed the threshold I heard the same tinkling of bells I'd heard in the other Paper Palace on the eighteenth. The Brooklyn shop had been small, but this one was even smaller, with the bulk of the merchandise stacked up on wooden shelves that extended all the way to the ceiling. Once again, there were no customers in the store. At first, I didn't see anyone, but a soft, tuneless humming was wafting up from somewhere in the vicinity of the front counter, as if someone were squatting behind it – tying his shoe, perhaps, or picking up a fallen pen or pencil. I cleared my throat, and a couple of seconds later Chang rose from the floor and put his palms on the countertop, as if to steady his balance. He was wearing the brown sweater this time, and his hair was uncombed. He looked thinner than he had before, with deep creases around his mouth and slightly bloodshot eyes.

'Congratulations,' I said. 'The Paper Palace is back on its feet.'

Chang stared at me with a blank expression, either unable or unwilling to recognize me. 'Sorry,' he said. 'I don't think I know you.'

'Of course you do. I'm Sidney Orr. We spent a whole afternoon together just the other day.'

'Sidney Orr is no friend of mine. I used to think he's good guy, but no more.'

'What are you talking about?'

'You let me down, Mr. Sid. Put me in very embarrassing position. I no want to know you no more. Friendship over.'

'I don't understand. What did I do?'

'You leave me behind at dress factory. Never even say good-bye. What kind of friend is that?'

'I looked everywhere for you. I walked all around the bar, and when I couldn't find you I figured you were in one of the booths and didn't want to be disturbed. So I left. It was getting late, and I had to go home.'

'Home to your darling wife. Just after you get blow job from the African Princess. How funny is that, Mr. Sid? If Martine walk in here now, you do it again. Right here on floor of my shop. You fuck her like a dog and love every minute of it.'

174

'I was drunk. She was very beautiful, and I lost control of myself. But that doesn't mean I'd do it again.'

'You not drunk. You horny hypocrite, just like all selfish people.'

'You said no one could resist her, and you were right. You should be proud of yourself, Chang. You saw into me and found my weakness.'

'Because I knew you think bad thoughts about me, that's why. I understand what's in your mind.'

'Oh? And what was I thinking that day?'

'You think Chang in nasty business. Dirty whore-man with no heart. A man who dream only of money.'

'That's not true.'

'Yes, Mr. Sid, it's true. It's very true. Now we stop talking. You give big hurt to my soul, and now we stop. Look around if you like. I welcome you as customer to my Paper Palace, but no more friend. Friendship dead. Friendship dead and buried now. All finished.'

I don't think anyone had ever insulted me more thoroughly than Chang did that afternoon. I had caused him a great sadness, unintentionally wounding his dignity and sense of personal honor, and as he lashed out at me with those stiff, measured sentences of his, it was as if he felt I deserved to be drawn and quartered for my crimes. What made the attack even more uncomfortable was that most of his accusations were correct. I had left him at the dress factory without saying good-bye, I had allowed myself to fall into the arms of the African Princess, and I had questioned his moral integrity about wanting to invest in the club. There was little I could say to defend myself. Any denials would have been pointless, and even if my transgressions had been relatively small ones, I still felt guilty enough about my session with Martine behind the curtain not to want to bring it up again. I should have said good-bye to Chang and left the store immediately, but I didn't. The Portuguese notebooks had become too powerful a fixation by then, and I couldn't

175

go without first checking to see if he had any in stock. I understood how unwise it was to linger in a place where I wasn't wanted, but I couldn't help myself. I simply had to know.

There was one left, sitting among a display of German and Canadian notebooks on a lower shelf at the back of the store. It was the red one, no doubt the same red one that had been in Brooklyn the previous Saturday, and the price was the same as it had been then, an even five dollars. When I carried it up to the counter and handed it to Chang, I apologized for having caused him any suffering or embarrassment. I told him he could still count on me as a friend and that I would continue to buy my stationery supplies from him, even if it meant traveling far out of my way to do so. For all the contrition I tried to express, Chang merely shook his head and patted the notebook with his right hand. 'Sorry,' he said. 'This one not for sale.'

'What do you mean? This is a store. Everything in it's for sale.' I removed a ten-dollar bill from my wallet and spread it out on the counter. 'Here's my money,' I said. 'The sticker says five dollars. Now please give me my change and the notebook.'

'Impossible. This red one the last Portuguese book in shop. Reserved for other customer.'

'If you're holding it for someone else, you should put it behind the counter where no one can see it. If it's out on the shelf, that means anyone can buy it.'

'Not you, Mr. Sid.'

'How much was the other customer going to pay for it?'

'Five dollars, just as sticker say.'

'Well, I'll give you ten for it and we'll call it a deal. How's that?'

'Not ten dollars. Ten thousand dollars.'

'*Ten thousand dollars?* Have you lost your mind?'

'This notebook not for you, Sidney Orr. You buy other notebook, and everybody happy. Okay?'

'Look,' I said, finally losing patience. 'The notebook costs five dollars, and I'm willing to give you ten. But that's all I'm going to pay.'

'You give five thousand now and five thousand on Monday. That's the deal. Otherwise, please buy other note-book.'

We had entered a domain of pure lunacy. Chang's taunts and absurd demands had finally pushed me over the edge, and rather than go on haggling with him, I snatched the notebook out from under his palm and started for the door. 'That's it,' I said. 'Take the ten and go fuck yourself. I'm leaving.'

I hadn't taken two steps when Chang jumped out from behind the counter to cut me off and block my way to the door. I tried to slip past him, using my shoulder to push him aside, but Chang held his ground, and a moment later he had his hands on the notebook and was yanking it away from me. I pulled it back and clutched it against my chest, straining to hold on to it, but the owner of the Paper Palace was a fierce little engine of wire and sinew and hard muscle, and he tore the thing from my grip in about ten seconds. I knew I would never be able to get it back from him, but I was so peeved, so wild with frustration, that I grabbed hold of his arm with my left hand and took a swing at him with my right. It was the first punch I'd thrown at anyone since grade school, and I missed. In return, Chang delivered a karate chop to my left shoulder. It crashed down on me like a knife, and the pain was so intense that I thought my arm was going to fall off. I dropped to my knees, and before I could stand up again, Chang started kicking me in the back. I yelled at him to stop, but he kept on sending the tip of his shoe into my rib cage and spine – one short brutal jab after another as I rolled toward the exit, desperately trying to get out of there. When my body was flush against the metal plate at the bottom of the door, Chang turned the handle; the latch clicked open, and I fell out onto the sidewalk.

177

'You stay away from here!' he shouted. 'Next time you come back, I kill you! You hear me, Sidney Orr? I cut out your heart and feed it to the pigs!'

I never told Grace about Chang or the beating or anything else that happened on the Upper East Side that afternoon. Every muscle in my body was sore, but in spite of the power of Chang's avenging foot, I had walked away from the pummeling with only the faintest bruises along the lower part of my back. The jacket and sweater I had been wearing must have protected me, and when I remembered how close I'd come to taking off the jacket as I roamed around the neighborhood, I felt lucky to have had it on when I entered the Paper Palace – although luck is perhaps an odd word to use in such a context. On warm nights, Grace and I always slept naked, but now that the weather was turning cool again, she had started going to bed in her white silk pajamas, and she didn't question me when I joined her under the covers in my T-shirt. Even when we made love (on Sunday night), it was dark enough in the bedroom for the welts to escape her notice.

I called Trause from Landolfi's when I went out for the *Times* on Sunday morning. I told him everything I could remember about my visit with Jacob, including the fact that the safety pins were gone from his son's ear (no doubt as a protective measure), and summarized each one of the opinions he'd expressed from the moment I arrived until the moment I saw him vanish in the bend of the staircase. John wanted to know if I thought he'd stay for the whole month or skip out before the time was up, and I answered that I didn't know. He'd made some ominous remark about having plans, I said, which suggested that there were things in his life that no one in his family knew about, secrets he wasn't willing to share. John thought it might have had something to do with dealing drugs. I asked him why he suspected that, but other than making a glancing reference to the stolen tuition money, he wouldn't say. The conversation hit a lull at that point, and in the short silence that followed, I finally mustered the courage to tell him about my misadventure on the subway earlier in the week and how I'd lost 'The Empire of Bones.' I couldn't have chosen a more awkward moment to bring up the subject, and at first Trause didn't understand what I was talking about. I went through the story again. When he realized that his manuscript had probably traveled all the way to Coney Island, he laughed. 'Don't torture yourself about it,' he said. 'I still have a couple of carbons. We didn't have Xerox machines in those days, and everyone always typed at least two copies of everything. I'll put one in an envelope and have Madame Dumas mail it to you this week.'

The next morning, Monday, I went back into the blue notebook for the last time. Forty of the ninety-six pages were already filled, but there were more than enough blanks to hold another few hours' work. I started on a fresh page about halfway in, leaving the Flitcraft debacle behind me for good. Bowen would be trapped in the room forever, and I decided that the moment had finally come to abandon my efforts to rescue him. If I had learned anything from my ferocious encounter with Chang on Saturday, it was that the notebook was a place of trouble for me, and whatever I tried to write in it would end in failure. Every story would stop in the middle; every project would carry me along just so far, and then I'd look up and discover that I was lost. Still, I was furious enough with Chang to want to deny him the satisfaction of having the last word. I knew I was going to have to say good-bye to the Portuguese *caderno*, but unless I did it on my own terms, it would continue to haunt me as a moral defeat. If nothing else, I felt I had to prove to myself that I wasn't a coward.

I waded in slowly, cautiously, driven more by a sense of defiance than any compelling need to write. Before long, however, I found myself thinking about Grace, and with the notebook still open on the desk, I went into the living room to dig out one of the photo albums we kept in the bottom drawer of an all-purpose oak bureau. Mercifully, it had been left untouched by the thief during the Wednesday afternoon break-in. It was a special album, given to us as a wedding present by Grace's youngest sister, Flo, and it contained over a hundred pictures, a visual history of the first twenty-seven years of Grace's life – Grace before I had met her. I hadn't looked at this album since coming home from the hospital, and as I turned the pages in my workroom that morning, I was again reminded of the story Trause had told about his brother-in-law and the 3-D viewer, experiencing a similar kind of entrapment as the pictures pulled me into the past.

There was Grace as a newborn infant lying in her crib. There she was at two, standing naked in a field of tall grass, her arms lifted toward the sky, laughing. There she was at four and six and nine – sitting at a table drawing a picture of a house, grinning into the lens of a school photographer's camera with several teeth missing, posting in the saddle as she trotted through the Virginia countryside on a chestnut-brown mare. Grace at twelve with a ponytail, awkward, funny-looking, uncomfortable in her skin, and then Grace at fifteen, suddenly pretty, defined, the earliest incarnation of the woman she would eventually become. There were group pictures as well: Tebbetts family portraits, Grace with various unidentified friends from high school and college, Grace sitting on Trause's lap as a four-year-old with her parents on either side of them, Trause bending forward and kissing her on the cheek at her tenth or eleventh birthday party, Grace and Greg Fitzgerald making comic faces at a Holst & McDermott Christmas bash.

Grace in a prom dress at seventeen. Grace as a twenty-year-old college student in Paris with long hair and a black turtleneck sweater, sitting at an outdoor café and smoking a cigarette. Grace with Trause in Portugal at twenty-four, her hair cut short, looking like her adult self, exuding a sublime confidence, no longer uncertain of who she was. Grace in her element.

I must have looked at the pictures for more than an hour before I picked up the pen and started to write. The turmoil of the past days had happened for a reason, and with no facts to support one interpretation or another, I had nothing to guide me but my own instincts and suspicions. There had to be a story behind Grace's dumbfounding shifts of mood, her tears and enigmatic utterances, her disappearance on Wednesday night, her struggle to make up her mind about the baby, and when I sat down to write that story, it began and ended with Trause. I could have been wrong, of course, but now that the crisis seemed to have passed, I felt strong enough to entertain the darkest, most unsettling possibilities. Imagine this, I said to myself. Imagine this, and then see what comes of it.

Two years after Tina's death, the grown-up, irresistibly attractive Grace goes to visit Trause in Portugal. He's fifty, a still vigorous and youthful fifty, and for many years now he's taken an active interest in her development – sending her books to read, recommending paintings for her to study, even helping her to acquire a lithograph that will become her most treasured possession. She's probably had a secret crush on him since girlhood, and Trause, who has known her all her life, has always been intensely fond of her. He is a lonely man now, still struggling to find his balance after his wife's death, and she is smitten, a young woman at the height of her loveliness, and ever so warm and compassionate, ever so available. Who can blame him for falling in love with her? As far as I was concerned, any man in his right mind would have fallen for her.

They have an affair. When Trause's fourteen-year-old son joins them in the house, he's revolted by their carryings-on. He has never liked Grace, and now that she's usurped his position and stolen his father from him, he sets out to sabotage their happiness. They go through a hellish time.

Ultimately, Jacob makes such a nuisance of himself that he's banished from the household and sent back to his mother.

Trause loves Grace, but Grace is twenty-six years younger than he is, the daughter of his best friend, and slowly but surely guilt wins out over desire. He is bedding down with a girl he used to sing lullabies to when she was a small child. If she were any other twenty-four-year-old woman, there wouldn't be a problem. But how can he go to his oldest friend and tell him he loves his daughter? Bill Tebbetts would call him a pervert and kick him out of the house. It would cause a scandal, and if Trause held his ground and decided to marry her anyway, Grace would be the one to suffer. Her family would turn against her, and he would never be able to forgive himself for that. He tells her she belongs with someone her own age. If she sticks with him, he says, he'll turn her into a widow before she's fifty.

The romance ends, and Grace returns to New York, crushed, disbelieving, brokenhearted. A year and a half goes by, and then Trause returns to New York as well. He moves into the apartment on Barrow Street and the romance starts up again, but much as Trause loves her, the old doubts and conflicts remain. He keeps their affair a secret (to prevent the news from getting back to her father), and Grace plays along, unconcerned about the question of marriage now that she has her man again. When male co-workers at Holst & McDermott ask her out, she turns them down. Her private life is a mystery, and the tight-lipped Grace never tells anyone a thing.

At first, all goes well, but after two or three months a pattern begins to emerge, and Grace understands that she's trapped in a machine. Trause wants her and he doesn't want her. He knows he should give her up, but he can't give her up. He vanishes and reappears, withdraws and comes back, and each time he calls for her, she goes flying into his arms. He loves her for a day or a week or a month, and then his doubts return and he withdraws again. The machine goes

182

off and on, off and on . . . and Grace isn't allowed near the control switch. There's nothing she can do to change the pattern.

Nine months after this madness begins, I enter the picture. I fall in love with Grace, and in spite of her connection to Trause, she is not wholly indifferent to me. I pursue her relentlessly, knowing there's someone else, knowing there's an unnamed rival competing for her affections, but even after she introduces me to Trause (John Trause, celebrated writer and longtime friend of the family), it never occurs to me that he's the other man in her life. For several months she goes back and forth between us, unable to make up her mind. When Trause waffles, I'm with Grace; when Trause wants her back, she's unavailable to see me. I agonize through these disappointments, continuing to hope things will turn my way, but then she breaks up with me, and I assume I've lost her forever. Perhaps she regrets her decision the moment she walks back into the machine, or perhaps Trause loves her so much that he begins to push her away, knowing that I represent a more promising future for her than the hidden, dead-end life she shares with him. It's even possible that he talks her into marrying me. That would account for her sudden, inexplicable change of heart. Not only does she want me back, but in the same breath she declares that she wants to be my wife, and the sooner we get married the better.

We live through a golden age of two years. I'm married to the woman I love, and Trause becomes my friend. He respects my work as a writer, he takes pleasure in my company, and when the three of us are together, I detect no signs of his former involvement with Grace. He's turned himself into a doting, quasi-paternal figure, and to the degree that he looks on Grace as an imaginary daughter, he looks on me as an imaginary son. He's partly responsible for our marriage, after all, and he's not about to do anything that could put it in jeopardy.

Then catastrophe strikes. On January 12, 1982, I collapse in the 14th Street subway station and fall down a flight of stairs. There are broken bones. There are ruptured internal organs. There are two separate head injuries and neurological damage. I'm taken to Saint Vincent's Hospital and kept there for four months. For the first several weeks, the doctors are pessimistic. One morning, Dr. Justin Berg takes Grace aside and tells her they've given up hope. They doubt I'll live more than a few days, and she should prepare herself for the worst. If he were in her shoes, he says, he'd begin thinking about possible organ donations, funeral homes, and cemeteries. Grace is appalled by the bluntness and coldness of his manner, but the verdict seems final, and she has no choice but to resign herself to the prospect of my imminent death. She goes reeling out of the hospital, blasted apart by the doctor's words, and heads straight for Barrow Street, which is just a few blocks away. Who else can she turn to at such a moment but Trause? John has a bottle of Scotch in his apartment, and she begins drinking the moment she sits down. She drinks too much, and within half an hour she's crying uncontrollably. Trause reaches out to comfort her, wrapping his arms around her and stroking her head, and before she knows what she's doing, her mouth is pressing against his. They haven't touched each other in over two years, and the kiss brings it all back to them. Their bodies remember the past, and once they begin to relive what they used to be together, they can't stop themselves. The past conquers the present, and for the time being the future no longer exists. Grace lets herself go, and Trause doesn't have the strength not to go with her.

She loves me. There's no question that she loves me, but I'm a dead man now, and Grace is falling to pieces, she's half out of her mind with misery, and she needs Trause to hold her together. Impossible to blame her, impossible to blame either one of them, but as I continue to languish in Saint Vincent's over the next few weeks, not yet dead, but not yet truly alive, Grace continues to visit Trause's apartment, and little by little she falls in love with him again. She loves two men now, and even after I defy the medical experts and begin my miraculous turnaround, she goes on loving both of us. When I leave the hospital in May, I'm only dimly aware of who I am anymore. I don't notice things, I stagger around in a half trance, and because a fifth pill is part of my daily regimen for the first three months, I'm in no shape to perform my duties as a husband. Grace is good to me. She's a model of kindness and patience, she's warm and affectionate, she's encouraging, but I can't give anything back to her. She continues her affair with Trause, hating herself for lying to me, hating herself for leading a double life, and the more my recovery advances, the worse her suffering becomes. In early August, two things happen that prevent our marriage from crumbling into ruin. They occur in quick succession, but neither event is related to the other. Grace finds the courage to break off with John, and I stop taking the fifth pill. My groin comes to life again, and for the first time since I left the hospital, Grace is no longer sleeping in two beds. The sky has cleared, and because I know nothing about the deceptions of the past months, I'm blissfully and ignorantly happy – an ex-cuckold who adores his wife and cherishes his friendship with the man who nearly stole her from him.

That should be the end of the story, but it isn't. A month of harmony ensues. Grace settles down with me again, and just when our troubles seem to be over, another storm breaks out. The disaster occurs on the day in question, September 18, 1982, no more than an hour or two after I find the blue notebook in Chang's store, perhaps at the very moment I sit down at my desk and write in the notebook for the first time. On the twenty-seventh, I open the notebook for the last time and record these speculations in an effort to understand the events of the past nine days. Whether they are sound or not, whether they can be verified or not, the story continues when Grace goes to the doctor and finds out she's pregnant. Glorious news, perhaps, but not if you don't know who the father is. She keeps going over the dates in her head, but she can't be sure if the baby is mine or John's. She puts off telling me about it as long as she can, but she's in torment, feeling as if her sins have come back to haunt her, feeling as if she's getting the punishment she deserves. That's why she breaks down in the cab on the night of the eighteenth and attacks me when I reminisce about the Blue Team. There's no fellowship of goodness, she says, because even the best people do bad things. That's why she begins talking about trust and weathering hard times; that's why she implores me to go on loving her. And when she finally tells me about the baby, that's why she immediately talks about having an abortion. It has nothing to do with our lack of money – it's about not knowing. The idea of not knowing nearly destroys her. She doesn't want to start a family that way, but she can't tell me the truth, and because I'm in the dark I lash out at her and try to talk her into keeping the child. If I do anything right, it's when I back down the next morning and tell her the decision is hers. For the first time in days, she begins to feel a possibility of freedom. She runs off to be alone, scaring the life out of me when she stays out all night, but when she returns the next morning she seems calmer, more capable of thinking clearly, less afraid. It takes her just a few more hours to figure out what she wants to do, and then she leaves that extraordinary message for me on the answering machine. She decides she owes me a gesture of loyalty. She wills herself to believe the baby is mine and puts her doubts behind her. It's a leap of pure faith, and I understand now what courage it's taken her to arrive at that decision. She wants to stay married to me. The episode with Trause is finished, and as long as she continues to want to stay married to me, I will never breathe a word to her about the story I've just written in the blue notebook. I don't know if it's fact or fiction, but in the end I don't care. As long as Grace wants me, the past is of no importance.

That was where I stopped. I put the cap on my pen, stood up from the desk, and carried the photo album back into the living room. It was still early – one, maybe one-thirty in the afternoon. I rustled up some lunch for myself in the kitchen, and when I'd finished eating my sandwich, I returned to my workroom with a small plastic garbage bag. One by one, I ripped the pages out of the blue notebook and tore them into little pieces. Flitcraft and Bowen, the rant about the dead baby in the Bronx, my soap opera version of Grace's love life – everything went into the garbage bag. After a short pause, I decided to tear up the blank pages and then shoved them into the bag as well. I closed it with a tight double knot, and a few minutes later I carried the bundle downstairs when I went out for my walk. I turned south on Court Street, kept on going until I was several blocks past Chang's empty, padlocked store, and then, for no other reason than that I was far from home, I dropped the bag into a trash can on the corner, burying it under a bunch of wilted roses and the funny pages from the *Daily News*.

Early in our friendship, Trause told me a story about a French writer he had known in Paris in the early fifties. I can't remember his name, but John said he had published two novels and a collection of stories and was considered to be one of the shining lights of the young generation. He also wrote some poetry, and not long before John returned to America in 1958 (he lived in Paris for six years), this writer acquaintance published a book-length narrative poem that revolved around the drowning death of a young child. Two months after the book was released, the writer and his family went on a vacation to the Normandy coast, and on the last day of their trip his five-year-old daughter waded out into the choppy waters of the English Channel and drowned.

The writer was a rational man, John said, a person known for his lucidity and sharpness of mind, but he blamed the poem for his daughter's death. Lost in the throes of grief, he persuaded himself that the words he'd written about an imaginary drowning had caused a real drowning, that a fictional tragedy had provoked a real tragedy in the real world. As a consequence, this immensely gifted writer, this man who had been born to write books, vowed never to write again. Words could kill, he discovered. Words could alter reality, and therefore they were too dangerous to be entrusted to a man who loved them above all else. When John told me the story, the daughter had been dead for twenty-one years, and the writer still hadn't broken his vow. In French literary circles, that silence had turned him into a legendary figure. He was held in the highest regard for the dignity of his suffering, pitied by all who knew him, looked upon with awe.

John and I talked about this story at some length, and I remember that I was quite firm in dismissing the writer's decision as an error, a misbegotten reading of the world. There was no connection between imagination and reality, I said, no cause and effect between the words in a poem and the events in our lives. It might have appeared that way to the writer, but what happened to him was no more than a horrible coincidence, a manifestation of bad luck in its cruelest, most perverse form. That didn't mean I blamed him for feeling as he did, but in spite of sympathizing with the man for his dreadful loss, I saw his silence as a refusal to accept the power of the random, purely accidental forces that mold our destinies, and I told Trause that I thought he was punishing himself for no reason.

It was a bland, commonsense argument, a defense of pragmatism and science over the darkness of primitive, magical thinking. To my surprise, John took the opposite view. I wasn't sure if he was pulling my leg or simply trying to play devil's advocate, but he said that the writer's deci-

188

sion made perfect sense to him and that he admired his friend for having kept his promise. 'Thoughts are real,' he said. 'Words are real. Everything human is real, and sometimes we know things before they happen, even if we aren't aware of it. We live in the present, but the future is inside us at every moment. Maybe that's what writing is all about, Sid. Not recording events from the past, but making things happen in the future.'

Roughly three years after Trause and I had that conversation, I tore up the blue notebook and threw it into a garbage can on the corner of Third Place and Court Street in Carroll Gardens, Brooklyn. At the time, it felt like the correct thing to do, and as I walked back to my apartment that Monday afternoon in September, nine days after the day in question, I was more or less convinced that the failures and disappointments of the past week were finally over. But they weren't over. The story was just beginning – the true story started only *then*, after I destroyed the blue notebook – and everything I've written so far is little more than a prelude to the horrors I'm about to relate now. Is there a connection between the *before* and the *after*? I don't know. Did the unfortunate French writer kill his child with his poem – or did his words merely predict her death? I don't know. What I do know is that I would no longer argue against his decision today. I respect the silence he imposed on himself, and I understand the revulsion he must have felt whenever he thought of writing again. More than twenty years after the fact, I now believe that Trause called it right. We sometimes know things before they happen, even if we don't know that we know. I blundered through those nine days in September 1982 like someone trapped inside a cloud. I tried to write a story and came to an impasse. I tried to sell an idea for a film and was rejected. I lost my friend's manuscript. I nearly lost my wife, and yet fervently as I loved her, I didn't hesitate to drop my pants in a darkened sex club and thrust myself into the mouth of a stranger. I was a lost man, an ill man, a man struggling to regain his footing, but underneath all the missteps and follies I committed that week, I knew something I wasn't aware of knowing. At certain moments during those days, I felt as if my body had become transparent, a porous membrane through which all the invisible forces of the world could pass – a nexus of airborne electrical charges transmitted by the thoughts and feelings of others. I suspect that condition was what led to the birth of Lemuel Flagg, the blind hero of *Oracle Night*, a man so sensitive to the vibrations around him that he knew what was going to happen before the events themselves took place. I didn't know, but every thought that entered my head was pointing me in that direction. Stillborn babies, concentration camp atrocities, presidential assassinations, disappearing spouses, impossible journeys back and forth through time. The future was already inside me, and I was preparing myself for the disasters that were about to come.

I had seen Trause for lunch on Wednesday, but aside from our two telephone conversations later that week, I had no further contact with him before I got rid of the blue notebook on the twenty-seventh. We had talked about Jacob and the lost manuscript of his old story, but that was the extent of it, and I had no idea what he was doing with himself during those days – except lying on the sofa and taking care of his leg. It wasn't until 1994, when James Gillespie published *The Labyrinth of Dreams: A Life of John Trause*, that I finally learned the details of what John had been up to from the twenty-second to the twenty-seventh. Gillespie's massive six-hundred-page book is short on literary analysis and pays little attention to the historical context of John's work, but it is exceedingly thorough when it comes to biographical facts, and given that he spent ten years working on the project and seemed to have talked to every living person who had ever known Trause (myself included), I have no reason to doubt the precision of his chronology.

After I left John's apartment on Wednesday, he worked until dinnertime, proofreading and making minor changes on the typescript of his novel *The Strange Destiny of Gerald Fuchs*, which he had apparently finished several days before the onset of his phlebitis attack. This was the book I had suspected he was writing but had never been certain about: a manuscript of just under five hundred pages that Gillespie says Trause had started during his last months in Portugal, which meant it had taken him over four years to complete. So much for the rumor that John had stopped writing after Tina's death. So much for the rumor that a once-great novelist had given up his vocation and was living off his early accomplishments – a has-been with nothing more to say.

That evening, Eleanor called with the news that Jacob had been found, and early the next morning, Thursday, Trause telephoned his lawyer, Francis W. Byrd. Lawyers seldom make house calls, but Byrd had been representing Trause for over ten years, and when a client of John's stature informs his attorney that he's laid up on the sofa with a bad leg and needs to see him on an urgent matter at two o'clock, the attorney will scrap his other plans and arrive at the appointed hour, equipped with all necessary papers and documents, which he will have pulled from his office files before heading downtown. When Byrd reached the Barrow Street apartment, John offered him a drink, and once the two men had finished their Scotch and sodas, they sat down to the task of rewriting Trause's will. The old one had been drawn up more than seven years earlier, and it no longer represented John's desires concerning the disposal of his estate. In the aftermath of Tina's death, he had named Jacob as his sole heir and beneficiary, appointing his brother Gilbert to serve as executor until the boy reached the age of twenty-five. Now, by the simple act of tearing up all copies of that document, Trause disinherited his son in front of his lawyer's eyes. Byrd then typed out a new will that bequeathed everything John owned to Gilbert. All cash, all stocks and bonds, all property, and all future royalties to be earned from Trause's literary works would henceforth be inherited by his younger brother. They finished at five-thirty. John shook Byrd's hand, thanking him for his help, and the lawyer left the apartment with three signed copies of the new will. Twenty minutes later, John went back to proofreading his novel. Madame Dumas served him dinner at eight, and at nine-thirty Eleanor called again, telling him that Jacob had been admitted to the program at Smithers and had been there since four o'clock that afternoon.

Friday was the day Trause was supposed to have his leg examined at Saint Vincent's Hospital, but he neglected to look at his calendar and forgot to go. In all the turmoil surrounding the business with Jacob, the appointment had slipped his mind, and at the precise moment when he should have been meeting with his doctor (a vascular surgeon named Willard Dunmore), he was on the phone with me, talking about his son's lifelong animosity toward Grace and asking me to go to Smithers for him on Saturday. According to Gillespie, the doctor called Trause's apartment at eleven-thirty to ask him why he hadn't shown up at the hospital. When Trause explained that there had been a family emergency, Dunmore delivered an angry lecture on the importance of the scan and told his patient that such a cavalier attitude toward his own health was irresponsible and could lead to dire consequences. Trause asked if it would be possible to go in that afternoon, but Dunmore said it was too late and they would have to put it off until Monday at four o'clock. He urged Trause to remember to take his medicine and to remain as still as possible over the weekend. When Madame Dumas arrived at one, she found John in his usual spot on the sofa, correcting the pages of his book.

On Saturday, while I was visiting Jacob at Smithers and tangling over the red notebook in Chang's store, Trause continued to work on his novel. His phone records indicate that he also made three long-distance calls: one to Eleanor in East

Hampton, a second to his brother Gilbert in Ann Arbor (who worked as a professor of musicology at the University of Michigan), and a third to his literary agent, Alice Lazarre, at her weekend house in the Berkshires. He reported to her that he was making good progress with the book, and if he didn't run into any unforeseen problems in the days ahead, she could expect to have a finished manuscript by the end of the week.

On Sunday morning, I called from Landolfi's and gave him the rundown on my brief visit with Jacob. Then I made my confession about having lost his story, and John laughed. If I'm not mistaken, it was a laugh of relief rather than of amusement. It's difficult to know for sure, but I think Trause gave me that story for highly complex reasons – and the talk about providing me with the subject for a film was no more than an excuse, a peripheral motive at best. The story was about the cutthroat machinations of a political conspiracy, but it was also about a marital triangle (a wife running off with her husband's best friend), and if there was any truth to the speculations I put down in the notebook on the twenty-seventh, then perhaps John gave me the story in order to comment on the state of my marriage – indirectly, in the finely nuanced codes and metaphors of fiction. It didn't matter that the story had been written in 1952, the year Grace was born. 'The Empire of Bones' was a premonition of things to come. It had been put in a box and left to incubate for thirty years, and little by little it had evolved into a story about the woman we both loved – my wife, my brave and struggling wife.

I say he laughed with *relief* because I think he regretted what he had done. When we were having lunch on Wednesday, he reacted with great emotion to the news of Grace's pregnancy, and immediately after that we found ourselves on the verge of an ugly quarrel. The moment passed, but I wonder now if Trause wasn't a good deal angrier at me than he let on. He was my friend, but he also must have resented me for having won back Grace. Breaking off their affair had been her decision, and now that she was pregnant, there was no chance that he would ever be with her again. If this was true, giving me the story would have served as a veiled, cryptic form of revenge, a churlish sort of one-upmanship – as if to say, You don't know anything, Sidney. You've never known anything, but I've been around a lot longer than you have. Perhaps. There is no way to prove any of this, but if I've misunderstood his actions, how then to interpret the fact that John never sent me the story? He promised to have Madame Dumas mail me a carbon of the manuscript, but he wound up sending me something else instead, and I took that thing not only as an act of supreme generosity but as an act of contrition as well. By losing the envelope on the subway, I had spared him the embarrassment of his momentary fit of pique. He was sorry for having let his passions run away from him, and now that my clumsiness had gotten him off the hook, he was determined to make it up to me with a spectacular, altogether unnecessary gesture of kindness and goodwill.

We had talked on Sunday somewhere between ten-thirty and eleven o'clock. Madame Dumas arrived at noon, and ten minutes later Trause handed her his ATM card and instructed her to go to the neighborhood Citibank near Sheridan Square and transfer forty thousand dollars from his savings account to his checking account. Gillespie tells us that he spent the rest of the day working on his novel, and that evening, after Madame Dumas had served him dinner, he dragged himself off the sofa and limped into his study, where he sat down at his worktable and made out a check to me for thirty-six thousand dollars – the exact sum of my unpaid medical bills. Then he wrote me the following short letter:

Dear Sid:
 I know I promised you a carbon of the ms., but what's

194

the point? The whole idea was to earn you some money, so I've cut to the chase and written you the enclosed check. It's a gift, free and clear. No terms, no strings, no need to pay me back. I know you're broke, so please don't get on your high horse and tear it up. Spend it, live on it, get yourself going again. I don't want you to have to waste your time fretting about movies. Stick with books. That's where your future is, and I'm expecting great things from you.

Thanks for taking the trouble to visit the brat yesterday. It's much appreciated – nay, more than much, since I know how unpleasant it must have been for you.

Dinner this coming Saturday? Can't say where yet, since it all depends on this damn leg. Strange fact: the clot was brought on by my own cheapness. Ten days before the pain started, I made a lightning trip to Paris – back and forth in thirty-six hours – to talk at the funeral of my old friend and translator, Philippe Joubert. I flew coach, slept both ways, and the doctor says that's what did it. All cramped up in those midget seats. From now on, I only travel first class.

Kiss Gracie for me – and don't give up on Flitcraft. All you need is a different notebook, and the words will start coming again.

J.T.

He sealed up the letter and the check in an envelope and then wrote out my name and address in block letters across the front, but there were no more stamps in the house, and when Madame Dumas left Barrow Street at ten o'clock to return to her apartment in the Bronx, Trause gave her a twenty-dollar bill and asked her to swing by the post office in the morning to stock up on a new supply of first-class stamps. The ever-efficient Madame Dumas took care of the errand, and when she showed up for work on Monday at 11 a.m., John was finally able to put a stamp on the letter. She served him a light lunch at one. After the meal, he pushed on with the proofreading of his novel, and when Madame Dumas left the apartment at two-thirty to shop for groceries, Trause handed her the letter and asked her to mail it for him while she was out. She promised to return by three-thirty, at which point she would help him down the stairs and into the town car he had ordered to take him to his appointment with Dr. Dunmore at the hospital. After Madame Dumas left, Gillespie tells us we can be sure of only one thing. Eleanor called at two-forty-five and informed Trause that Jacob had gone missing. He'd walked out of Smithers sometime in the middle of the night, and no one had heard from him since. Gillespie quotes Eleanor as saying that John became 'extremely upset' and went on talking to her for fifteen or twenty minutes. 'He's on his own now,' John finally said. 'There's nothing we can do for him anymore.'

Those were Trause's last words. We have no idea what happened to him after he hung up the phone, but when Madame Dumas returned at three-thirty, she found him lying on the floor at the foot of his bed. That would seem to suggest he'd gone into the bedroom to begin changing his clothes for the appointment with Dunmore, but that is only conjecture. All we know for certain is that he died somewhere between three o'clock and three-thirty on September 27, 1982 – less than two hours after I tossed the remains of the blue notebook into a garbage can on a street corner in South Brooklyn.

The initial cause of death was presumed to be a heart attack, but on further investigation by the medical examiner that verdict was changed to pulmonary embolism. The blood clot that had been sitting in John's leg for the past two weeks had broken loose, traveled upward through his system, and found its target. The little bomb had finally gone off inside him, and my friend was dead at fifty-six. Too soon. Too soon by thirty years. Too soon to thank him for sending me the money and trying to save my life.

John's death was reported in a late bulletin at the end of the local six o'clock news broadcasts. Under normal circumstances, Grace and I would have turned on the television as we were setting the table and preparing our dinner, but we didn't have a television anymore, so we went through the evening without knowing that John was lying in the city morgue, without knowing that his brother Gilbert was already on a plane from Detroit to New York, without knowing that Jacob was on the loose. After dinner, we went into the living room and stretched out on the sofa together, talking about Grace's upcoming appointment with Dr. Vitale, a female obstetrician recommended by Betty Stolowitz, whose first baby had been delivered in March. The visit was scheduled for Friday afternoon, and I told Grace I wanted to be there with her and would show up at the office on West Ninth Street at four o'clock. As we were going over these arrangements, Grace suddenly remembered that Betty had given her a book about pregnancy that morning – one of those big paperback compendiums filled with charts and illustrations – and she hopped off the sofa and went into the bedroom to retrieve it from her shoulder bag. While she was gone, someone knocked on the door. I assumed it was one of our neighbors, coming to borrow a flashlight or a book of matches. It couldn't have been anyone else, since the front door of the building was always locked, and a person without a key had to push an outside buzzer and announce himself through the intercom before he could get in. I remember that I wasn't wearing any shoes, and when I climbed off the sofa and went to open the door, I picked up a small splinter in the sole of my left foot. I also remember looking at my watch and seeing that it was eight-thirty. I didn't bother to ask who it was. I simply opened the door, and once I did that, the world became a different world. I don't know how else to put it. I unlocked the door, and the thing that had been building inside me over the past days was suddenly real: the future was standing in front of me.

It was Jacob. He had dyed his hair black, and he was bundled up in a long dark overcoat that hung down to his ankles. Hands thrust into his pockets, bouncing impatiently on the balls of his feet, he looked like some futuristic undertaker who'd come to carry away a dead body. The green-headed clown I'd talked to on Saturday had been disturbing enough, but this new creature scared me, and I didn't want to let him in. 'You've got to help me,' he said. 'I'm in real trouble, Sid, and there's no one else to turn to.' Before I could tell him to go away, he pushed himself into the apartment and shut the door behind him.

'Go back to Smithers,' I said. 'There's nothing I can do for you.'

'I can't go back. They found out I was there. If I go back to that place, I'm dead.'

'Who's *they*? Who are you talking about?'

'These guys, Richie and Phil. They think I owe them money. If I don't come up with five thousand dollars, they're going to kill me.'

'I don't believe you, Jacob.'

'They're the reason I went to Smithers. It wasn't because of my mother. It was to hide from them.'

'I still don't believe you. But even if I did, I wouldn't be able to help. I don't have five thousand dollars. I don't even have five hundred dollars. Call your mother. If she turns you down, call your father. But leave Grace and me out of this.'

I heard the toilet flush down the hall, a signal that Grace would be coming back to the room at any moment. Distracted by the noise, Jacob turned his head toward that area of the apartment, and when he saw her walk into the living room with the pregnancy book in her hand, he broke into a big smile. 'Hiya, Gracie,' he said. 'Long time no see.'

Grace stopped in her tracks. 'What's he doing here?' she

said, addressing her words to me. She looked stunned, and she spoke in a kind of suppressed rage, refusing to turn her eyes back in Jacob's direction.

'He wants to borrow money,' I said.

'Come on, Gracie,' Jacob said, in a half petulant, half sarcastic tone of voice. 'Won't you even say hello to me? I mean, it doesn't cost anything to be polite, does it?'

As I stood there watching the two of them, I couldn't help thinking about the torn-up photograph that had been left on the sofa after the break-in. The frame had been stolen, but only someone with a deep, long-standing grudge against the person in the portrait would have gone to the trouble of ripping it to pieces. A professional burglar would have left it intact. But Jacob wasn't a professional; he was a frantic, drug-addled kid who'd gone out of his way to hurt us – to hurt his father by going after two of his closest friends.

'That's enough,' I said to him. 'She doesn't want to talk to you, and neither do I. You're the person who robbed us last week. You crawled in through the kitchen window and smashed up the place, and then you walked off with every valuable thing you could find. Do you want me to pick up the phone and call the cops, or do you want to leave? Those are your two choices. Trust me, I'll make that call with great pleasure. I'll press charges against you, and you'll wind up going to jail.'

I was expecting him to deny the accusation, to pretend to be insulted that I would dare to think such a thing about him, but the boy was much cleverer than that. He let out a beautifully calibrated sigh of remorse, and then he sat down in a chair, slowly shaking his head back and forth, acting as if he were shocked by his own behavior. It was the same kind of self-loathing performance he'd mentioned to me on Saturday when he'd bragged about his theatrical talents. 'I'm sorry,' he said. 'But what I told you about Richie and Phil is true. They're after me, and if I don't give them their five thousand bucks, they're going to put a bullet in my head. I came here the other day thinking I'd borrow your checkbook, but I couldn't find it. So I took some other things instead. It was a dumb move. I'm really sorry. The stuff wasn't even worth that much, and I shouldn't have done it. If you want, I'll give it all back to you tomorrow. I still have it in my apartment, and I'll bring everything back first thing in the morning.'

'Bullshit,' Grace said. 'You've already sold what you could, and then you threw out the rest. Don't play that sorry-little-boy routine, Jacob. You're too big for that now. You ripped us off last week, and now you're back for more.'

'Those guys are fixing to shorten my life,' he said, 'and they need their money by tomorrow. I know you two are strapped for cash, but Christ, Gracie, your dad's a federal judge. He's not going to flinch if you ask him for a loan. I mean, what's five thousand dollars to an old southern gentleman?'

'Forget it,' I said. 'There's no way we're going to drag Bill Tebbetts into this.'

'Get him out of here, Sid,' Grace said to me, her voice tight with anger. 'I can't stand it anymore.'

'I thought we were family,' Jacob replied, staring hard at Grace, almost forcing her to look at him. He had begun to pout, but in a curiously insincere way, as though he were trying to mock her and twist her dislike for him to his own advantage. 'After all, you're sort of my unofficial stepmom, aren't you? At least you used to be. Doesn't that count for something?'

By then, Grace was already moving across the room, on her way to the kitchen. 'I'm calling the police,' she said. 'If you won't do it, Sid, I will. I want this slimeball out of here.' In order for her to reach the phone in the kitchen, however, she had to pass in front of the chair Jacob was sitting in, and before she managed to get there, he had already stood up to block her way. Until then, the confrontation had consisted entirely of words. The three of us had been talking, and no matter how distasteful that talk had been, I wasn't prepared for those words to erupt into physical violence. I was standing near the sofa, a good eight or ten feet from the chair, and when Grace tried to slip past Jacob, he grabbed hold of her arm and said, 'Not the police, stupid. Your father. The only person you're going to call is the judge – to ask for the money.' Grace tried to squirm out of his grip, bucking around like an incensed animal, but Jacob was five or six inches taller than she was, which gave him superior leverage and allowed him to bear down on her from above. I rushed toward him, slowed by my sore muscles and the splinter in my foot, but before I got there, Jacob had already locked his hands onto her shoulders and was slamming her into the wall. I jumped him from behind, trying to wrap my arms around his torso and pull him away from her, but the kid was strong, much stronger than I had expected, and without even bothering to turn around, he sent his elbow straight into my stomach. It blew the wind out of me and knocked me down, and before I could make another charge at him, he was punching Grace in the mouth and kicking her in the belly with his thick leather boots. She tried to fight back, but each time she stood up, he slugged her in the face, banged her against the wall, and threw her to the floor. Blood was pouring out of her nose when I was ready to attack again, but I knew that I was too weak to have any effect, too debilitated to stop him with my sad and frail fists. Grace was moaning and nearly unconscious by then, and I felt there was a real danger that he would beat her to death. Instead of going straight for him, I rushed into the kitchen and pulled out a large carving knife from the top drawer next to the sink. 'Stop it!' I yelled at him. 'Stop it, Jacob, or else I'm going to kill you!' I don't think he heard me at first. He was completely lost in his fury, an insane destroyer who scarcely seemed to know what he was doing anymore, but as I advanced toward him with the knife, he must have caught a glimpse of me out of the corner of his eye. He turned his head to the left, and when he saw me there with the knife raised in my hand, he suddenly stopped hitting her. His eyes had a wild, unfocused look, and sweat was sliding off his nose and falling onto his narrow, trembling chin. I felt certain he was going to come after me next. I wouldn't have hesitated to stick the knife into his body, but when he glanced down at the bleeding and immobilized Grace, he dropped his arms to his sides and said, 'Thanks a lot, Sid. Now I'm a dead man.' Then he turned around and left the apartment, vanishing into the streets of Brooklyn a few minutes before the police cars and the ambulance pulled up in front of the house.

Grace lost the baby. The blows from Jacob's boot had torn up her insides, and once the hemorrhaging began, the tiny embryo was dislodged from the wall of her uterus and came washing out in a miserable stream of blood. Spontaneous abortion, as the term goes; a miscarriage; a life that was never born. They drove her across the Gowanus Canal to Methodist Hospital in Park Slope, and as I sat beside her in the back of the ambulance, wedged in among the oxygen tanks and two paramedics, I kept looking down at her poor battered face, unable to stop myself from trembling, seizing up in continual spasms that shuddered through my chest and down the entire length of my body. Her nose was broken, the left side of her face was covered with bruises, and her right eyelid was so swollen it looked as if she would never see out of that eye again. At the hospital, they wheeled her off for X rays on the ground floor and then took her upstairs to an operating room, where they worked on her for more than two hours. I don't know how I did it, but as I waited for the surgeons to finish their job, I managed to pull myself together just long enough to call Grace's parents in Charlottesville. That was when I found out John was dead. Sally Tebbetts answered the phone, and at the end of our exhausting, interminable conversation, she told me that

Gilbert had called earlier that evening with the news. She and Bill were already in shock, she said, and now I was telling her that John's son had tried to kill their daughter. Had the world gone crazy? she asked, and then her voice choked up and she started to cry. She handed the phone to her husband, and when Bill Tebbetts came on, he got right to the point and asked me the only question worth asking. Was Grace going to live? Yes, I said, she was going to live. I didn't know that yet, but I wasn't about to tell him that Grace was in critical condition and might not pull through. I wasn't going to hex her chances by speaking the wrong words. If words could kill, then I had to keep a careful watch over my tongue and make sure never to express a single doubt or negative thought. I hadn't come back from the dead in order to watch my wife die. Losing John was terrible enough, and I wasn't going to lose anyone else. It simply wasn't going to happen. Even if I had no say in the matter, I wasn't going to allow it to happen.

For the next seventy-two hours, I sat by Grace's bed and didn't budge from my spot. I washed and shaved in the adjoining bathroom, ate meals as I watched the clear liquid in the IV line drip into her arm, and lived for those rare moments when she opened her good eye and said a few words to me. With so many painkillers circulating in her blood, she seemed to have no memory of what Jacob had done to her and only the dimmest awareness that she was in a hospital. Three or four times, she asked me where she was, but then she'd drift off again and immediately forget what I'd told her. She often whimpered in her sleep, groaning softly as she swatted at the bandages on her face, and once she woke up with tears in her eyes asking, 'Why do I hurt so much? What's wrong with me?'

People came and went during those days, but I have no more than the faintest memories of them, and I can't recall a single conversation I had with anyone. The assault occurred on a Monday night, and by Tuesday morning Grace's parents had already flown up from Virginia. Her cousin Lily drove down from Connecticut that same afternoon. Her younger sisters, Darcy and Flo, arrived the next morning. Betty Stolowitz and Greg Fitzgerald came. Mary Sklarr came. Mr. and Mrs. Caramello came. I must have talked to them and left the room every now and then, but I can't remember anything but sitting with Grace. For most of Tuesday and Wednesday, she was in a semiconscious torpor – drowsing, sleeping, waking for just a few minutes at a stretch – but by Wednesday evening she seemed to be a little more coherent and was beginning to remain conscious for longer periods of time. She slept soundly that night, and when she woke up on Thursday morning, she finally recognized me. I took hold of her hand, and as our palms touched, she muttered my name, then repeated it to herself several more times, as though that one-syllable word were an incantation that could turn her from a ghost into a living being again.

'I'm in a hospital, aren't I?' she said.

'Methodist Hospital in Park Slope,' I answered. 'And I'm sitting next to you, holding your hand. It's not a dream, Grace. We're really here, and little by little you're going to get better.'

'I'm not going to die?'

'No, you're not going to die.'

'He beat me up, didn't he? He punched me and kicked me, and I remember thinking I was going to die. Where were you, Sid? Why didn't you help me?'

'I got my arms around him, but I couldn't pull him off you. I had to threaten him with a knife. I was ready to kill him, Grace, but he ran off before anything happened. Then I called Nine-one-one, and the ambulance brought you here.'

'When was that?'

'Three nights ago.'

'And what's this stuff on my face?'

'Bandages. And a splint for your nose.'

'He broke my nose?'

'Yes. And gave you a concussion. But your head is clearing now, isn't it? You're starting to come around.'

'What about the baby? There's this big pain in my gut, Sid, and I think I know what it means. It can't be true, can it?'

'I'm afraid it is. Everything else is going to get better, but not that.'

One day later, Trause's ashes were scattered in a meadow in Central Park. There must have been thirty or forty of us in the group that morning, a gathering of friends, relatives, and fellow writers, with no official from any religion present and not one mention of the word *God* made by any of the people who spoke. Grace knew nothing about John's death, and her parents and I had decided to keep it from her as long as we could. Bill went to the ceremony with me, but Sally stayed behind at the hospital to be with Grace – who had been told I was accompanying her father to the airport for his flight back to Virginia. Grace was gradually getting better, but she still wasn't well enough to handle a blow of that magnitude. One tragedy at a time, I said to her parents, but no more. Like the single drops of liquid that fell from the plastic bag into the IV tube attached to Grace's arm, the medicine would have to be parceled out in small doses. The lost child was more than enough for now. John could wait until she was strong enough to bear a second onslaught of grief.

No one mentioned Jacob at the service, but he was present in my thoughts as I listened to John's brother and Bill and various other friends deliver their eulogies under the blazing light of that autumn morning. How rotten for a man to die before he had a chance to become old, I said to myself, how grim to contemplate the work he still had in front of him. But if John had to die now, I felt, then surely it was better that he had died on Monday, and not Tuesday or Wednesday. If he had lived another twenty-four hours, he would have found out what Jacob had done to Grace, and I was certain that knowledge would have destroyed him. As it was, he would never have to confront the fact that he had sired a monster, never have to walk around with the burden of the outrage his son had committed against the person he loved most in the world. Jacob had become the unmentionable, but I burned with hatred against him, and I was looking forward to the moment when the police finally caught up with him and I would be able to testify against him in court. To my infinite regret, I was never given that opportunity. Even as we stood in Central Park mourning his father, Jacob was already dead. None of us could have known it then, since another two months went by before his decomposing body was found – wrapped in a sheath of black plastic and buried in a Dumpster at an abandoned construction site near the Harlem River in the Bronx. He had been shot twice in the head. Richie and Phil had not been phantoms of his imagination, and when the forensic report was placed in evidence at their trial the following year, it showed that each bullet had been fired from a different gun.

That same day (October 1), the letter sent from Manhattan by Madame Dumas reached its destination in Brooklyn. I found it in my mailbox after I went home from Central Park (to change my clothes before setting out for the hospital again), and because there was no return address on the envelope, I didn't learn who it was from until I'd carried it upstairs and opened it. Trause had written the letter by hand, and the script was so jagged, so frenzied in its execution, that I had trouble deciphering it. I had to go through the text several times before I managed to crack the mysteries of its illegible curls and scratches, but once I began to translate the marks into words, I could hear John's voice talking to me – a living voice talking from the other side of death, from the other side of nowhere. Then I found the check inside the envelope, and I felt my eyes watering up with tears. I saw John's ashes streaming out of the urn in the park that morning. I saw Grace lying in her bed in the hospital. I saw myself tearing up the pages of the blue notebook, and after a while – in the words of John's brother-in-law Richard – I had my face in my hands and was sobbing my guts out. I don't know how long I carried on like that, but even as the tears poured out of me, I was happy, happier to be alive than I had ever been before. It was a happiness beyond consolation, beyond misery, beyond all the ugliness and beauty of the world. Eventually, the tears subsided, and I went into the bedroom to put on a fresh set of clothes. Ten minutes later, I was out on the street again, walking toward the hospital to see Grace.